As the daughter of an officer in the Royal Air Force, Sandra Wilson has travelled and lived in various parts of Europe. She now lives in Gloucestershire with her family, where all her spare time is spent writing.

THE ABSENT WIFE

A proper young lady must hide her love for a lord who has even more to hide. Miss Roslyn Meredith knew so little about Lord James Atherton. Why had this handsome, charming, aristocrat married the notorious Vanessa, society's most heartless and scheming beauty? Seemingly vanished off the face of the earth, what had happened to her? And now, why did Atherton invite Roslyn and her improvident father to his estate in Foxcombe? One question overshadowed all others. Could Roslyn trust this man who had no right to make her lose her heart to him — and could she trust herself?

Books by Sandra Wilson
Published by The House of Ulverscroft:

THE CHALBOURNE SAPPHIRES

SANDRA WILSON

THE ABSENT WIFE

Complete and Unabridged

ULVERSCROFT
Leicester

First published in Great Britain in 2007 by
Robert Hale Limited
London

First Large Print Edition
published 2008
by arrangement with
Robert Hale Limited
London

The moral right of the author has been asserted

British Library CIP Data

Wilson, Sandra, *1944 –*
   The absent wife.—Large print ed.—
   Ulverscroft large print series: historical romance
   1. Missing persons—Fiction
   2. Love stories 3. Large type books
   I. Title
   823.9'14 [F]

   ISBN 978–1–84782–483–7

Published by
F. A. Thorpe (Publishing)
Anstey, Leicestershire

Set by Words & Graphics Ltd.
Anstey, Leicestershire
Printed and bound in Great Britain by
T. J. International Ltd., Padstow, Cornwall

This book is printed on acid-free paper

1

There should have been six at the small but elegant dinner party that cold January evening in 1811, but there were only four. The hosts were Lord and Lady Elgin, and their two guests were Sir Owen Meredith, the fashionable portrait artist, and his niece, Miss Roslyn Meredith, who had only recently come to London from the country. The two exceedingly interesting absentees were Lord and Lady Atherton, who were at present the cause of a great deal of gossip and speculation. Lady Atherton had apparently vanished off the face of the earth, and her husband was being strangely reticent about her disappearance. It was the talk of Mayfair, but so far tonight the Elgins' dinner party hadn't touched upon it at all.

Candlelight cast a soft glow over the blue-and-gold dining room, and over the faces of those at the gleaming mahogany table. Their meal was almost over, the tablecloth had been removed, and liqueurs, nectarines, and walnuts placed before them. The fire in the wide marble hearth glowed brightly as the winter wind moaned dismally around the mansion on the corner of Piccadilly and Park Lane.

Sir Owen Meredith was a round little man with impish hazel eyes and receding light-brown hair. He had been laced into his fashionably tight black velvet evening coat and satin waistcoast, and the frills of his shirt stuck out like the feathers of a ruffled hen. His was a jovial personality, and it was impossible from his manner to tell that he was actually in dire financial straits. Tonight his monetary problems were far from his mind. He had dined well and had now decided the conversation needed enlivening. Up to this point it had concentrated rather on the imminence of a regency due to the king's apparently incurable mental illness, and Sir Owen was tired of such a dismal topic; how much better to twit Thomas Bruce, seventh Earl of Elgin, on the subject of controversial Greek antiquities he had for some time been bringing back from Athens and placing on display at the back of the house in a museum known sarcastically throughout society as Lord Elgin's stone shop.

'Come on, Thomas,' Sir Owen urged in his deep, melodic voice, 'admit that those wretched lumps of stone belong on the Acropolis and not in your London back yard.'

Lord Elgin, a tall angular Scot, had very

little sense of humor where his antiquities were concerned. 'If I'd left them where they were, Owen, they'd have become dust and memory, the Turkish occupation would have seen to that! Good heavens, man, the Ottomans keep an arsenal in the Parthenon and have already managed to blow part of it to perdition!' He tapped an irritated finger on the shining table.

'The Turks have occupied Greece for centuries and haven't decimated the place yet,' pointed out Sir Owen, enjoying himself immensely. There was nothing he liked more than to get poor old Thomas going.

'Give them a little more time and they'll no doubt attend to the oversight. I was quite right to bring those items back to safety, where they can be admired by future generations.'

'Ah, I see what you mean. So the same thing applies to the Stone of Scone, does it?'

'There isn't any comparison, and you know it.'

'Why isn't it the same thing? The English removed the stone upon which the kings of Scotland sat to be crowned, and they've kept it in Westminster Abbey ever since — to be admired by generations.' Sir Owen grinned. 'Be honest, Thomas. The Scots, your good self included, have positively fumed about

3

that lump of stone, saying it belongs in Scotland, so how can you possibly justify your stone shop, eh?'

Lord Elgin glared at him. 'There's no similarity whatsoever. You're arguing for the sake of it.'

'It's something I happen to be very good at.'

'So I've noticed. The Welsh are born troublemakers.'

Sir Owen laughed. 'It helps to pass the time while we regroup to drive the rest of you back into the North Sea, where you belong.'

Lord Elgin glowered at him and pushed the silver dish of fruit and nuts across the table. 'Have another nut and chew on that instead of on me.'

Still grinning, Sir Owen picked up the nutcracker and demolished one of the nuts with a satisfying crunch.

Lady Elgin had been listening to the exchange, and smiled. She was a poised woman of the world, and very handsome with her clear blue eyes and slender figure. She wore a pale-green silk dress with a very low décolletage, and in her short dark hair there was a fine emerald-set comb from which sprang a tall ostrich plume. A delicate white lace shawl rested over her graceful arms, and her closed fan lay on the table beside her glass of liqueur. She knew that Sir Owen's teasing was finding its mark. Poor Eggy, he was foolish to rise so easily to the bait.

Roslyn smiled as well, knowing her uncle's propensity for 'getting 'em going,' as he put it. Tonight she was enjoying herself for the first time since coming to London six months earlier to live with him after the sudden death of her widowed father. Sir Owen was her father's brother and her only living relative, and she loved him very much, but she was in awe of the lofty circles in which he moved. She was used to the quiet, simple life of a remote Monmouthshire manor house, where the highlight of her social year had been the annual subscription ball in Monmouth; now she was plunged into the hothouse whirl of London's *haut ton*, and it was an ordeal for a country mouse of retiring disposition.

She was an attractive rather than beautiful young woman of twenty-two, with an oval face, clear complexion, and generous mouth. Her large eyes were green and long-lashed, and her hair a rich tawny-blond, like spun bronze. She wore it in a knot at the back of her head, with several heavy ringlets falling to the nape of her neck, and her gown had a very high waist and low scooped neckline. It was an elegant gown, made of figured French gauze over white satin, and had long, diaphanous sleeves gathered daintily at her slender wrists. Her only piece of jewelry was the golden locket on a black velvet ribbon at her throat; it had belonged to her mother, who had died at her birth. Tonight there was animation in her likable face, for she had relaxed under the kind wing of Lady Elgin, who had been determined to somehow bring Sir Owen's quiet little niece out of her shell. Instead of the pale, rather withdrawn countenance she'd shown the world during the last six months, there was now a little color in her cheeks and a brightness in her green eyes. But it was her smile that transformed her: it was a refreshing, open smile, revealing her to be far from the dull nonentity society had thought her.

Lady Elgin surveyed Roslyn, thinking that the little Meredith was blessed with good looks and a charming disposition, and that it was a great shame that her uncle's financial ineptitude was denying her the fortune necessary to attract the right sort of husband. Sir Owen Meredith might be very successful indeed, and his order book might be filled to overflowing, but the fat fees he received from his many wealthy patrons seemed to trickle through his fingers at alarming speed. The genius of brush and canvas was a half-wit with pounds, shillings, and pence. Every investment he made turned out to be a disaster, and the situation had now become so bad that he was secretly reduced to selling possessions to fend off his creditors. Very few people knew the truth; he was not a man to bemoan his misfortunes, and as far as most of society was concerned, he was doing very nicely. His rented house in Conduit Street was a handsome property. He was a teacher of perspective at the Royal Academy, and his studio in the Strand bustled with pupils and assistants. Last year alone he had completed seven full-length portraits, including one of the queen, five half-lengths, and innumerable heads, but his bank balance was sunk far into the red. No one could guess it, though; he remained outwardly as buoyant as ever, and the wardrobe he had provided for his niece was elegant and fashionable enough for a duchess.

Looking at Roslyn again, Lady Elgin thought it was sad that she wasn't quite lovely enough to be another Vanessa Atherton. Lady Elgin's glance then moved thoughtfully to the two empty chairs, and she wondered anew about the intriguing mystery of Lady Atherton's disappearance. It was the chatter of every drawing room in town. She'd just vanished, and her handsome husband was refusing to say anything about it. Vanessa had been in a rather agitated state getting into her carriage outside their Grosvenor Square house, then the carriage had speedily driven away and she hadn't been seen or heard of since. Lady Elgin sighed wistfully, wishing she'd managed to lure Lord Atherton to her dinner table that evening. What a social coup it would have been, being the first hostess to have succeeded in enticing him into accepting any invitation since Vanessa had disappeared.

The gentlemen's lively discourse on Greece had been continuing, and Roslyn had been listening, but now she turned toward her hostess and smiled. 'I do believe our existence has been forgotten, my lady.'

'Mm?' Thoughts of Vanessa Atherton still prevailed.

'I said the gentlemen have forgotten us.'

Lady Elgin drew herself back to the present. 'You're quite right, and it's time to remonstrate with them.' Picking up her fan, she rapped it peremptorily on the table, causing the two men to break off in midsentence and look inquiringly at her. She gave them a stern look. 'Sirs, this isn't your club, it's a private dinner party and there are ladies present, or have we slipped your minds completely?'

Her husband smiled a little sheepishly, knowing that his passion for his antiquities was apt to override everything else. 'Have we been neglecting you, my dear?'

'You know perfectly well that you have. You should also know by now when Sir Owen is deliberately rattling your foolish cage to make you squawk.'

'Squawk?' His eyes were blank for a moment and then he darted a quick, accusing look at his grinning friend. 'You wretched Welshman,' he said, beginning to smile himself. 'She's right, I *should* know you by now.'

Sir Owen gave a delighted laugh. 'I'm sorry, Thomas, but you make such splendid sport. *Duw*, you rise as sweetly as the finest trout!'

Lord Elgin poured himself another glass of liqueur and then replenished the others on the table. 'I don't know why I agree to invite you to my house.'

Lady Elgin sat back. 'Miss Meredith and I were just discussing your horrid stones, Thomas,' she said with a very straight face, 'and we've decided that since they've caused so much trouble, we'll go down directly to your stone shop and topple everything over. That will end the argument once and for all.'

He was appalled. 'You wouldn't do such a thing!'

Sir Owen almost choked with laughter.

'You're squawking again, Thomas!'

Lord Elgin looked reproachfully at them all. 'Well, I *have* had a great deal to put up with since I brought those antiquities back here,' he grumbled. 'Half London would hang me for a thief, the rest say I'm history's savior.'

Sir Owen took a deep breath to stop his laughter and then nodded sympathetically. 'I know, my friend, and so I won't provoke you anymore tonight. Mind you, that doesn't mean I won't set about you again the next time we meet.'

'I've no doubt.'

'Actually, it so happens that I agree with what you've done, for those marbles would indeed soon cease to exist if left to the Turks' tender mercies. Now, then, shall we talk about something less contentious?' Sir Owen raised his eyebrows and surveyed the table.

Lady Elgin smiled sleekly. 'Oh, yes, *do* let's change the subject. I'm tired of ancient stones and regencies.'

Her husband reached over to put his hand over hers. 'Forgive me ten times over, my dear. What would you like to talk about?'

Her eyes became almost feline and she glanced deliberately at the two vacant chairs. 'How about absent friends?' she murmured.

He drew a long breath. 'I don't think

there's very much to talk about, is there? Vanessa's disappeared and James is keeping mum. *Finis*.'

'Oh, come now, Eggy,' she protested. 'I've been very good all evening. I haven't mentioned them once, even though I've been *dying* to. I did so hope James would come. I thought I'd worded the invitation quite perfectly, but I suppose we're acquaintances really, not close friends.' She looked at Sir Owen. 'You know them both quite well, don't you?'

'Ah! So that's why I've been dragged here tonight.'

'Don't be silly, of course it isn't.'

'Fibber.'

She smiled. 'Well, maybe it was, just a little.'

'I suppose I do know them quite well. I first met them shortly after their marriage when James commissioned me to paint three portraits of them together at Foxcombe.'

Roslyn hadn't met either of the Athertons and knew very little about them, in spite of all the recent gossip. 'Where's Foxcombe?' she inquired.

Her uncle smiled at her. 'In the hills above Cheltenham in Gloucestershire.'

Lady Elgin was impatient to get on with it. 'Would you have said they were in love, Sir Owen?'

He hesitated. 'He was in love with her,' he said at last.

She was triumphant. 'Ha! But *she* wasn't in love with *him*!'

'I don't think so, but perhaps my judgment has always been clouded by all that fuss before she finally accepted James instead of Sir Benedict Courtenay.'

Lady Elgin was scornful. 'What do you mean instead of? It wasn't like that at all. James's was the only honorable offer she had; Benedict's intentions were far more base. He's a handsome, dissolute rakehell, steeped in every vice imaginable. If he ever takes a wife, it will have to be a rich one, he's gambled away his entire fortune. Vanessa was, and is, penniless without James's wealth.' She glanced at Roslyn. 'Have you ever met Courtenay?'

'Yes, unfortunately.' Roslyn hadn't liked him in the slightest, finding him swaggering, vain, and far too aware of his devastating good looks. He had the build and figure to wear the most fashionable and excellent of clothes, and the sort of curling brown hair and flashing dark eyes that many women seemed to find irresistible. No doubt he could charm most birds down from the trees, but Roslyn Meredith wasn't one of them.

Nor, apparently, was Lady Elgin, who

smiled approvingly at her. 'I perceive that you are a woman of taste, Miss Meredith. He's a conceited coxcomb, and a dangerous one for any woman to fall in love with. He gambles to excess, isn't afraid to provoke quarrels because he's such a renowned shot, and is a libertine of the meanest order. How Vanessa could have dithered about accepting James because of a wretch like him I'll never know.'

Roslyn was curious. 'What happened?'

Lady Elgin drew a deep breath, eager to tell her everything. 'Vanessa came to London as an adventuress — '

Her husband interrupted with a protest. 'Oh, come now, she's of good family.'

'But impoverished.' She looked a little crossly at him and then continued. 'She came to London from Westmorland and took society by storm — much in the same way an actress can become the toast of Town. There were men in plenty eager to admire her, but very few equally as eager to make an honest woman of her. I'll warrant she had offers to set her up somewhere, but only one to put a ring on her finger first — from James.'

'Is she very lovely?'

Sir Owen nodded. 'Divine. She's the most magnificent woman I've ever seen, with shining black hair and eyes, and a complexion like porcelain. And her figure, oh, *duw*, it must have been fashioned in heaven.'

Lady Elgin didn't care to hear such praise. 'I grant you she has looks, but some who know her say she's quite obnoxious. She's a selfish, callous, attitudinizing *chienne*, and I only wish poor James had seen it before he so rashly asked her to marry him.' She paused dramatically. 'She only married James so that she could keep Benedict.'

Lord Elgin laughed scoffingly. 'That's rubbish!'

'It isn't.'

'Oh, yes it is. You claimed earlier that she came to London as an adventuress. If she did, she couldn't have done better than James Atherton, could she? He mightn't have the loftiest title in the realm, but he has one of the greatest fortunes, and he's young, handsome, dashing, and charming — in short, he's everything any adventuress worth her salt would make a beeline for. I don't think Benedict Courtenay entered into it. Besides, how could marrying James mean keeping Courtenay? It doesn't make sense.'

'It makes very good sense,' she replied. 'Benedict always has huge gambling debts, and when those debts begin to catch up with him, he begins an affair with the wife of a wealthy man. I've noticed the pattern, even if you haven't. There was the Duchess of

Strathame, the Countess of Lisbyrne, Lady Jennington, the Comtesse de la Vaire.' She marked them off with her fingers. 'Shall I go on?'

Lord Elgin stared at her. 'I hadn't thought — '

'You're too trusting in your fellow man, my love. Benedict likes married mistresses. Oh, he wouldn't be above an affair with Vanessa; he'd bed her without any intention of putting a ring on her finger, but she wouldn't do as a wife, she didn't have a fortune of her own. What if the duns began to close in on him while he was seeing her? He'd have to look elsewhere, wouldn't he? That's why she accepted James, so that she could dip into the Atherton thousands to help Benedict settle his debts, and in the process hold on to him.'

They were all staring at her now. Lord Elgin sat back, exhaling slowly. 'It has a horrid ring of truth about it, doesn't it?' he murmured.

Sir Owen gave a long, low whistle. 'It does indeed,' he said. 'And I think I know something that proves it to be the truth.'

It was a dramatic statement, and said with such overwhelming conviction that they all stared at him. A pin could have been heard to drop in the ensuing silence.

15

2

Then Lady Elgin sat up urgently. 'Tell us. Please.'

'Well, as you know, I was commissioned by James to go to Foxcombe not long after their marriage to paint three portraits of them together. For one of them he wanted her to wear his late mother's favorite topaz necklace and earrings — it seems that Vanessa had been given the use of the Atherton jewels on her wedding day, every new Lady Atherton has them.'

Lady Elgin was impatient. 'Yes, yes. Oh, do go on! What happened?'

'Vanessa became quite upset at the request, although James was most reasonable and didn't press the point. She said that she'd decided to wear her mauve silk gown and topazes wouldn't go with it at all. Maybe she was right, I couldn't say, but sometimes the most unexpected shades blend very sweetly. All I know is that it would have been the simplest thing in the world for her to oblige him and just wear a different gown — heaven knows, she had enough in her wardrobe. But no, she refused to wear the topazes and

16

insisted on the mauve gown. The gown wasn't one of her finest, by any means, and I'm sure she knew it, but she wouldn't be moved. In fact, she became worked up about it out of all proportion.' He paused, looking around at them all. 'With hindsight, I think that her reason for behaving like that was that the topazes were no longer in her possession, but had been given to her lover.'

Lord Elgin wasn't totally convinced. 'I admit that it's very pat and could indeed be the truth, but it doesn't explain why Vanessa dashed off as she did. Why did she go? And where? She can't have taken the jewels with her, the story would have got out if she had; they form far too important a part of the Atherton estate. Besides, Courtenay is hardly living like Croesus at the moment, is he? Oh, I admit he's had a winning streak at the green baize and isn't looking over his shoulders for the duns, but he's living on what he's winning, I'm sure of it. If Vanessa had rushed off to him with the jewels, I'd expect more sign of it, wouldn't you?'

Lady Elgin pouted a little disappointedly. 'Yes, I suppose I would.'

'So we have a very fine theory, but there are things about it that don't ring true.'

'I suppose you're right,' she conceded reluctantly.

Sir Owen pursed his lips. 'I'm still convinced that what Lady Elgin says is what happened. I was there when James asked her to wear those topazes, and I *know* she was frightened. It didn't strike me at the time, but it most certainly does now.'

Lord Elgin grinned. 'Well, don't let Lady Gallermayne hear you say it or she'll breathe fire and brimstone over you.'

'*Duw*, is she in Town?'

'Brought posthaste by the scandal. She can't abide scandal, as you probably know.'

Roslyn looked at Lord Elgin. 'Who is Lady Gallermayne?'

'James Atherton's paternal aunt, a dragon of a woman who abhors any sly whispering about her family. She'll be appalled by all this, you mark my words. Lord help anyone she overhears mentioning it, that's all I can say. Lord help James too, for his attitude hasn't helped. He could have silenced the whispers by inventing some plausible reason for Vanessa's absence, but instead he's held his tongue and fueled speculation. His aunt will not be best pleased, of that you may be sure.'

'You make it sound as if Lord Atherton goes in fear of his aunt,' said Roslyn rather curiously.

Lord Elgin smiled. 'Oh, no, it isn't like

that. James isn't afraid of anyone, but he does respect Lady Gallermayne, and he treats her very handsomely indeed, considering she's the difficult woman she is.'

Roslyn wanted to know more. 'What's he like?' she ventured.

Lady Elgin looked at her in astonishment. 'Your memory is amazingly short, Miss Meredith.'

'Is it? Why? Have I met him?' Roslyn was taken aback, for she was sure Lord Atherton had never been presented to her.

'Met him? No, but you've spent an entire evening gazing wistfully at him.'

Color leapt into Roslyn's cheeks. 'I — I have?'

'At the theater last week. He was the divine gentleman in the box opposite, the one you couldn't tear your eyes from throughout the performance.'

Now Roslyn's cheeks were burning. She remembered the gentleman very well. He'd caught her eye the moment he'd sat down alone in the other box. He'd been tall and elegant, with golden hair and eyes so clear and blue she could see their color across the auditorium. He'd been wearing formal black, a tight velvet evening coat that suited his fine figure very well, and there had been a particularly costly solitaire diamond sparkling

19

in the folds of his lace-edged cravat. He'd lounged in his chair, staring down at the stage without really seeing the performers. When the audience had laughed at the amusing comedy, he'd seemed unaware of anything. An air of melancholy surrounded him, drawing her full attention. She'd thought him devastatingly handsome, easily the most attractive man she'd seen since coming to the capital. Somewhat embarrassed at having been observed by Lady Elgin watching him so intently, she gave a flustered smile. 'That — that was Lord Atherton?'

'The very same.'

'I would have thought that with all the rumors he would have attracted more attention.'

'He would, if people had known he was there. Our box was one of the few from where he could be seen. He pulled the draperies forward, if you recall, and he arrived after the performance had begun, and left before it ended. To be perfectly honest, I was rather surprised he attended at all.'

'I wasn't,' inserted Sir Owen. 'The play was the one he and Vanessa attended on the eve of their wedding.'

'Oh.'

Roslyn lowered her eyes. 'No wonder he looked so sad.'

Lady Elgin's sharp eyes moved toward her. 'He's amazingly good-looking, isn't he?' she murmured.

'Yes.'

'And you can't believe that his wife would prefer someone like Benedict Courtenay?'

'No.'

Lady Elgin smiled, glancing at Sir Owen. 'Sir, I do believe your niece is smitten, and understandably so, for James Atherton is without a doubt the most delicious man in England. Present company excepted, of course,' she added, leaning over to put her cool hand over her husband's.

Roslyn's cheeks were now aflame.

Lord Elgin looked displeased, not liking the way his wife praised the attractions of another man. 'Oh, to be sure, Atherton's a veritable angel, but can't we talk about something else? Such as the forthcoming excursion to Greece that Sir Owen is now persuaded to undertake with Miss Meredith?'

Lady Elgin was taken aback. 'They're off to Greece?'

Lord Elgin nodded.

Roslyn looked askance at her uncle. 'Uncle Owen?'

'It's true, *cariad*. Thomas here has persuaded me.'

'But . . . ' Her voice died away. She longed

21

to see Greece, but had recently discovered how desperate her uncle's financial situation was. A visit abroad was surely out of the question.

He read her thoughts. 'It's all right, sweetheart,' he said reassuringly. 'I can manage it without too much difficulty, and besides, Thomas has recommended some excellent investments that should come to handsome fruition by the time we return.'

'But what about your studio?'

'I'm tired of the drudgery of face-painting and would much prefer the joy of sketching classical landscapes. It's something I've always wanted to do, but have denied myself until now. My pupils and assistants can get on with things in my absence, rattling off backgrounds, et cetera, so that all I'll need to do on my return is perform the physogs.' He chuckled then. 'Besides, it would suit me handsomely to scuttle away from London for a while. I'm being pursued by Lady Ferney to perform her likeness.'

Lady Elgin raised an eyebrow. 'Courtenay's sister? I thought she and her dolt of a husband were still in Ireland.'

'They're very much in Town, and she's determined to be daubed for posterity, as Britannia, would you believe?'

Lord Elgin smothered a laugh. 'Good God.

That's not how *I* see her.'

'Nor I,' agreed Sir Owen. 'I think her much more in the mold of a Lady Macbeth. Dagger and all,' he added.

Lady Elgin was highly amused. 'She's certainly a Courtenay to her fingertips, as sharp-clawed as they come. No wonder she and dear Vanessa got on so famously. But we digress, we were talking about the visit to Greece. When do you leave, Sir Owen?'

'Early next month, on the frigate *Volage*, at least so I understand.' He looked inquiringly at Lord Elgin.

That gentleman nodded. 'Yes, the *Volage*. I happen to know she's sailing then. You'll have a month or so in Greece then before returning on the *Hydra*.'

His wife smiled. 'Isn't that the transport ship bringing back your last shipment of antiquities?'

'From Pireaus on April the eleventh. I shall give Sir Owen a letter of introduction to my agent there, Giovanni Lusieri.'

Rosyln was amused. 'That's not a Greek name, sir.'

'No, he's a Neapolitan painter I've engaged to draw the Parthenon for me. He lives in Athens with his family and is a very helpful and reliable fellow.'

She looked at her uncle again. 'Are you

sure it's all right for us to go? The lease on the house — '

'Runs out next month. Yes, I know. Thomas has very kindly offered us this house on our return.'

Lady Elgin clapped her hands delightedly. 'Of course! Thomas and I are going to Scotland for the summer. Oh, how excellent. You mustn't worry, Miss Meredith, for you'll have a fine roof over your head, and I'm sure the investments Thomas has recommended will come sailing in.'

Roslyn smiled then, suddenly reassured about the whole thing. Greece! It was a land she'd always wanted to see, and now, quite out of the blue, she was going to go there.

Lady Elgin sat back, toying with her fan. 'Isn't Lord Byron in Greece now?'

Her husband's smile faded. 'I really couldn't say,' he said stiffly, revealing his dislike for the rising young poet. 'Why do you ask?'

'Oh, I suddenly remembered that night at Melbourne House when Vanessa Atherton set herself up as critic extraordinary and positively shredded his volume of poems. What was it called now? *Hours of Idleness*? Yes, that was it. Well, what Vanessa knows about poetry could be written on the back of my hand, but she had the impudence and

24

audacity to stand up in front of the whole assembly and cut him into tiny pieces. Poor Lord Byron, he'd already suffered excruciating reviews in the *Monthly Mirror*, the *Satirist*, and the *Edinburgh Review*, and then he had to stand there and listen to that vain, opinionated chit pronouncing her idiotic verdict as well. I thought poor James would die of embarrassment. As for Lord Byron, well, I didn't think he'd manage to keep his hands from her silly throat.'

'He had to,' interposed her husband. 'Prinny was present.'

'Oh, yes, so he was. What a pity, Lord B. might have rid us of her right there and then. Do you remember that night, Eggy? She posed this way and then that, holding court as if every word she uttered was of profound importance. Conceited creature. Lord Byron was beside himself. He can't take criticism at the best of times, and she really went beyond the pale. I heard him say later that he'd have his revenge, no matter how long he had to wait. He meant it too, he won't let her get away with that.' Lady Elgin chuckled. 'His vanity matches hers, I fancy.'

'I'll agree with you there,' said Lord Elgin, who disliked the poet because he more than anyone else had been responsible for the furor and debate surrounding the marble antiquities now reposing at the back of the house. He had written scathing words on the matter and had set the whole argument in motion. Lord Elgin drew a long breath. 'Athens is going to be rather crowded, isn't it, *mes enfants?*'

Sir Owen looked inquiringly at him. 'What do you mean?'

'Well, you and Miss Meredith will be there, so will Lord Byron — and so will James Atherton.'

Lady Elgin stared at him. 'James is going to Greece?'

'I saw him at White's recently. He told me then that he intended to go.'

Lady Elgin's lips pursed knowingly and her clever glance slid toward Roslyn. 'Well, well,' she murmured, 'just think, you might encounter him there, Miss Meredith.' Then she tossed her napkin on the table, picked up her fan, and got to her feet. 'But for the moment we must leave the gentlemen to their port.' She swept out in a rustle of pale-green silk, the draft she caused making the candles sway.

As Roslyn followed her, she hoped that she would encounter Lord Atherton in Greece, for he'd made more than a small impression upon her the night she'd looked across the auditorium and seen him for the first time. She wanted to meet him. She wanted to know him better.

3

Athens extended from the foot of the Acropolis in a sea of white, red-roofed houses, and was very bright in the clear, early-April sun. It was a city of some ten thousand inhabitants, mostly a mixture of Greeks, Turks, and Albanians, and was ruled by the infamous Ali Pasha, absolute overlord of Albania, from his fortress at Jannina. Ali Pasha's domains extended over macedonia and western Greece, and he was a cruel, much-feared man; but to Europeans like Roslyn and her uncle, he was magnanimous and almost gracious.

Roslyn sat on the dry, springy grass of the Acropolis, in the shade of a cypress tree close to the Parthenon itself. Sir Owen was at his easel a little distance away. He was her only chaperone because her maid had left her service to marry just before the *Volage* had set sail. It was a little awkward being without a maid, especially when it came to putting up her hair. There were surprisingly many social gatherings for the small European community and she found it difficult to achieve a suitably elegant coiffure. By coincidence, her uncle was without his valet, his man having in the past proved such a poor traveler that it was decided on this occasion that he should remain behind in London. If the truth were known, Sir Owen was quite self-sufficient and enjoyed looking after himself from time to time, but then balding gentlemen did not have to greatly concern themselves with the latest hairstyles.

Roslyn felt good as she sat beneath the tree in her short-sleeved lilac muslin gown, her wide-brimmed gypsy hat discarded on the grass beside her next to her portable writing case. Her tawny-blond hair shone in the dappled sunlight and she felt pleasantly warm. She'd expected the Greek spring to be much more advanced than England's, but not quite as much as this. It was like an English June. Everyone had commented upon the unusually fine weather, so that the few rainy days there had been had been much more noticeable.

The *Volage* had set sail at the beginning of February. England had been cold and frosty, and London had still been buzzing about Vanessa Atherton's disappearance. Lady Gallermayne's presence in the capital hadn't silenced the rumors in the slightest, and James Atherton's departure for Greece had done nothing to help. Benedict Courtenay had been loudly expressing his mystification concerning the whole business, and everyone had been convinced he was indeed innocent. So where was Lady Atherton? It was a puzzle that promised to simmer indefinitely, and it had certainly occupied Roslyn's thoughts a great deal during the stormy, month-long voyage to Piraeus.

When she and her uncle had arrived in Athens at the beginning of March, they'd repaired immediately to the residence of Lord Elgin's agent, Lusieri. On their behalf he'd approached a certain Mrs Tarsia Macri, widow of the former British vice-consul, a lady who often provided lodgings for British visitors in her spacious double house near the foot of the Acropolis. She'd gladly offered them comfortable accommodations.

The moment they'd settled in, it had been Sir Owen's purpose to climb the Acropolis and commence sketching, but this hadn't been possible because they were refused permission to set foot on the hill until they'd sent a suitable present to the *disdar*, the Turkish governor's subordinate in charge. Only when such a present had been sent was permission given, and almost a week after their arrival they'd at last climbed the fabled rock and gazed upon the most famous classical ruins in the world. They'd made the climb every day since.

Now it was the beginning of April, and in barely a week's time they would be leaving for England again. Roslyn drew a long breath. Soon this visit of a lifetime would be over. She glanced down at the portable writing case she'd brought with her. Usually she read, but today she'd been intermittently engaged upon a long-overdue letter to Mrs March, the cook-housekeeper at the manor house in Monmouthshire. This lady had been almost a mother to her, but had declined to leave the seclusion of the countryside for the rigors of the capital, and so had retired to live with a married sister in Chepstow. Roslyn had been sad to part from her, and had been determined not to lose touch. She'd written regularly, but the voyage and the excitement of being in Greece had been a considerable distraction. Now she was attempting to make amends, but there was so much to look at that her pen was frequently idle.

There was evidence of Turkish occupation everywhere; the Parthenon even sported a minaret. Fierce-eyed, turbaned janissaries were on guard in their baggy pantaloons and embroidered shirts, with awesome scimitars and daggers thrust into their wide sashes. There were strings of camels waiting by the scaffolding that had been erected around the Parthenon by Lord Elgin's men, so that the stonework could be sketched in detail or removed entirely and taken down to Piraeus by the camels to the transport ship *Hydra*, on which Roslyn and her uncle were to leave for England again in a few days' time. The scaffolding had caused much difficulty in the beginning, the Turks objecting to it because infidels working there could look down into the garden of the harem ensconced in the nearby Erechtheum. The problem had been solved to everyone's satisfaction by the prudent use of large canvas sheets around the outside of the scaffolding, shutting off the view.

Roslyn smiled as she looked at it, for on several occasions there had been disturbances because one of the watchful janissaries had been convinced that the workmen were more interested in the harem than the Parthenon, and Lusieri had been hard put to calm the situation so that work could continue. She glanced at her fob watch. Soon it would be time to return to Mrs Macri's for dinner. She pulled a face, for Greek cooking wasn't to her taste, being much too oily, and Mrs Macri's seemed particularly so.

The landlady's last British guests had been a party including Lord Byron, who had suffered at Vanessa Atherton's hands at Melbourne House. He had earned himself a considerable reputation in Athens for his adventures with the fair sex, and this side of his nature had led to a major upset in the Macri household when he'd been accused of a misdemeanor with the youngest of the landlady's three nubile daughters. He'd been abruptly requested to leave and had done so the week before Roslyn and her uncle had arrived. Now he resided in the nearby Capuchin monastery. The incident had been much talked about at the various functions Roslyn had attended, and from her own observations of the handsome lord, she was inclined to believe him guilty. She found him oddly disturbing. He was vain and prone to being unnecessarily sarcastic, and she'd done her utmost to avoid him, but such conduct on her part only seemed to attract him the more. He'd pursued her at every opportunity when they happened to find themselves at the same venue. She didn't know why he did it, she was sure he didn't have her seduction in mind. Maybe he was simply trying to irritate her; he was quite capable of amusing himself in such a way.

But if Lord Byron was being disagreeably attentive, James, Lord Atherton, was proving completely elusive. The scandal of his wife's disappearance rang through Athens drawing rooms as loudly as those in London, but he'd given no answers to the questions and had now left the city to travel south. Roslyn hadn't encountered him and was resigned to the fact that she simply wasn't destined to meet the man who'd so caught her attention that night at the theater.

She leaned back against the tree. The scent of orange blossom drifted over her from a grove farther down the hill. It was an alien scent, but there wasn't anything alien about the noise of the rooks circling above the Parthenon. Their raucous cries evoked memories of other rooks that had called in the elms near her Monmouthshire manor house.

Nearby, Sir Owen shifted his position on his little stool. She glanced toward him, smiling. He'd been in his element since they'd arrived, and his financial problems had become but a vague memory. Each morning after breakfast he climbed the Acropolis with his various implements, one of Mrs Macri's many menservants carrying the more cumbersome easel. The janissaries were used to him now, taking little notice as he put on his green eyeshade and dark-lensed spectacles to protect his eyes from the glare of the Greek sun. He then sat at the easel all day, sketching and painting until the light began to fade and it was time to go down once more, and he became so engrossed in what he was doing that he was completely oblivious to everything else around him.

Taking a deep breath, Roslyn applied herself to her letter again, dipping her pen in the little silver inkwell, but as she did so, a shadow suddenly fell across the paper, making her gasp and look up.

Lord Byron stood there. 'Good afternoon, Miss Meredith. Athens may be infested with the British, but you are so delightful an infestation that I shall forgive you.' He smiled, his melting brown eyes warm and knowing.

He cut a very extravagant figure in a brilliant red-and-gold Albanian costume that had been a gift from Ali Pasha himself. A scarflike matching hat was wound around his profusion of reddish-chestnut curls, and draped down over the shoulder of his crimson velvet jacket. His waistcoat was embellished with gold lace, and he had on a long white kilt. There were silver-mounted pistols and daggers thrust into his sash, and there was a swagger about him which told that he was well aware of how handsome and dashing he looked, and how important with his constant entourage of Albanian servants. They stood nearby now, peering secretly over Sir Owen's unknowing shoulder and whispering together.

The artist remained engrossed in his work, as if he were totally alone on the hill.

Lord Byron continued to hold her gaze. At twenty-three he was a practiced poseur, with a very high opinion of his looks and talent. He strove always to convey an impression of smoldering passion, and had perfected an intense way of glancing from beneath his curving, lowered lashes, at the same time making his voice sound low, musical, and caressing. Amused by her startled silence, he spoke again. 'I said good afternoon, Miss Meredith.'

'Good afternoon, Lord Byron,' she replied reluctantly.

His shrewd glance moved over her. 'I cannot believe you find it stimulating to sit there writing letters when you have the Parthenon itself upon which to feast your eyes.'

'I've been feasting my eyes on the Parthenon for many days now, sir.'

'And now you're tired of it?'

'Now I'm trying to get on with my letter,' she replied, hoping he'd take the hint.

He didn't, but a light passed through his magnificent eyes and she knew he was well aware of her thoughts. 'I came here for inspiration for my next poem,' he said, turning to glance deliberately toward the scaffolding on the Parthenon, 'and I do believe I've found it. Yes, I think I shall condemn that rapacious despoiler of Greece, your friend Thomas Bruce.'

She sighed inside. This wasn't the first time he'd taunted her about her connection with Lord Elgin. 'Sir, are you suggesting that Lord Elgin has been stealing the antiquities?'

'Yes, as surely as any low brigand makes off with booty.'

'But he paid a very good price for them,' she pointed out.

'To the Turks, who have no right to sell. Those stones belong to Greece, Miss Meredith, not to Constantinople, or to Thomas Bruce, God rot his cold Caledonian soul.'

'Better they be preserved by a cold Caledonian soul than not preserved at all,' she answered.

'Miss Meredith,' he chided, wagging a pale finger, 'you're a wicked Elginite and therefore quite beyond redemption. Beware, for the curse of Minerva will soon be upon him, and upon his supporters.'

She wished he'd go away. 'You have Minerva's ear, I suppose,' she inquired dryly.

This amused him. 'No, I don't claim direct contact with Olympus.'

'You do surprise me.'

He grinned broadly at that. 'Oh, no, Miss

36

Meredith, *you* surprise *me*.'

'I do?'

'Yes. I was given to understand that you were a retiring country mouse with a dread of society, but you don't seem that to me, you're a drawing room creature if I ever met one. And you have a way of looking at me that suggests most strongly you've been paying attention to the old witch Macri.'

She flushed a little. 'And what could Mrs Macri have to say about you, my lord?'

'A great deal, since I refused to purchase her youngest daughter. The old harridan wanted thirty thousand piasters, a fortune to make a lady of a Macri. *She* should have offered to pay *me*!'

It was interesting to hear his side of the story, but what he was saying wasn't very proper. 'Are you trying to shock me, sir?'

'Am I succeeding?'

'Not particularly.'

'Then I'm not trying.' He grinned again and his face was suddenly boyish, as if he'd relaxed in some way and become more natural. 'Tell me, Miss Meredith, has the old witch been drowning your food in oil? She did mine. At the monastery I now dine handsomely on red mullet and woodcock, and with hardly a drop of oil in sight. It's most agreeable. I'll warrant there's a horrendous oily fish pilaf waiting for you on your return. Sir Owen will soon be lamenting the absence of good roast beef and beer, all her British guests do in the end.'

Reluctantly she smiled, because her uncle had been doing that for some time.

Suddenly Lord Byron turned and waved his entourage away to a discreet distance. They obeyed immediately, and Sir Owen continued painting, still unaware that anyone else was nearby. Then the poet sat down beside Roslyn, leaning back against the tree, his shoulder brushing hers. She moved uneasily away and he smiled. 'Don't be alarmed, Miss Meredith, I'm not about to assault your virtue. I've merely decided that I like you and that therefore I should be more polite to you.'

'I'm honored,' she replied guardedly. She didn't trust him; he was quite capable of saying one thing and meaning another.

'Don't be suspicious, I promise you I'm being perfectly honest.' He looked beyond her toward the Parthenon. 'What's your opinion of Greece?' he asked.

'It's very beautiful.'

'Beautiful? Yes, I suppose it is, but beyond that outer beauty is the decay of something that was once perfect. Greece is being crushed beneath the Turkish heel, but will one day rise against her oppressors and be free again. It may interest you to know that until I came here I too supported Elgin for removing the Parthenon marbles to safety. I can't feel that way now, because I can't be indifferent to Greece. She needs her treasures, Miss Meredith, they belong to her, not to us.'

She didn't say anything.

With a sudden change of mood, he glanced toward Sir Owen, who still remained blissfully unaware of anything but the painting on his easel. 'Good Sir Owen appears to be enjoying himself.'

'He is. He's always wanted to come here. As I have, I suppose.'

'When you say here, do you mean just Athens? Or the whole of Greece?'

There was an odd note in his voice and she looked curiously at him. 'Greece in general. Why?'

'Because if that's the case then there's one place you must see before you leave, the temple of Poseidon at Ayios Georghios, about twenty miles south of here on the coast of Attica. It stands on a cliff overlooking the Aegean, and the sunsets have to be seen to be believed.' His voice took on a dreaming tone. 'The eye sees forever through a golden haze, past a score or more of melting islands into infinity itself,' he murmured. 'It's a moving experience, Miss Meredith, one that everyone should know at least once in their life.'

'It sounds very lovely. I wish we'd gone there now.'

'You still have time.'

She shook her head. 'The *Hydra* leaves on the eleventh.'

'No, she doesn't sail until the twenty-fourth now. I believe there was some difficulties with the Caledonian brigand's stolen stones.' He smiled a little. 'You have more than enough time to visit Poseidon's roost if you wish.'

'How do you know about the *Hydra*'s sailing date?' she asked.

'I'm sailing on her myself, and word was sent to me at the monastery this morning. No doubt a similar missive awaits you at Witch Macri's. Please consider Ayios Georghios, Miss Meredith, you won't regret it if you go. And if anyone should attempt to deter you by talking of pirates — '

'Pirates?'

'They aren't of any consequence at the moment, especially at Ayios Georghios, where some armed Turkish ships are at anchor in the next bay and keep danger well and truly away. If you go, you must be certain to stay with Constantin Niphakos. He's the *cogia basha*, the governor of the district, and he owns the only house of consequence in the town, an extremely large and elegant villa on the hillside between the sea and the clifftop where the temple stands. He's a wealthy Greek, and although he has Turkish masters, you won't find much Turkish influence in his district. It's an enclave of old Greece. You'll find it quite perfect, I promise you.' His dark eyes rested almost intensely on her.

He seemed inordinately anxious that she and her uncle should go to this place.

'Lord Byron — ' she began, but he got up immediately, halting her question by speaking again of her uncle.

'Doesn't he fear catching a fever sitting in the sun like that?'

'It seems not. Lord Byron — '

He looked down at her. 'Go to Ayios Georghios, Miss Meredith, and remember that it is at Constantin Niphakos's house that you must stay. You'll find the company, er, interesting.'

She looked at him in some confusion. 'Company? What do you mean?'

'James Atherton's staying there. Providentially without his *chienne* of a wife.'

She stared at him, caught completely off guard.

A knowing smile touched his lips, and before she could say anything more, he left her to go over to her uncle, making him jump by suddenly placing a hand on his shoulder.

They spoke together for a while. She couldn't hear what they were saying but she knew that Lord Byron was now busily engaged upon persuading the artist that he simply *had* to visit Ayios Georghios before returning to England.

When the poet and his strange entourage at last walked away, Roslyn stared after them. She was quite shaken that somehow Lord Byron knew about her interest in James Atherton. Of what possible concern was it to him? Why was he so keen that she and her uncle should go to Ayios Georghios? Why did he want her to meet James Atherton?

4

Whatever Lord Byron had said to Sir Owen certainly fired him with enthusiasm, for two days later he and Roslyn set off on horse-back for Ayios Georghios and the house of the governor, Constantin Niphakos, who had been notified to expect them. They left Athens early on the morning their *firman* was issued, it being impossible to travel anywhere in Greece without a Turkish travel permit, and they took with them two mounted Greek guides and two packhorses carrying all they'd need for a short visit. The rest of their belongings they left with Mrs Macri.

From the moment Sir Owen had learned about Ayios Georghios, its temple and miraculous sunsets, he'd talked of little else. It had occupied him over Mrs Macri's oily fish pilafs and while he enjoyed a final glass of retsina on the vine-hung balcony afterward. His mind was made up, and now that the *Hydra's* sailing date had been postponed, nothing was going to stop him from traveling south to see the glories for himself.

Roslyn had remained uneasy about the whole thing, because she knew full well that there was something behind Lord Byron's recommendation, something that had nothing to do with a desire to assist her uncle in the furtherance of his artistic quest, and everything to do with a wish to see Sir Owen's niece making James Atherton's acquaintance. No matter how much she thought about it, she couldn't arrive at a satisfactory explanation. And she was ashamed to admit, even to herself, that she was making very little protest about the whole business, because she so very much wanted to meet the mysterious Lord Atherton.

And so here they were two days later, leaving Athens far behind as they rode through the warm Greek countryside. In front of them, leading the packhorses, the two guides laughed and talked together. They looked very dashing with their flowing black hair, red jerkins, and flapping white skirts, and they maneuvered their nimble ponies easily along the dusty road. Their cheerfulness only vanished when they encountered Turks, which happened quite frequently because there were garrisons along the way. Sometimes Turkish horsemen rode past, and when they'd passed, the guides spat in unison on the ground.

The higher the sun rose in the morning sky, the hotter and more uncomfortable

Roslyn began to feel in her dark-green wool riding habit and veiled beaver hat. Such clothes were far from practical in such a climate, but were all she had for riding. Sir Owen looked scarcely less hot as he bounced along on his sturdy gray mount, occasionally removing his hat to waft it to and fro before his rosy face.

They passed soft, whitewashed villages lying among protective hills, and pretty churches surrounded by walls. Washing dried on trees and shrubs in gardens, and outside the tavernas, men sat in the sun enjoying glasses of ouzo.

Rich vineyards stretched up from the side of the track, and silver-green olive groves were scattered on the slopes farther up, mingling with terraces of ancient cypresses. Occasionally a turreted dovecote shone white among the trees, and from time to time they rode past wayside shrines adorned with flowers.

The morning passed in a haze of sunshine, scenery, and flowers, for this was the season of flowers in Greece. They carpeted the ground in swirls of fresh, clear colors, from the drifts of creamy narcissi blooming in the hollows, to the pools of blue grape-hyacinths growing among the sun-warmed rocks. Tall gray-white asphodel, the immortal flower of

Elysium, spread across the open hillsides, and sweet-smelling pink oleanders marked the beds of streams. There was an endless echoing of birdsong and sometimes the babble of hidden water, while in the distance the air was punctuated now and then with the tinkle of goat bells.

Pine-clad mountains, snow-capped against the clear blue of the sky, rose ahead as they broke their journey to rest the horses and eat by an isolated ruined sanctuary shaded by tall cypress trees. A tiny stream flowed softly between banks of ferns, and the horses gladly dipped their muzzles in its coolness. The guides had brought their own food and sat apart, talking easily. Roslyn and Sir Owen sat beneath one of the cypresses and opened the covered wicker basket Mrs Macri had provided for them. For a moment they feared they might find it contained something horribly oily, like stuffed vine leaves, but to their relief there was fresh-baked bread, thick slices of ham, and two kinds of cheese. There was also an earthenware jar of white wine, mercifully not retsina, which Roslyn disliked because of its harsh resin taste, and two cups to drink it from.

It was good to sit there in such peaceful but different surroundings. England seemed another world. But England was evidently very much on Sir Owen's mind as he helped himself to a slice of ham. 'Oh, *duw*, how I wish this was good roast beef,' he grumbled.

She smothered a smile, remembering what Lord Byron had said.

'And what are you grinning at, may I ask?'

'Oh, nothing.'

'Only Bedlamites grin at nothing.'

'All right, I was recalling something Lord Byron said to me.'

'And what, pray, was that?'

'That Mrs Macri's British guests soon lamented the absence of good roast beef and beer.'

Sir Owen chuckled. 'He would appear to be a most perceptive fellow.'

She had to look away. Perceptive? He was positively psychic!

They rode on through the afternoon, the mountains looming ever nearer until at last the horses were making their way up through a pass where the air was fresh and cool and pine needles cushioned the sound of their hooves.

Evening shadows were beginning to lengthen when they emerged from the pass on to the ridge of a high escarpment facing south toward the peacock-blue Aegean. The islands Lord Byron had talked of floated indistinctly in the shimmering haze, seeming almost to sway toward the distant horizon. Ayios Georghios spread steeply up the lower slopes of a promontory that stood out sharply into the sea. At the seaward tip of this promontory, above cliffs two hundred feet high, stood the ruined temple of Poseidon, its columns a stark white against the blue of the sea and the sky, while at the landward end the undulating, sun-drenched hills rolled gradually up toward the escarpment. Ayios Georghios itself was a cluster of whitewashed houses spilling down toward a sheltered bay and a harbor in the very lee of the promontory. A maze of narrow streets and alleyways, it was approached from the north by the track from the escarpment, and from the east by another track that led down from the promontory through a tree-choked valley, emerging by a white church with a cupola from which radiated four red-tiled roofs, like a cross. From the church the track meandered on down the lower slopes toward the town, passing the only large house in evidence, a beautiful villa set in its own magnificent grounds, with terraced gardens, tall poplars, and lemon groves. Roslyn knew instinctively that it was the residence of the governor, Mr Niphakos.

The air was heady with the pungent scent of wild thyme and marjoram, and she thought she could taste the sea on her lips. Far out on the water, close to the nearest islands, she could see a small fleet of Turkish ships beating south toward the horizon. The church bell began to ring, the sound carrying so clearly that there was no sensation of distance at all. She drank in the magnificence of it all. This was surely one of the most beautiful places on earth.

The evening shadows were lengthening all the time as they rode down through another pine wood, emerging at last into a grove of yellow broom. They reached the first houses of the town about half an hour after this, the horses' hooves clattering on the cobbles that now studded the way. The houses and walled gardens kept the low sun out as the small party followed the street down toward the harbor. A small crowd of wide-eyed children came after them, and women seated in doorways watched curiously, looking at Roslyn in particular, for it wasn't every day that fine foreign ladies ventured to this part of Greece.

The leafy square by the harbor was the place where the men mended their yellow-and-brown fishing nets or attended to any repairs on their caïques. They all paused to watch as the party rode across the square and up the narrow lane leading from the other side. Even the donkeys standing beneath the trees with their empty panniers turned their heads to watch. There were other eyes too, Roslyn noticed, the feline eyes of the cats that seemed to have taken up residence on the caïques.

They left the town behind again, riding past a taverna where someone was singing and dancing inside, accompanied by much clapping. The final house and garden slipped away as they rode up the shrub-edged track toward the villa. Two waiting men flung open the villa gates as the weary horses turned off the track and on to the dusty drive that swept up through the gardens to the house, which had a fine terrace before it, commanding a panoramic view over the town and bay.

The villa was larger than Roslyn had thought. It was a wide, white building of two floors, and it had a vine-hung balcony extending across the whole of the upper floor. The main entrance appeared to be through a wide archway to the right of the terrace, and as Roslyn rode toward it, she was sure she could see a galleried courtyard beyond. The house was protected on the seaward side by a windbreak of dark-green poplars that shielded it from the violence of the winter storms that sometimes swept in against this southern edge of Greece. Like the country-side Roslyn had ridden through that day, the villa's gardens were a riot of flowers.

The scent of lemon blossom hung in the evening air as the small party passed below the edge of the terrace. Roslyn glanced up and saw a trellis of roses climbing up from the rough stone balustrade on the top. The roses were of a kind she'd never seen before, pretty single flowers with clear white petals blushing to a frill of deep pink around the edges. A wicker cage had been hung on the trellis and two canaries hopped from perch to perch in the fading evening light, singing whenever they paused.

Then the archway swallowed the travelers, and the horses' hooves rattled on cobbles as they emerged into the enclosed courtyard Roslyn had seen earlier. It was a large, airy place, shadowy now, where fountains splashed and servants hurried immediately to attend the weary guests and their mounts.

Sir Owen dismounted a little stiffly and then assisted Roslyn down. She shook out her heavy, dusty riding habit and swept the veil back from her face to look around. Terracotta pots of flowers and herbs stood around the sides of the courtyard, and the gallery above was leafy with vines. There was a cool peacefulness about everything, a very welcome change from the heat and the dust of the journey from Athens.

James Atherton was very much on her

mind in that brief moment, so much so that she turned with an expectant gasp as she heard male footsteps approaching a nearby doorway. But the man who emerged wasn't an English lord; he was a huge Greek dressed so finely in his national costume that he could only be their host, Mr Constantin Niphakos.

He was a mountain of a man in an embroidered white shirt, scarlet jerkin, and full white skirt. Thick black hair fell about his broad shoulders and he had a drooping mustache that had been combed and twisted very carefully into place. He was about forty-five years old, with brown, patrician eyes, and there was a likable ease in the way his full lips curved quickly into a welcoming smile.

'Yássas! Welcome! Welcome to Ayios Georghios and my house, which is now your house.' His voice was deep and guttural, and his English was good. He saluted them in the Turkish style, inclining his head and placing his hand upon his heart.

Sir Owen went to him, extending his hand. 'Sir Owen Meredith. Your servant, sir.'

'Constantin Niphakos, governor of this district.'

Sir Owen drew Roslyn forward. 'May I present my niece, Miss Meredith?'

The Greek bowed. 'Miss Meredith.'

'Sir.' She curtsied.

As servants led the horses away and a maid beckoned the two guides toward the kitchens, Mr Niphakos ushered his two guests into the house. 'Come this way, please. You must take some refreshment and be welcomed in the way of my country.'

The house was furnished in a mixture of Greek and Turkish styles, and was cool and airy. They were led into a large room with slatted doors standing open onto the terrace. The canaries could be heard singing in their cage on the rose trellis. The room was furnished with Eastern sofas and low tables, and there was a smell of sandalwood.

When they were all seated, their host clapped his hands and a young woman of about Roslyn's age came in with a silver tray on which stood a jar of preserves, some cups of thick black coffee, and glasses of water. She was dressed in a pale-blue robe and her braided black hair was coiled beneath a gold-embroidered blue cap. She was attractive, with flashing dark eyes and a clear olive complexion. As she set the tray carefully down, Mr Niphakos introduced her.

'This is my daughter, Christina. She is the mistress of this house now that her mother is no longer of this world.' He made the sign of the cross.

Christina smiled at them. 'Welcome to Ayios Georghios,' she said, her English evidently as good as her father's.

Roslyn was used to the welcoming custom of preserves, coffee, and water, having first come across it when arriving at Mrs Macri's house. The water was drunk first, then the preserves were taken, and finally the coffee was sipped at leisure. Both Mr Niphakos and his daughter were attentive and kindly, and their command of English was such that conversation with them was very easy indeed. Mr Niphakos had learned while staying at the house of a British diplomat in Athens, and he had sent his daughter there to learn the language as well.

When the coffee had been finished, Mr Niphakos informed his new guests that dinner would be served in an hour's time, and then he took Sir Owen up to his room. Christina led Roslyn to hers, and as they ascended the wide staircase, Roslyn brought herself to mention James Atherton. 'Is — is Lord Atherton still staying here?'

Christina halted. 'Yes. Do you know him?'

'I don't, but my uncle does. Will we be dining with him tonight?'

'I think so. He goes out riding each day and returns at about this time. He is very strange; he does not smile and he says very little.'

Christina looked apologetic. 'Maybe I should not say such things about another guest, but you see, I do not think he will be very pleased when he discovers that you have come to stay here.'

Roslyn stared at her. 'Doesn't he know about us?'

'No, the message from Athens was delayed and didn't reach here until after he'd gone for his ride this morning.' Christina met her gaze. 'When he came here, he told my father that he wished to escape for a while from everything that reminded him of England. And now you are here. I'm afraid he will not like it at all.'

5

Feeling decidedly uncomfortable, Roslyn said nothing more about James Atherton, and Christina continued up the staircase.

The rooms that had been prepared for her were at the front of the house, opening onto the balcony she'd seen when arriving. There was a bedroom and adjoining dressing room, their slatted doors standing open to the fading evening light and the soft breeze stirring the vines growing so profusely over the balcony. There was a magnificent view over the town and bay. The sun was setting fast now and the sea was a blaze of crimson and gold. The white-walled rooms were comfortably furnished, with thick, patterned rugs on the polished wooden floor. The ceiling was inlaid with wickerwork for coolness in summer, while the chill days of winter were provided for by an earthenware brazier in a corner. The bed had a blue-and-white coverlet, and there were matching curtains at the windows. A bowl of oranges stood on a table next to the bed, together with a bowl of the unusual white-and-pink roses she'd seen on the terrace where the canaries' cage had been hanging. The dressing room contained a table with a mirror on it and a stool that fitted neatly out of the way underneath. The wardrobe was so large that it took up a whole wall, and could have held three times the clothes Roslyn had brought with her.

As they entered the rooms, the men were still carrying her luggage into the dressing room, but when they'd gone, Christina looked a little questioningly at Roslyn. 'Excuse me, but you do not have a maid?'

'No, I'm afraid she left my service just before we sailed from London. She wanted to get married.'

'Then I must be your maid.'

Roslyn was. startled. 'Oh, no, I wouldn't dream — '

'My father will insist. It is *sostó*, it is what is correct.' Christina smiled. 'Maybe you will not mind so much if I say that you can help me by letting me be your maid.'

'I can? How?'

'By assisting me with my English and by telling me all about the fashions in London. I wish to be fashionable, Miss Meredith, and I do not like dressing like this.'

'But you look lovely like that.'

'I look plain, and from the country.'

Roslyn could sympathize with the latter

57

sentiment, for in the few weeks before she'd acquired her fashionable wardrobe, she'd felt exactly the same.

Christina looked hopefully at her. 'I can be your maid?'

'If you really wish to.'

'Oh, I do.'

'Then of course.'

'I shall be your second maid to be getting married.'

'You will?'

'Yes. I marry Theo next week. You and Sir Owen must come to the wedding.'

'It's very kind of you to ask.'

'It would not be *sostó* to leave you out. I do not think Lord Atherton will come, though,' she added.

Roslyn drew a long breath, wondering what James Atherton's reaction was going to be when he found that he had fellow guests.

Christina glanced at her. 'Lord Atherton hates weddings. He told my father.'

'He, er, has had some personal problems,' said Roslyn.

'Yes, I think you are right. He has been hoping for some news from England, but nothing has arrived so far. He isn't pleased when he asks each morning if the messenger has arrived from Athens and my father has to tell him there hasn't been any word. Lord

Atherton isn't pleased about anything,' she added almost as an aside.

Roslyn decided that James Atherton sounded a very uncomfortable guest.

Christina's thoughts returned to her wedding. 'So, you and Sir Owen will come?'

'We'd love to.'

'It will be in the church above here, and afterward there will be a feast in the lemon grove behind the house. It will be a great occasion, *ólos o kózmos*, all the world, will come.'

'It sounds very exciting.' Roslyn smiled at her.

'It will be the greatest day of my life. I love Theo.' Christina glanced at the roses on the table by the bed. 'Do you like them?'

'They're lovely. I haven't seen any like that before.'

'They are the Ayios Georghios rose, they only grow here. The priests say they began to grow when Saint George passed this way and was given shelter. Ah, here is the maid with the water for you to wash.'

A serving girl carried a bowl of warm water into the dressing room and then withdrew. Christina helped Roslyn out of the uncomfortable riding habit. It was good to wash away the dust and stickiness of the journey, and Roslyn took her time, savoring every refreshing moment.

Christina began to unpack her things, hanging the clothes up in the wardrobe, exclaiming with admiration at each one. It was almost dark now, the Greek twilight was short, and so she lit candles.

For dinner Roslyn elected to wear a dainty cream lawn gown with little petal sleeves. She soon discovered that Christina's interest in fashion went as far as hair-styles, and that when her father didn't know, she practiced dressing her hair in modish knots and curls instead of the strict braids he insisted upon. She soon had Roslyn's tawny-blond hair up into a creditable knot and had teased soft little curls around her face.

When she had finished, she surveyed her work rather proudly. 'I think that looks very nice, Miss Meredith. I shall have my hair like you have on the day of my wedding, whether my father wishes it or not.' There was determination in the dark eyes. 'And if he thinks my wedding gown is going to be Greek, he is wrong. Theo and I have talked and we are decided — I shall wear a dress like the Empress Josephine's at her coronation. It will be made of white muslin, with a brocade overrobe, and it will not look at all like the gown my mother wore, and her mother before her, and her mother before her.'

Christina grimaced. 'Now, then, I will leave you to be on your own for a while. I think you will be glad of a few minutes. Dinner will be served on the terrace in about a quarter of an hour. Will you remember how to get to the terrace, or would you like me to come back to lead you?'

'I'll remember. Thank you.'

Christina smiled and then went out.

Roslyn got up from the stool and went out onto the balcony. The bay was a deep indigo and the sky stained a full, fading crimson. On the headland the ruined temple was a black silhouette, while down below the town was beginning to twinkle with lights. The onset of darkness released the scent of flowers from the gardens, particularly the Ayios Georghios rose growing on the terrace immediately below.

As she looked down, she saw some maids putting the finishing touches to the dinner table, which stood close to the trellis and the canaries' cage. Shaded candles had been lit, casting a soft glow over the white cloth, gleaming glass, and silver cutlery. She noticed that it had been set for three; her uncle and herself, and presumably James Atherton.

She glanced along the balcony. On either side of her rooms a line of other slatted doors stretched away. One of the rooms was candlelit and she could hear her uncle humming to himself.

Drumming hoofbeats sounded through the gathering dusk and she saw a horseman riding swiftly toward the house. His top hat was tilted back on his head and she could see his bright golden hair. She recognized James Atherton immediately. He was a consummate rider, easily managing a mount that was very spirited indeed, tossing its head and fighting the bit every inch of the way. He wore a dark riding coat and breeches that clung to his thighs like a second skin. In the few seconds before he reached the terrace and the archway, she saw his face quite clearly. It was set and cold, as if all warmth had died within him. Then he passed out of her sight.

She heard the horse's hooves clattering in the courtyard as he dismounted, then there was a brief exchange of voices as he handed the reins to a groom. Shortly after this she heard him pass her door. A moment later candlelight appeared in a window beyond her uncle's room.

She remained where she was, gazing out at the sea. Apprehension filled her now that she was on the point of meeting him. From her own observation of his face as he'd ridden back to the house, and from what she'd heard from Christina, she was no longer sure she wanted to know the man she'd been so drawn to that night across the London theater.

A crashing noise suddenly pierced the silence, making her start and turn. The crash was followed by the muffled tinkle of breaking glass or crockery. The sounds had come from James Atherton's room. His shadow moved briefly past the window, a movement as abrupt and furious as the noises. Then there was silence again. Her uncle had evidently heard something; his humming had stopped, but after a moment he began again.

Roslyn stared at the candlelit window. What had happened? It had sounded as if something had been hurled against a wall with as much force as possible. The silence continued. It was as if she'd imagined everything.

Uneasily she returned to her own room to pick up her reticule and shawl and extinguished the candles. Christina was right about Lord Atherton, he appeared to be very strange, very strange indeed.

Going down through the house, she emerged onto the terrace just as a maid was placing an unexpectedly fashionable epergne in the center of the table. The canaries were still singing in their cage, and the scent of roses was stronger than ever. The maid smiled and bobbed a quick curtsy before hurrying away. The smell of cooking drifted from the kitchens, and Roslyn heard a man singing. The food smelled appetizing, more so than it ever had at Mrs Macri's. She hoped that the Niphakos household did not relish quite as much oil as her previous hostess.

She'd been standing there for some time when she heard footsteps approaching. Then James Atherton was silhouetted in the doorway, lamplight burning brightly behind him. He saw her immediately and halted, evidently taken completely by surprise. His hair was a brighter gold than she'd been expecting. It was tousled and rather unruly, and he wore it a little longer than present fashion dictated. It suited his fine-boned, aristocratic looks. He was dressed for dinner, but not formally so. His tight coat was the color of dark claret and had velvet facings and buttons. His gray waistcoat was made of costly figured silk, and his close-fitting trousers were cut from the very best charcoal corduroy. A jeweled pin glittered in the complex folds of his neck-cloth, flashing more brightly as he came toward her. His eyes were a cold, piercing blue as he addressed her in fluent Greek.

She didn't understand and smiled a little apologetically. 'F-forgive me, sir, but I'm British.'

A flash of deep displeasure leapt into his eyes. 'British?'

She could only nod.

'God damn it,' he snapped, his lips thin and bitter. 'I came here to avoid London, not to have it pursue me!'

She drew back, not having expected quite such a rude outburst, but before she could say anything more, he'd turned abruptly on his heel and was striding away. Her first encounter with James Atherton was over before it had begun.

6

Dumbfounded, Roslyn stared after him. All she could think was that although his looks were divine, his manners were those of the devil himself.

But then his departure was suddenly halted by the bustling figure of Sir Owen, who was hurrying out, thinking himself late for dinner.

James stared at him as if at a ghost. 'Sir Owen?' he inquired lamely.

'James, my boy! We meet again at last.'

'What on earth are you doing here?'

'We're staying for a while.'

'We?' James glanced uneasily back at Roslyn, belatedly wondering who she was.

Sir Owen followed the glance. 'Ah, I see you've already met my niece.'

'Your niece?' James drew a long breath and then shook his head. 'Er, no, we haven't been formally introduced.'

'Then allow me to do the honors.' Sir Owen took him firmly by the arm and ushered him back across the terrace. 'Roslyn, my dear, allow me to present Lord Atherton. James, this is my niece, Miss Meredith.'

James' blue eyes were cool and veiled and

he made no apology for his previous conduct; indeed, he behaved as if they hadn't spoken before. 'I'm pleased to make your acquaintance, Miss Meredith,' he murmured, reluctantly taking her hand and drawing it fleetingly toward his lips.

She accorded him the merest nod of her head. 'Sir.' The single word spoke volumes about her opinion of him.

Her uncle looked at her in surprise, but James gave no flicker of reaction, looking past her at the canaries, as if he found them infinitely more interesting. At last Sir Owen began to sense the atmosphere, realizing that something had happened in the few moments before he'd come onto the terrace. He cleared his throat uncomfortably, wondering what to say or do next.

Roslyn looked coldly at James and then turned away. His conduct was inexcusably bad and at the very least he should apologize for it, but she knew that he had no such intention. He resented the presence of his fellow guests and was making that resentment only too plain. He fell far short of her expectations, and if this was a fair sample of his general character, then her sympathies began to veer toward his wife, who maybe had excellent reason for leaving him.

To Sir Owen's relief, at that moment Mr

Niphakos appeared with a tray on which stood a bottle of ouzo, a jug of water, and a number of glasses. He was followed by Christina carrying a dish of *mezedes*, the appetizing tidbits always served before a Greek meal.

With great care and ceremony, Mr Niphakos poured the ouzo into the glasses, topping each one with water to turn the liquid milky, then he handed one to each of his guests. Taking one himself, he raised it to them in salute. '*Stiniyiá*. Your health!'

They returned the salute, but then James withdrew a little from the rest of them, going to stand by the balustrade to gaze down at the lights of the town. Mr Niphakos was evidently used to the English milord's uncommunicative manner, as was Christina, who shrugged expressively at Roslyn, but Sir Owen found it a great change after the warmer James Atherton he'd known at Foxcombe a few years before. For a moment he considered going to stand with him, but then Mr Niphakos began to talk to him about what he might like to sketch at the temple of Poseidon, and James's disagreeable behavior was set aside for the time being.

Christina left to attend to her duties shortly after this, and Roslyn found herself at liberty to study James without him knowing. Sipping her glass of ouzo, she looked at the silent figure by the balustrade. She was disappointed that he hadn't lived up to her secret expectations; at least, he hadn't as far as character was concerned, but when it came to looks, he was by far the most devastatingly handsome man she'd ever seen. The blue blood of centuries was evident in the fine-boned strength of his profile, and there was a sensuality about him, especially his lips, a suggestion of hidden depths that, once stirred, would more than melt their present coldness. But what would kindle that warmth? As she looked at him now, he seemed frozen, as if something deep within him had withered. She found herself wondering anew about his wife's disappearance. What had really happened? Was Lady Elgin right? Had Vanessa married him in order to pay Benedict Courtenay's debts?

Her thoughts were interrupted at that moment by the serving of the first course. Mr Niphakos departed, and as the three British guests sat down at the table, an uncomfortable silence descended over the terrace. Sir owen wasn't usually a reticent man, but even he was deterred by James's manner, which did not invite conversation of any kind.

As far as Roslyn was concerned, the only good thing about the meal was the dearth of oil. The thought of sitting at the table with James Atherton for the next week was too odious to contemplate.

By the time the dessert was served, Sir Owen could bear the silence no more and felt he had to make some attempt at conversation. He glanced at James. 'And how are you finding Greece, my friend?' he inquired in his rich Welsh voice.

'It does well enough.'

'Is that all you have to say about the land of the Hellenes?'

The blue eyes became irritated. 'What would you have me say?'

Roslyn glanced coldly at him. He really was the rudest person she'd ever come across.

Sir Owen sat back, studying him for a moment. 'What would I have you say? Well, the truth, I suppose.'

'Very well. I find Greece tedious.'

'I seem to recall you once telling me you longed to come here.'

'The reality has fallen far short of the dream.'

'I'm relieved to say that I haven't suffered the same disillusionment.'

'Being a single man, sir, there are many disillusionments you've been spared.'

'And many happinesses I've been denied. Come, now, James, aren't you being a little cynical?'

'I'm merely being truthful.'

'You've changed a great deal, and not for the better, I fear.' Sir Owen's voice was sad.

'I've changed because I'm no longer the dull-witted, blind fool I once was.' James tossed his napkin onto the table and got up. 'Nor am I in the mood to be drawn into discussing my private affairs in order to satisfy your unwarranted curiosity. That is what you've come here for, isn't it? My private life is my business, Sir Owen, not yours or your niece's, and I'll thank you to remember and respect that fact from now on.' Turning angrily on his heel, he strode away.

Like Rosyln before, Sir Owen now stared after him in utter amazement. 'Whatever's got into the fellow? If I hadn't seen and heard that for myself, I'd never have believed it. In fact, I still can't believe it. He's changed beyond all recognition. He was always a perfect gentleman, with wit and charm and an infinite capacity for making others enjoy his company. Now he appears to be sadly deficient in all those qualities.'

'Well, since I've already been exposed to his notion of gracious conduct, this latest episode doesn't surprise me in the slightest. He was unnecessarily rude to me before you came.'

'I guessed that something had happened.'

'Did you hear that crash earlier?'

'From his room? Yes. What was it, do you know?'

'No, but I'd say that James, Lord Atherton, doesn't only hurl insults, he hurls inanimate objects as well. I think he's most peculiar and can't imagine now why I ever wanted to meet him.'

'If you'd known him before, you'd have been very agreeably impressed, I promise you.'

'I'll have to take your word for that,' she replied dryly.

'Yes, well, if you *had* known him then, you'd have understood why everyone was so amazed when Vanessa hesitated before accepting him. Everyone knew Benedict Courtenay was her reason, and they all thought her quite mad.'

'After tonight's little performance, I begin to think that *I* would prefer Benedict Courtenay as well, obnoxious as he is. I can't help feeling that if this is a sample of how James Atherton goes on, then his wife was probably justified in leaving him.'

At that moment someone walked past the terrace where they sat. Roslyn recognized James' steps and got up quickly just in time to see him walking away down the drive. She sat down again. He must have heard what she'd said.

Sir Owen looked at her, his eyebrow raised. 'Is that your dainty foot in the proverbial, *cariad*?'

'I think so. But to be perfectly honest, I don't really care if it is. He doesn't deserve anything else after the way he's behaved tonight.'

'Maybe he doesn't, but I still remember the man he was before. This isn't the real James Atherton, Roslyn. Something has happened to make him like this, and until I know the facts, I'll not judge him. You shouldn't either. He was desperately in love with his wife, and I'd say that love hasn't diminished.'

★   ★   ★

Whatever the reason for James Atherton's poor behavior, and no matter how strongly Roslyn had reacted, he wasn't on her mind when she went to her bed that night; she was too tired for anything but rest. More weary than she'd realized after the journey from Athens, she slept very deeply, not stirring until quite late the next morning. She was awakened by the sound of voices in the garden. Slipping from the bed, she put on her green-and-white-spotted wrap, brushed her hair, and then stepped out onto the deserted balcony.

The morning sun was high in the sky and the sea a bright, glorious blue. In the distance the islands shimmered, and on the headland the temple was a glaring white. Ayios Georghios spilled down the hillside toward the bay, and she could see some caïques leaving the harbor. The voices drew her attention back to the gardens. Mr Niphakos was talking to two of his gardeners. His long white skirt moved a little in the light breeze, and his crimson jacket shone with golden embroidery. He looked very impressive and not altogether pleased about something, for the gardeners appeared to be receiving a ticking-off.

As she watched, another figure approached the group. It was James. He was elegantly Bond Street in a light-blue riding coat and tight buckskin breeches, and his top boots were as highly polished as if he were about to take a ride in Hyde Park. His top hat was pulled forward, throwing his face in shadow, but he removed it as he reached his host. 'Good morning, sir.'

The Greek turned. 'Good morning, my lord.'

'Is there any word for me from Athens?'

'I'm sorry, my lord, there is nothing.'

James ran his fingers through his golden hair. It was a curious gesture, and at once disappointed and angry.

Mr Niphakos looked apologetic. 'Perhaps tomorrow?' he ventured.

'Perhaps. Could a horse be saddled for me?'

'*Aiginai*! It is done!' Mr Niphakos hurried away, much to the undisguised relief of the two gardeners, who had been rescued from further admonishment by the English milord's provident arrival. They moved quickly away in the opposite direction, leaving James standing where he was. He had his eyes lowered, and then he turned to look down at the bay. He took a Spanish cigar from his pocket and a Lucifer flared as he lit it. A moment later the sweet smoke was curling up into the air.

Roslyn was suddenly aware of how she was staring at him, and she drew quickly back from the edge of the balcony in case he should turn and see her. It was then that she saw the door of his room was open. Curiosity drew her inexorably toward it. The room was very like her own, furnished in the same fresh blue-and-white, but there was evidence everywhere that it was occupied by a man. Gloves and a riding crop lay upon a table, with beside them an out-of-date copy of *The Times*. A paisley dressing gown made from the finest silk had been tossed casually upon the bed, and there were Turkish slippers on the rug beside it. In the dressing room the door of the wardrobe stood slightly ajar, revealing the beautifully tailored clothes of a gentleman of taste and fashion.

She wouldn't have dreamed of going inside had it not been for the broken porcelain miniature lying on the floor in the corner, where it had been thrown the night before. There were marks on the wall above that bore silent witness to the violence with which the delicate little portrait had been smashed against it. The elegant filigree porcelain surround that had once framed the little likeness had been shattered into a thousand fragments, and the face itself, that of a dark-haired woman, was disfigured by an ugly crack that had broken it in two.

Filled with an irresistible and unwise urge to see it more closely, Roslyn stepped hesitantly into the room. What if James should return? But no, he was waiting for a horse, and anyway was smoking a cigar. Her silk wrap rustled as she went to the corner and crouched to pick up the two pieces of the face. The woman was breathtakingly beautiful, with a sweet, heart-shaped face and large, lustrous dark-brown eyes. Her complexion was pale and flawless, and her lips were curved into a gentle, wistful smile. Her hair was a shining glory of almost black curls, and the low neckline of her lace-frothed pink gown revealed a creamy, curving bosom of perfect proportion. Her name was painted clearly. Vanessa, Lady Atherton.

She didn't hear the door open quietly behind her; she knew nothing until James' icy voice addressed her. 'Are you much given to entering gentlemen's rooms in your undress, Miss Meredith?'

She dropped the miniature with a gasp and straightened, guilty color flooding into her cheeks.

He closed the door, surveying her with a cold, contemptuous glance. 'I trust you have a suitable explanation for this gross intrusion.'

'Sir, I . . . ' She couldn't think of anything to say; she was too mortified at having been caught in such a situation.

'I'm waiting, madam.'

She stared miserably at him, wishing the floor would open up and swallow her. She'd never felt more embarrassed in her life.

'Your silence is most instructive, Miss Meredith, for it reveals your reason for coming in here to be your vulgar and base curiosity about my private affairs.'

'I didn't mean to — '

'You didn't *mean* to come in and examine my wife's likeness? I suppose you sleepwalk.'

She fell silent again. She had no defense, and they both knew it.

'You are no lady, madam.'

She was stung into retaliation then. 'And you, sirrah, are no gentleman.'

He picked up the gloves and riding crop he'd come back for, his glance still cold and disdainful. 'If I'm no gentleman, I suggest you remove yourself from my room immediately.'

Her cheeks on fire, she gathered her skirts and fled to her own room. Her heart thundered with shame as she sat weakly on the bed. How could she have been so foolish? What on earth had possessed her? How was she going to be able to face him across the dinner table that night? Oh, how she wished she'd never come to this place. A plague on Lord Byron and his deviousness; if it hadn't been for him, she and her uncle would be in the calm serenity of Athens. Instead, they were here, and she'd just committed a *faux pas* so dreadful that she felt ill just to think of it.

7

She still felt dreadful as she dressed in her lilac muslin gown and prepared to go down to breakfast. She knew she wouldn't have to face James; he'd ridden away shortly after finding her prying in his room, and he wasn't expected back until dusk.

She couldn't bring herself to tell her uncle what had happened; she felt too ashamed. He put her quiet mood down to lingering tiredness after the previous day's long ride, and wouldn't hear of her accompanying him up to the temple. Not that she wished to see the temple just yet, there was time enough and for the moment she'd prefer to get to know Christina better, and find out all about the forthcoming wedding. And so Sir Owen went up to the headland alone with a man Mr Niphakos provided to help carry the various things required for a day's sketching. There was a pouch of black lead pencils, pens, bottles of ink, sticks of charcoal, a painting box of watercolors, a quiver of brushes, a wooden drawing block, a satchel of paper, and a wicker basket containing a picnic luncheon.

Roslyn passed the day in Christina's agreeable company, being shown the gown copied from the coronation apparel of the Empress of France, and meeting Theodore Mavrocordatos, Christiana's future husband. He was a good-looking young man, dark-haired and dark-eyed, and extremely shy. He didn't dress in the Greek style, and wouldn't have looked out of place in Paris or London; it wasn't hard to see why Christina was chafing so much at her father's insistence upon her wearing Greek clothes. Theo came from a good family, with estates farther up the coast, and he was considered quite a catch, even for the governor's daughter. The wedding in a week's time did indeed promise to be a grand affair, with *ólos o kózmos* there to see Christina Niphakos and her bride-groom show them all that there was much more to the world than just Ayios Georghios.

As evening approached, James Atherton was very much on Roslyn's mind. She was dreading seeing him again, so much so that she even contemplated pleading a headache and staying in her room. But she couldn't do that for the whole of her stay and so decided that the sooner she got the awful moment over, the better. As it happened he didn't say a word to her. He didn't mention the morning's events or hint at it by so much as a

80

glance. He remained silent throughout the meal and left immediately afterward, much to her and Sir Owen's immense relief.

Over the following days the pattern remained the same. Roslyn stayed at the villa with Christina, with whom she had swiftly become on first name terms, while Sir Owen went up to the temple to sketch to his heart's content. Each evening they dined on the terrace with James, hardly a word being uttered.

Preparations for the wedding began in earnest several days before the event, with guests arriving from all over the district. There was noise, bustle, and excitement throughout the house, and Christina began to succumb to nerves, worrying about everything that might possibly go wrong.

Roslyn and her uncle racked their brains about what gift to give. The problem was solved by Sir Owen's suggestion that he paint the wedding feast, with all the principal guests. He couldn't do it straightaway, of course — such a painting would take time — but he could sketch it on the day and then perform it properly on his return to England. Christina and Theo didn't object to the delay; they were only too delighted and flattered by his kind offer.

On the afternoon before the wedding

Christina began to worry about the flowers for the church, and so Roslyn accompanied her there to see that all was well. Christina was particularly anxious about some yellow lilies that had failed to arrive from a nearby village, and she wasn't consoled by Roslyn's reassurance that the church must look very lovely indeed judging from the number of donkeys she'd seen toiling up the hill, their panniers laden with beautiful blooms of every color.

It was a very warm day and Roslyn wore an apricot seersucker gown with little puffed sleeves. The broad white ribbons of her high-crowned stray bonnet fluttered prettily loose, and a fringed white parasol twirled above her head. She carried a brown velvet reticule, and there was a brightly colored shawl over her arms, its vivid crimson, gold, and white pattern set off to perfection by the demure shade of the gown.

The bay spread out grandly below, a deep, clear blue that was very different indeed from the cold gray of the waters around Britain. Ahead of them the church was brightly white against the hillside, and beyond it was the vale of trees that swallowed the track leading to the summit. Roslyn glanced toward the temple, but she couldn't see her uncle. She hoped he would remember that dinner was going to be much earlier that evening because the wedding celebrations were to begin at dawn the next day.

Entering the church through a low archway in the perimeter wall, the first thing she saw inside was a dazzling array of wall mosaics. Rich in blue and purple, they depicted the feasts of the Orthodox calendar, and were a breathtaking display of intricacy and skill. Above, on the inside of the cupola's golden vault, a painting of Christ gazed compassionately down at the cool marble rosette in the center of the floor below. Separating the altar and sanctuary from the rest of the church was a particularly fine iconostasis, a screen bearing the glittering icons so venerated in this part of the world. It blazed with gold and jewels, its richness almost hazy in the candlelight that illuminated everything. The scent of incense vied with that of the wedding flowers that had been arranged in every conceivable place. There were bowls of them before the iconostatis, garlands around the stalls, and spilling down the walls. One glance was sufficient to tell Roslyn that the absent yellow lilies would not be missed.

Christina evidently realized the same. She smiled a little ruefully. 'I think maybe I have been a little silly.'

'All brides worry. They're expected to.'

'Do you think it looks nice?' asked Christina, looking around.

'Beautiful.'

'Do you see the Ayios Georghios rose?'

'No. Where?' Rosyin glanced around at the flowers.

'Not there. Up there.' Christina pointed up at the ceiling and Roslyn saw that the painting of Christ wore a garland of the unusual little roses. Christina sighed then, looking around for a last time. 'The next time I come here, I will be a bride.'

'A very happy bride.'

'Yes. I love Theo very much and he loves me. We are fortunate. I went to the wise woman in Ayios Georghios, to have my fortune read. She said that we will be happy and I will have five children, three boys and two girls.' Christina paused. 'I do not think the milord was very fortunate, and if he'd had his fortune told, he would not have married. Marriage has been unhappy for him.'

'Yes. So it seems.'

'It is sad that one so very handsome should have such a sad heart.'

Roslyn didn't say anything.

'*Ela*, come, we go back to the house and I will make a drink of lemons and honey, to refresh us.' Christina linked her arm through Roslyn's and they walked from the church.

As they emerged into the daylight again, Roslyn became sharply aware of the thunderous pounding of hooves descending the hillside from behind the church. A horse was being ridden at breakneck speed! She'd just stepped out onto the track from the church when James Atherton rode around the corner at a gallop, his horse foam-flecked and sweating. She froze with shock, and he didn't see her. She heard Christina scream a terrified warning, but she couldn't move; she was mesmerized by the horse as it flew toward her. The thunder of its hooves filled her ears, drumming like frantic heartbeats.

At the very last second James became aware of Christina's scream, and saw Roslyn. Desperately he tried to rein in, but it was too late; the horse cannoned into her, sending her reeling heavily against the church wall. Her untied bonnet was dislodged, rolling beneath the horse's capering hooves, where it was trampled and crushed, and her parasol bounced a short way down the track, coming to a halt against the hedge and rocking slowly to and fro. She felt consciousness slipping away, receding into a deep, velvety blackness. All sound began to fade around her and she sank to the ground.

Christina cried out anxiously and went to her, while James at last managed to steady his frightened horse and dismount. His boots crunched on the track as he ran to where Roslyn lay. He took off his gloves and crouched beside her, putting his hand to her dusty cheek. 'Miss Meredith?'

Her green-gray eyes opened, but she couldn't speak. It was as if all strength had been drained from her.

He looked quickly at Christina. 'Is there any water in the church?'

'Yes!' She hurried away through the archway.

He looked down at Roslyn again, his hand still warm and surprisingly gentle against her cheek. 'Can you hear me, Miss Meredith?'

Her lips moved as she struggled to answer. At last her voice obeyed. 'Yes.'

Relief flooded into his eyes. 'Are you in any pain?'

'I — I don't know.' She felt too winded and confused to really know.

'May God forgive me,' he muttered, turning as Christina returned with a dish of water. Supporting Roslyn's head, he put the dish to her lips. The water was cool and refreshing. It seemed to clear her head.

He handed the dish back to Christina, still looking anxiously at Roslyn. 'Do you think you can move?'

'I think so.'

'Be sure now, because if you've broken any bones — '

'I think I'm all right.' She reached up to him and he took her hands to draw her gently into a sitting position. Her hair tumbled down from its pins and she felt momentarily dizzy, but apart from that, she wasn't in any pain.

'Is that all right?' he asked.

She nodded. 'I think I'm just winded.'

'I'll carry you into the church, it'll be cooler in there.'

'There's no need . . . '

'There's every need.' He picked her up as if she was weightless, carrying her easily out of the blaze of the sun into the shade of the church. The smell of incense seemed somehow stronger, and for a moment the candles began to spin, but then they were steady again. He sat her gently down on a stone bench before the wall mosaics. 'Is that better?'

She nodded.

He straightened then, taking off his top hat and running his fingers through his disheveled hair. He was shaken by the accident, which could so easily have been much, much worse.

Christina looked accusingly at him. 'You could have killed her, my lord.'

'Do you think I don't know that?'

'You were riding like a madman.'

'I'm more than aware that I was at fault.'

'Is that all you can say?' Christina was angry because she'd had such a fright.

'I apologize. I know that I was entirely to blame for what happened.'

'Should you not be saying that to the one you hurt?'

He met Christina's angry gaze for a moment and then nodded, turning to Roslyn. 'Forgive me, Miss Meredith, I'm truly sorry for what happened. I wasn't thinking.'

She raised her eyes to his face. 'Of course you're forgiven, my lord, for I don't imagine you rode me down deliberately; you can't possibly dislike me that much.'

'Dislike you? I don't dislike you, Miss Meredith.' He looked away, a strange expression passing through his eyes. 'Are you recovered enough for me to take you back to the house?'

'Take me?'

'You don't imagine I'll let you walk, do you?'

'I hadn't thought,' she replied.

'I'll take you on the horse. Are you well enough?'

'Yes.'

Christina hurried to the door. 'I'll go ahead

and tell them what's happened.'

Roslyn looked anxiously after her. 'Please, Christina, there's no need!'

Christina had already dashed out, pausing only to retrieve the crushed bonnet and dusty parasol before running on down the track.

James held his hand out and hesitantly Roslyn took it. He drew her to her feet, steadying her for a moment. 'Are you still all right?'

She nodded.

He seemed aware of her hand suddenly, and released it.

She looked at him. Surely now was the time to apologize for going into his room. His behavior may not have been perfect, but she shouldn't have done that. 'I'm sorry for what happened the other morning.'

'The other morning?'

'When you found me in your room. I didn't mean to pry; truly I didn't. At least, not in the way you thought. I heard the miniature breaking the night before, and when I saw it still lying there . . . it was just a stupid whim and I regret it most deeply.'

'I know you didn't mean to pry, Miss Meredith.'

'You do?' She couldn't hide her surprise.

'Yes. And if apologies are the order of the day, then I think I owe you far more than you

owe me. I've behaved boorishly since you and
Sir Owen arrived, and today I nearly killed
you.' A faint smile touched his lips. 'Your
small indiscretion pales into insignificance, I
fancy.'

'It doesn't for me.'

'Then I assure you that you are forgiven,
Miss Meredith. Please don't give the matter
another thought.' He smiled again and it
reached his eyes.

The sunlight almost dazzled Roslyn as they
came out of the church. The horse was quiet
now, pricking its ears as they approached.
James lifted her lightly up before the saddle
and then mounted behind her, his arm firm
about her waist. He maneuvered the horse on
down the hill toward the house.

8

Christina had alarmed the household a great deal, and everyone was most concerned about Roslyn when she and James arrived in the courtyard. All the Niphakos and Mavrocordatos families and the other wedding guests gathered around, anxious to see that she hadn't been too badly hurt. James received a number of disapproving glances, although no one said anything; they were too polite for that. His strange conduct since arriving in Ayios Georghios had evidently been much discussed, and Roslyn's accident was regarded as the worst example yet of his eccentric behavior.

She was able to reassure them all that she felt quite all right, although she gave in at last to Christina's insistence that she go to her room and lie down; it was easier to do that than to keep saying she felt quite well. When she was in the quiet of her room, however, she found that she felt a little more tired than she'd thought, and before she knew it, she'd fallen asleep.

When Sir Owen returned from the temple, she was still asleep. He was at first most concerned about the accident, but by then everyone was sure that she was all right, and so his fears were allayed. It was almost time for the early dinner, but it was decided that Roslyn should be left to sleep, as that would be best for her, and so Sir Owen and James dined alone.

Sir Owen was already on the terrace when James joined him. The older man had a lighted cigar and was standing by the balustrade looking down over the bay. Sunset was still several hours away and the evening light was warm and bright. The canaries were singing their hearts out and the roses filled the air with perfume.

James wore an indigo velvet coat and elegant cream trousers, and as he approached, the sunlight shone on the ruby pin in his neckcloth and upon the pale-gray satin of his waistcoat. 'Sir Owen?'

The other turned. 'James?'

'If you do not wish me to join you tonight, I'd quite understand.'

Sir Owen surveyed him a moment. 'Tell me, did you deliberately ride my niece down?'

James was taken aback. 'Of course not. Surely you don't believe — '

'No, I don't believe you did, my boy. It's just that I'm surprised you should think your presence might not be welcome.'

'My presence has hardly been agreeable of late.'

'I won't argue with that; in fact, you've been downright oppressive.'

James nodded, going to the balustrade and leaning both hands upon it. 'I've been guilty of allowing my private problems to rule my life.'

'Do you want to talk about them?'

James shook his head. 'They're better left.'

'If you're sure?'

'Quite sure.'

'As you wish, but if you change your mind — '

James smiled at him. 'I'll remember your offer.'

'See that you do. I don't profess to know what's happened to you, James, but I do profess to be a man who stands by his judgment. I liked and respected you when first we met, and I haven't changed that opinion.'

'In spite of my atrocious conduct?'

'In spite of that.'

'I don't deserve it.' James glanced at the table then and saw that it had only been set for two. 'Isn't Miss Meredith joining us?'

'She's sleeping.'

'She's all right, I trust?' James straightened in concern.

'It was just decided to let her sleep on. It won't do her any harm, and probably a great deal of good. She was quite shaken, I fancy.'

James drew a long breath. 'I'm truly sorry it happened, Sir Owen.'

'I know.'

'I was riding like a madman, I could have killed her.'

'But you didn't. Don't dwell upon how dreadful it might have been, that won't do any good.'

James smiled a little wryly. 'I'm afraid that of late I've only been able to look on the dark side.'

'That much has been patently obvious.'

'I know. I'm sorry for inflicting it all upon you.'

'I venture to hope that you'll be more agreeable from now on.'

'I intend to be.'

'Good, for when you're in fine fettle, James, my boy, I don't know anyone who's better company. So, we can look forward to a pleasant last few days, can we?'

'Last few days? You're leaving?'

'On the twenty-third. The *Hydra* sails the day after.'

'I hadn't realized.'

'Are you here for much longer?'

'I doubt it.'

'Don't you know?'

James smiled a little wryly. 'Oh, I think I've known all along that I was wasting my time and might just as well have remained in London facing the proverbial music. Greece hasn't provided real escape, nor has it seen the solving of my problems. I'm no further forward now than I was in the very beginning.'

Sir Owen drew a long breath. 'James, I don't even begin to understand what you're talking about.'

'It doesn't matter, it's not important.' But everything in his manner suggested the very opposite.

Sir Owen decided it would be more tactful to change the subject. He glanced up at the sky, which was still clear and bright, with the first hint of gold as the sun began its long descent. 'I fancy tomorrow is going to be as fine as today. The wedding will go off well.'

'No doubt.'

Sir Owen glanced at him. 'I'm looking forward to it; it promises to be quite an occasion.'

'Does it?' There was no mistaking the irony with which this was said.

'I take it that you're not looking forward to it.'

'I abhor weddings, and I remember my

95

own only with bitterness.'

'I'm sorry to hear that, but surely you will not wish to offend our hosts by shunning their big day?'

'My presence would undoubtedly be a damper on the proceedings.'

'Nevertheless — '

'No, Sir Owen, I will not be attending.'

Nothing more was said on the matter because Mr Niphakos and Christina came out with the ouzo and *mezedes*, and shortly after that the first course was served.

Throughout the meal the two men conversed on all manner of subjects, but no more mention was made of James's private life, or of the wedding the following day. They lingered on the terrace after the meal, and then James withdrew, saying he had a letter he wished to write.

Sir Owen remained where he was, sipping a leisurely glass of retsina and enjoying another cigar. He drew a long breath. Soon he would be leaving this lovely place behind, to return to London and his financial problems. He only hoped that the new investments he'd made at Thomas Bruce's suggestion did indeed prove as fortunate as that gentleman had predicted. The cigar smoke curled up into the warm, still air. One things was certain; if they did, he'd change his ways. He had Roslyn to think of now, and she was as important to him as if she were his daughter. It was his duty to provide for her, to see that she had an inheritance that would ensure her the sort of dazzling match she deserved.

At that moment he heard light steps approaching and the rustle of taffeta. He looked up to see Roslyn coming toward him. She wore a pale-green high-waisted gown with a low neckline, and her mother's golden locket was at her throat on a thin black velvet ribbon. Her hair was brushed loose and tied back, and a white shawl rested over her bare arms. She smiled a little reproachfully. 'You should have woken me. Now I won't be able to sleep tonight.'

'How are you feeling, *cariad*?' he asked, getting quickly to his feet.

She hugged him, kissing his cheek. 'I'm quite all right, truly I am. I really don't know why I slept like that, it isn't like me at all.' The taffeta rustled again as she sat down.

'Have you had anything to eat?'

'Yes, Christina brought me something in my room a short while ago.' She glanced at James' place. 'How was he?'

'He? Oh, you mean James. He was much improved. I think the accident brought him up rather sharply.' Sir Owen sat down again. 'He's very sorry about it, you know.'

She nodded.

'He hasn't improved completely, though.'

'Oh?'

'He has absolutely no intention of attending the wedding tomorrow.'

'His absence will be rather glaring.'

'He won't be moved on it, that's for sure.' Sir Owen raised his cigar to his lips, gazing thoughtfully into the middle distance. 'He's a very unhappy young man, very unhappy indeed. I can still hardly believe that he's come to this after being so different at Foxcombe. But I suppose, he then had the two things he loves most in this world: his wife and his estate. Now he only has his estate.'

'What's Foxcombe like?' she asked curiously.

'Ah, it's paradise on earth,' he said softly, 'and if you think I'm exaggerating, let me tell you that in my eyes there is nowhere to compare with it. Oh, maybe the house is a little old-fashioned for today's tastes, but to me it's quite perfect. It's centuries old — parts of it date back to the time of Henry the Third — and it's a rambling place, Cotswold stone and architecture at its very best. It has mullioned windows, beautiful finials on the gables, and arched doorways beneath solid stone porches. It stands at the head of two valleys, one leading down to the broad vale and Cheltenham, the other down to a lake formed by the small river dividing Foxcombe from the adjoining estate, Grantby Place. The studio where I painted the portraits of James and Vanessa was in a converted boathouse by the lake. James's great-grandmother was a talented artist and spent a great deal of her long widowhood there. Her paintings hang in many rooms of the house. Landscapes, and good ones at that.' He smiled at Roslyn. 'I could have stayed there forever, *cariad*. It was beautiful, peaceful, and timeless. But Vanessa did not like it.'

'Why?'

'It wasn't modern enough for her. She much preferred the classical splendor of nearby Grantby Place, which has been fashionably improved and is very imposing.' He gave a wry laugh. 'For someone from a middling Westmorland family, she had very fine and grand notions. She did her damnedest to persuade James to 'improve' Foxcombe, but to his eternal credit he denied her such a sacrilege. She sulked, but was consoled by the gift of a very fine emerald necklace.'

'Did you like her?'

He paused and then shook his head. 'No,

although at the time I could not have really said why. She was charming, vivacious, and a fine hostess, and to me she was always gracious. But there was something — I can't quite put my finger on it — that made me draw back from liking her. Do you know what I mean?'

'I think so.'

'James I liked wholeheartedly; he was genuine and open.'

'But she wasn't?'

'I don't know. I don't think so. Oh, to be truthful, I don't know how much my opinion now is colored by what's happened since.'

'She's very beautiful, isn't she? I — I've seen a portrait of her.'

'She has a matchless beauty, the sort no artist would tire of painting. But you know what they say about beauty, don't you?'

'What?'

He grinned. 'That it's only skin deep. There must be an inner glow too, and I'm afraid Vanessa didn't have it.'

She smiled. 'Maybe you just didn't see it.'

'It wasn't there to see.' He took out his fob watch. 'Good Lord, is that all the time is? I'm so tired I could sleep right now.'

'It's all the fresh sea air up at the temple.'

'Probably. I suppose you're feeling bright and perky after your disgracefully long afternoon snooze.'

'Yes.' She sighed. 'It'll be ages before I'm tired again.'

'Perhaps a walk up to the temple would be the best thing,' he said jokingly. 'You've been so engrossed in Christina's wedding preparations that you've been disgustingly lazy and haven't been up there once since we arrived.'

He only said it teasingly, but it suddenly struck her as an excellent idea. 'You're quite right, a walk up to the headland would be the very thing.'

'I didn't mean it,' he said quickly.

'I know, but I really should have made the effort before now. It's most remiss of me, especially as Lord Byron told me how wonderul the sunsets are from up there.'

'I don't think I could manage that walk again today, *cariad*,' he said apologetically.

'I don't expect you to. I'll ask Christina if she can spare a maid to accompany me.'

'They're all very busy with the wedding,' he warned.

'If they are, I won't go,' she replied, getting up and dropping a kiss on his head. 'I promise to be back before it's completely dark, and you mustn't worry because I won't be on my own.'

'Oh, all right, off you go, then. But take care.'

'I will.'

She hurried away. But when she tried to find Christina, she found the whole house was in such a commotion with wedding preparations that she knew they would find it difficult to do without even one maid. She gave up all thought of the walk, until she happened to glance from a window and see the temple gleaming so white on the headland. She so wanted to go up there and see the sunset that she hesitated. She could go on her own, and her uncle need never know. She'd be back without anyone being any the wiser.

With sudden resolution, she slipped from the house by a side door, hurrying along the path through the screen of poplars and emerging through a wicket gate onto the track leading up toward the church. At the gate she halted, looking back toward the house. The terrace was hidden from view and there was no sign that anyone had seen her leaving. Drawing her shawl closer, she began to walk up the track.

9

The shadows were lengthening as she walked past the deserted church and entered the cool, leafy valley beyond. Pine trees released the scent of resin into the air, and wild purple lupins swayed beside the track. There was a light breeze in this high place, cool and refreshing as it rustled through the bushes.

She emerged at last onto the open, rock-strewn headland, where clumps of blue-mauve sea lavender made bright splashes of color. The temple rose ahead, its columns very clear and white on the edge of the sheer cliff. Beyond it the sea was an intense peacock-blue, and the islands shimmered in the haze of gold that was beginning to spread from the horizon as the sun continued its slow desent.

Poseidon's temple was a splendidly ruinous ruin, little more now than a line of eight columns facing defiantly out from the land. Others lay broken and forlorn among the paving slabs and weather-beaten bushes. In ancient times this place had been a look-out point because of its position guarding the sea approaches to Athens, and from the top of the temple it had been possible to see all the way to the capital, where the spear point of the bronze statue of Athena on the Acropolis had just been visible as a fleck of gold on the northern horizon. There was no statue now — it had been removed to Constantinople and destroyed in the thirteenth century — and there were no sentries to keep watch for enemy fleets, for the enemy had long since taken over the land.

Roslyn paused. From where she stood she could see the land on either side of the promontory. Ayios Georghios and its bay lay down to her right, while to the left there was another great bay, its shores uninhabited, its water sheltering the Turkish ships Lord Byron had said were keeping the pirates away from these parts. A twist of smoke rose from a field inland and she could just make out a young shepherd seated among the poppies. His evening meal was turning on a spit and his sheep were browsing on the shrubs edging the field, their bells tinkling now and then as they moved.

Slowly she walked on. The closer she came to the temple, the less white the columns became, taking on their true silver hue, for the white was only an illusion. The evening light was changing swiftly now, making the columns seem almost alive and breathing as they soared toward a sky that was visibly turning to amethyst. Where she walked there were fragments of mosaic floor among the tufts of wiry grass, and yellow-flowered cacti growing in the shelter of fallen masonry.

She was aware of an air of magic and mystery. Was this the witching hour, the moment each day when Poseidon, god of the sea and protector of mariners, might again make his presence felt in his high place? She smiled at her thoughts, but there did indeed seem to be some ancient enchantment all around her, an echo from the distant past when the gods and goddesses of Olympus had ruled the world.

Reaching the foot of the line of columns, she stepped up onto what was left of the temple's stylobate. On the side away from the sinking sun, the marble was ice-cold as she rested her hand upon it. Holding on to the nearest column to steady herself, she gazed out to sea. The cliffs fell away below, dotted here and there with tufts of blue bellflowers, and gentle waves lapped the rocks at the foot.

The Aegean was almost ethereal in its intense beauty as she stood there watching the glory of the sunset beginning to blaze against the sea and sky. The islands lacked all substance as the sun sank closer and closer to the edge of infinity, the sky passing through the full gamut of colors, from the palest of

green-blues to the most fiery and incandes-
cent of crimsons, with in between the
richness of purple, orange, and gold. She had
seen the sunset from the villa balcony, but it
was as nothing to the glory she witnessed now
from the top of Poseidon's cliff. The
magnificence of the show held her spellbound. She was unaware of time, moved by
what she saw, and knew that it was a sight she
would never forget.

She didn't know how long she'd been
standing there; she was unaware of anything
until a slight sound nearby made her turn
with a sharp, stifled gasp. Chill fears of pirates
swept through her until she saw James a little
distance away to her left, leaning back against
a huge slab of fallen column, his hands thrust
deep into his pockets. He was watching the
sunset and had no idea she was there.

His hair was burnished to copper-gold by
the rays of the dying sun, and the breeze
toyed with the soft folds of his neckcloth. He
seemed oddly vulnerable and unguarded, and
she felt that she was intruding upon his
privacy. She didn't want him to know she'd
seen him. Maybe she could creep away
without him knowing. But as she tried to step
stealthily down from the stylobate, she
dislodged a few tiny stones and he heard.

He straightened immediately, turning toward

her. 'Good evening, Miss Meredith.'

Slowly she went to him. 'G-good evening, my lord.'

He glanced around and realized that she was on her own. 'You're alone up here?'

'Yes.'

'Isn't that a little unwise?'

'I — Yes, I suppose it is,' she admitted unwillingly. 'I only wanted to see the sunset, and for one reason or another there wasn't anyone to accompany me.' She shouldn't have done it, and she knew it.

He didn't make any more of the point. 'I trust you aren't suffering any ill effects from this afternoon.'

'None at all.'

'I'm truly sorry about it. I was venting my anger upon the world, and you became a victim.'

'There's no need to apologize again. The matter is closed.'

He nodded and then glanced at the sunset again. 'So, this is what has lured you up here?'

'Lord Byron promised me that it was a magnificent sight, and he was right.'

'You've made the acquaintance of the poet?'

'In Athens.' If you did but know it, he was the author of our meeting.

'Do you admire his work?'

'I have to confess that I haven't read any of it, but I understand it shows more than small promise.'

'It does.' A faint smile touched his lips. 'My wife wouldn't agree, though.'

It was the first time he'd mentioned Vanessa. Roslyn remembered the story Lady Elgin had told of the very high-handed, public, and ill-informed criticism Vanessa Atherton had made of Byron's work in front of everyone at Melbourne House, including the Prince of Wales, or rather the Prince Regent, as he now was.

He glanced at her. 'From your silence I deduce that you've heard the tale.'

'Lady Elgin did mention something.'

'I'll warrant she did. It was a story that was much in circulation for a while. My wife can be rather impetuous, Miss Meredith, and on this occasion her impetuosity served her badly.' He looked at the sunset again. 'Do you know your islands?' he inquired with a sudden change of subject.

'Islands? What do you mean?'

'Can you identify them?' He waved a hand toward the sea and the dark outlines that seemed to be sinking into molten gold as the sun touched the horizon. 'No, I'm afraid I can't,' she replied.

'Do you mean to tell me you've come all

this way without boning up?'

'Yes.'

'Shame on you.'

She looked at him. 'Well, since you evidently possess infinitely greater knowledge, perhaps you should enlighten me.'

'Do you really want to know?'

She nodded. 'Yes.'

He smiled a little and then began to point. 'Very well. Over there to the right is Aegina, and then the hills of Argolis, with the island of Hydra beside them. Due south is Saint George.'

'Another Ayios Georghios?'

'Yes, one of many.' He pointed further on. 'Over there, to the southeast, is the double row of the Cyclades, while the long low island just across the channel from where we stand is called Helena.'

She followed his finger. 'Long low island? Oh, the one with what looks like a ruin on the hill in the center?'

'It's a ruined monastery. I hope to see it before I leave. The island's named after Helen of Troy herself.'

'Is it? Why?'

'As I understand it, the story goes that it was there that she first gave herself to Paris on their way to Troy.'

She colored a little. 'Really?'

'Maybe it's a slightly improper story for polite conversation. Shall we move on?' He pointed away toward the east. 'Do you see that huge rock over there?'

'Yes.'

'It's said that Aegeus threw himself into the sea from it on seeing his son Theseus' ship returning from Crete with black sails. He knew from those sails that Theseus had been killed by the Minotaur.'

'That's very sad.'

'My first story was improper and the second sad. I don't think I should say any more, do you?' He smiled. It was a smile that, like that in the church, reached his eyes. She was aware of how very great his charm could be, just as her uncle had claimed. She felt suddenly hot and looked at the sea. 'When — when I look at a view like this, it's hard to remember England, isn't it?' she said awkwardly.

'I remember England all the time, Foxcombe in particular. It grieves me to be here when all along I could have been there.'

'My uncle says it's a place he could gladly stay in forever.'

'It has that effect upon many, but I fear that there are others it leaves completely cold.'

She couldn't help remembering what her

uncle had told her about Vanessa's yearning for Foxcombe to be more like neighboring Grantby Place.

The sun had almost vanished beyond the horizon now, leaving the sky a majestic sweep of deep gold and cerise. The breeze was becoming noticeably cooler, making her draw her shawl even closer.

He noticed. 'Perhaps it's time to retrace our steps.'

'I think so.' She looked at him. 'Would you be returning now if it weren't for me?'

'Yes, Miss Meredith, I assure you that I would. You're not imposing upon me, I promise you.'

'I know I shouldn't have come up here on my own, it was very foolish indeed. Are you going to tell my uncle?'

'Tell tales? Miss Meredith, I'm not the school sneak.' He smiled.

'He might know already, of course.' She bit her lip regretfully.

'I doubt it, for someone would have come looking for you before now. Come on, I'll take you safely back down.' He offered her his arm.

They walked quickly back across the open promontory. The hills inland were a dark, dusky purple, and the pine trees in the vale were black silhouettes that stirred in the cool air. She could smell the sea lavender she'd noticed earlier, but now its flowers were a dull gray.

The vale folded over the track and the shadows deepened. She glanced nervously around, glad that she wasn't alone. Oh, how very silly she'd been to ever think of coming up here on her own.

He sensed her thoughts and put his hand reassuringly over hers. 'You're quite all right, Miss Meredith. I'll slay any dragon that leaps out at you.'

His fingers were warm on hers, and her skin tingled beneath them. She was sharply aware of everything about him. Today she'd been exposed to the fatally attractive side of his character, and she was drawn like a moth to a flame. She didn't want to be, but she couldn't help it.

They reached the wicket gate and entered the villa grounds. There was no sign of any alarm; her absence hadn't been noticed. A sound from the track made her look back through the poplar trees just in time to see a man and woman driving a donkey up toward the church. The beast's panniers were filled with yellow blooms; Christina's lilies had arrived, after all.

Rosyln smiled gladly and James looked at her. 'Why are you smiling?'

'The lilies have come for the church. Christina will be so pleased.'

'Lilies?'

'She wanted them for the wedding.'

'It seemed to me this afternoon that there were more than enough flowers already.'

'These few more will make the bride happy.'

'No doubt.' His tone had altered.

She looked at him. 'My uncle says you don't intend to be at the wedding.'

'That is correct.'

'But — '

'Don't attempt to change my mind, Miss Meredith, for you will not succeed.'

'Why won't you go?'

'Because I despise weddings.'

'It would look very rude if you stay away.'

He met her gaze, and his eyes had become cool. 'Then so be it,' he said quietly.

'My lord — '

'I think I've escorted you safely back,' he interrupted. 'Good night, Miss Meredith.'

She stared after him as he walked away. 'G-good night,' she murmured.

10

Sir Owen remained unaware of the true circumstances of her walk to the temple, and she didn't correct his belief that she'd been accompanied by one of the maids. When she at last retired to her bed, she was kept awake by the *kéfi*, the high spirits and merry-making of the many guests who'd descended on the house, and she was awakened at dawn to the sound of the men carrying trestle tables out to the lemon grove in readiness for the feast.

For Christina's wedding day, Roslyn chose to wear her lilac muslin gown because it went particularly prettily with the Ayios Georghios rose she'd decided to put on her gypsy hat. She'd picked the buds the night before and kept them in a glass of water beside her bed. This morning they'd just opened and their petals were crisp and fresh. Putting her hair up into a simple knot, she combed one long, curling ringlet down over her right shoulder and then tied on the hat, fluffing the wide ribbons out beneath her chin. The roses were tucked under the ribbon as it passed over the crown of the hat, and they looked as becoming as she'd thought they would.

Picking up her reticule and light shawl, she looked at her reflection in the mirror. Yes, she looked well enough, and the hat would shade her from the sun in the absence of her parasol, which looked a little the worse for wear after its mishap the day before. She pulled a slight face at herself, for in spite of all her efforts the sun had still managed to burn her skin; instead of looking fashionably pale, she looked disgustingly healthy.

As she went down the stairs, she saw Mr Niphakos approaching the doorway of the terrace room. He addressed someone inside. 'My lord, I fear there is still no word from Athens, but the horse you requested is saddled and waiting in the courtyard.'

'Thank you,' James replied from within.

The Greek gave what Roslyn thought was a decidedly cool bow and then walked away. He evidently did not think highly of his guest's intention to absent himself from the day's celebrations.

James emerged from the room in his riding clothes, striding quickly away in the direction of the courtyard.

Roslyn hesitated only a moment before hurrying after him. She felt she had to try once more to persuade him to stay, because she didn't like to think of the snub the Niphakoses must think he was dealing them.

She caught up with him just as he was about to mount. 'May I speak with you for a moment?'

He turned to look at her. 'Good morning, Miss Meredith.' His face did not offer any encouragement; it was set and determined.

'Good morning.'

'What is it you wish to say?' he inquired, although he knew perfectly well.

'I merely wanted to ask you not to go out today.'

'As you can see, my plans have already been made.' He indicated the horse.

'You could change them.'

'If I wished to, yes, I could. But I don't wish to, Miss Meredith, as I thought I'd made quite plain last night.'

'I hoped you'd thought again.'

'You hoped in vain.' He turned to the horse again. Stung a little by his intransigence, she went quickly to catch the animal's bridle. 'Please reconsider,' she said, holding his angry gaze.

'Release my horse, Miss Meredith.'

Abruptly she obeyed. 'Last night I began to think you were agreeably human, after all,' she said stiffly, 'but it seems I was wrong. You're as much a boor as ever.'

His blue eyes flashed coldly, and without a word he mounted, turning the horse toward the archway and riding quickly out.

She watched him for a moment and then turned to go back into the house. The old James Atherton was back, it seemed, and was as odious as before.

★ ★ ★

The whole population of Ayios Georghios and the surrounding district seemed to have climbed the track to wait by the wicket gate for the wedding procession to leave the villa and proceed to the church. It was as Christina herself had said, *ólos o kózmos* had come to see her marry her beloved Theo.

Above the noise of the crowd the church bell rang out gladly over the hillside and the bay, where the sun flashed on the water like a scattering of diamonds.

Roslyn stood outside the wicket gate with her uncle, who looked rather hot and uncomfortable in his formal black coat and tight white trousers. He was busily sketching, his drawing block resting on the gatepost. He was engaged upon a likeness of an old lady on a donkey. Her black clothes were a perfect foil for the lovely bunch of flowers she carried, ready to strew them before the bride and groom after the church ceremony. Many people in the crowd carried flowers, from the smallest posy of wild poppies carried by a little girl, to a rather grand, ribboned bouquet held by a man who claimed a blood tie with the groom.

The lemon grove was in readiness, the trees garlanded with bunting and more flowers. The trestles were covered with white tablecloths and laden with all manner of food and drink for the feast, which was expected to go on until well into the night. There were several rectangular pits in the ground beneath the trees, filled with charcoal over which whole lambs were being spit-roasted. Roslyn could smell the sweet smoke drifting in the air.

At last Christina and her father emerged from the house and approached along the path through the poplars. They were followed by six little girl attendants, all in white and carrying large candles tied with white ribbons. Christina's gown transformed her into a lady of supreme Parisian elegance, and caused the sort of stir all brides desire.

Roslyn smiled as she heard the astonished whispers passing through the crowds, for this wasn't how everyone had expected the governor's daughter to look on her wedding day. It wasn't what Constantin Niphakos had expected either, but from the proud look in his dark eyes, he'd been won over.

A priest went through the wicket gate toward the wedding party, scattering holy water in their path. Sir Owen's pencil moved like lightning over his page as he tried to commit as many details as possible to posterity. The priest began to chant, moving slowly in front of the bride and her father as they came through the gate and began to move up the hillside toward the church. The crowd joined in, streaming up the track behind, and Roslyn and her uncle went too.

Not everyone could squeeze into the church, but they were fortunate. The flowers looked magnificent, and there were so many candles flickering that the air was warm. The icons and mosaics glowed with gold and color. Roslyn watched breathlessly as floral crowns joined with ribbon were placed alternately on the bride's and groom's head, to signify their joining together in holy matrimony. Shivers passed through her at the sweet, emotional singing of the congregation, singing that was echoed on the hillside outside, and Roslyn breathed the headiness of the incense as the bride and groom were led from left to right around the glittering altar.

When the happy couple proceeded down the hillside again afterward, their path was strewn with thousands of flowers and the air hissed with the sound of scattering rice. Their arrival in the lemon grove for the feast was greeted by music played by three men with mandolinlike instruments, and the huge party of guests prepared to enjoy the lavish and costly hospitality expected of the governor.

Ouzo and retsina flowed as if from a spring, as did triandáfilla, a pink rose-leaf liqueur that Roslyn learned was considered essential at weddings. The smell of roasting lamb was appetizing as the spits turned and the meat was basted with oil and lemon before being sprinkled with oregano. The trestles groaned with food, from cheese and cold meats to fish and bread baked in the shape of lovers' knots. There were fruit, yogurts, honeyed white cakes, and sugared almonds, and if a dish was emptied, it was filled again immediately from a seemingly endless supply in the kitchens.

Morning drifted into afternoon, and the feast was in full swing. Roslyn and her uncle sat beneath a tree by the entrance to the grove, not far from the house, and Sir Owen was still busily sketching. Many sheets of paper lay on the grass beside him as he drew anything that caught his eye, especially the floral bower where the bride and groom sat with their closest family.

Some men had been dancing for a while now, leaping, stamping, and slapping the soles of their shoes in time to the music, but Roslyn looked away from them as suddenly Christina and Theo got up to cross the grove to where she and her uncle sat.

Christina was delighted with Sir Owen's drawings, clapping her hands and smiling. 'Oh, they are so clever.'

'Thank you, my dear,' he replied, pleased.

'And you will put them together and make a painting for me?'

'I will indeed.'

'Come, you and Roslyn must dance with Theo and me. Not a dance like this . . . ' she waved a hand toward the Greek men, 'but a dance like they do in Paris or London. They dance the minuet again now in Paris, don't they?' She glanced a little conspiratorily over her shoulder at her father, and then smiled at Sir Owen again. 'My father does not know, but I have been teaching the musicians how to play a minuet, and so now I wish to dance it, with you.'

'But I dance like an elephant,' he protested.

'I like elephants,' she replied irrepressibly.

Grinning, he got to his feet. Roslyn did too, accepting the hand Theo held shyly out to her. Christina waved the dancing men away and made a prearranged signal to the musicians, who immediately began to play a minuet. The lemon grove became very quiet as the two couples began to dance. At first Mr Niphakos looked a little cross with his daughter, but then he smiled, spreading his hands and shrugging expressively; today Christina had shown him that she was determined to be a woman of the world, not just of Ayios Georghios.

Sir Owen was proving to be every bit the elephant he'd said he was, but he wasn't crushed by his clumsiness, and delighted everyone with his willingness to laugh at himself.

Afterward he pleased them all still more by proving that although he couldn't dance, he could sing with all the rich feeling of his nation. He held their rapt attention while he sang a Welsh love song in his fine tenor voice, making Christina blush very prettily as he took her hand and sang just to her. As the final notes died away over the grove, appreciative applause broke out and then he was cheered loudly as he toasted the bride and groom with a large glass of ouzo, which he promptly drained.

His song was the signal for others, led by Mr Niphakos himself. Sir Owen and Roslyn stood with them all for a while, and then he took her arm and led her back to their place by the tree. 'That's got 'em going, eh?'

'You've pleased them very much.'

'It doesn't hurt to enter into the spirit of things, *cariad*.'

'I wish James Atherton felt the same way.'

They resumed their places and Sir Owen picked up his pencil and sketchbook again and continued drawing. Roslyn sat back against the lemon tree, watching the feast.

It was some time later, with evening upon them, that she glanced up the hillside and saw James riding down past the church. He passed from her sight behind the poplar trees. She wondered if he would still pointedly avoid the celebrations, even though he was back earlier than usual.

Several minutes later her question was answered, for she turned to look back at the house and saw him approaching. He'd changed out of his riding clothes and was dressed in his tight black evening coat and cream trousers. A diamond flashed in his neckcloth, and he wore a particularly elegant white satin waistcoat over his frilled shirt. He didn't appear to see her or Sir Owen as he passed and crossed the grove toward the bridal bower, where Christina and Theo were once again seated with their families. By now many of the guests had noticed him, and there were many whispers and nudges as he went up to the bower.

Christina saw him then, gazing in obvious

astonishment as he bowed to her, taking her hand and drawing it gallantly to his lips. He said something, and whatever it was pleased her, for she dimpled and smiled shyly. Theo looked a little bemused, and Mr Niphakos stared for a long moment before suddenly getting to his feet and grinning. He clapped James on the back and pressed a glass of ouzo into his hand. When James chose to use it, the Atherton charm was a devastating weapon, and he employed it upon them now, smiling and conversing in flawless Greek. They warmed to him immediately, and it was as if his past behavior had never been.

Roslyn watched in amazement, and Sir Owen paused in his sketching. 'So, he's thought better of it, eh?'

'It would seem so.'

'You don't look very pleased.'

'I could kick him for not behaving like this earlier. It wouldn't have hurt him to make the effort just this once. It's a wedding day; it means everything to Christina and Theo, but James Atherton puts his own grievances first.'

'If you're in that sort of mood, I think I'll make myself scarce.'

'Why do you say that?'

'Well, I believe he's about to come over and join us, and I shrink from the lashing your tongue seems set upon giving him.'

Before she could say anything else, he'd gathered his drawings together and was hurrying away, pausing for a moment to speak to James, who was carrying a small tray.

Then James continued toward her. 'Good evening, Miss Meredith.'

'Sir.'

'Ah, I see I'm definitely in your bad books.'

'You are.'

'I've tried to make amends.'

'Belatedly.'

'It is said that things are better done late than never at all.' He smiled at her. 'May I join you?'

'If you wish.'

'Oh, I do.' He crouched down to place the tray on the grass. On it stood a small jug of retsina, a bowl of greengages, two glasses, and a fork.

She looked at it all in surprise. 'What's this?'

'A peace offering,' he replied, sitting down beside her and putting a greengage into each glass before pouring the retsina on top. Then he sat back. 'I've behaved badly, Miss Meredith.'

'Yes, you have.'

'And you aren't going to spare me, are you?'

'No. It wouldn't have hurt you to stay here today.'

'I'm trying to redeem myself now. You're right to be angry with me. I shouldn't have allowed my own sour memories to cloud my judgment and manners where other weddings are concerned. I've made amends as best I can with our hosts, and now I am hoping to do the same with you.'

'By being charm personified again?'

'Is that how it seems?'

'Yes.'

'I don't mean it to, please believe me. I'm not being false or shallow, Miss Meredith. I'm truly sorry for being a bear and I wish to be in your good books again.'

She looked at him, hesitating.

He took the fork and speared one of the greengages soaking in the retsina, then he held it out to her, smiling. 'Pax, Miss Meredith?'

Unwillingly she smiled too, accepting it. 'Pax, Lord Atherton.'

★   ★   ★

Darkness fell and lanterns were lit among the lemon trees. The wedding feast came to a temporary halt, for it was time to escort the bride and groom down to the harbor, and the caïque that was to take them up the coast to their new home on the Mavrocordatos estate.

126

Candles and lanterns bobbed down the hillside toward the town as the guests streamed down behind the wedding party. Roslyn lost sight of her uncle, but James remained with her, holding her hand safely amid the crush and excitement.

The noise set all the dogs in Ayios Georghios barking wildly. In the harbor the lights winked on the glossy water, and the caïques rocked gently on the barely discernible swell of high tide. The vigilant taverna owner flung open his doors, having done no trade because of the wedding, but now he did very handsomely indeed.

By the bridal craft, rice and flowers were thrown as the bride and groom were cheered on board. The caïque had been decorated with garlands, streamers, and variegated lanterns. Christina and Theo stood on the low deck as the ropes were untied and the prow pushed away from the quay. The caïque slid silently out into the harbor, its sails hoisting to catch the breeze crossing the dark bay.

Roslyn stood beside James watching until the caïque's lights were only a faint glimmer in the distance. Turning, James noticed a man he wanted to talk to. They spoke together for a moment and then the man nodded and James turned back to her.

'Who was that?' she asked.

'Constantin Niphakos' cousin. He owns the caïque over there.'

'The *Andros*?' she said, following his pointing finger and struggling to read the Greek lettering on the prow.

'Yes. I've engaged him to take me across to Helena in the morning.' The guests were beginning to make their way back up the hill and he drew her hand through his arm. 'Maybe we should return as well.'

When they reached the house, she declined to go back to the lemon grove and rejoin the merrymaking. 'I'm very tired,' she explained. 'I had very little sleep last night and I seem to have been up forever today.'

'Up forever enduring my disagreeable conduct?'

She smiled. 'You've been tolerable for the last few hours.'

'That's praise indeed,' he answered, returning the smile.

Her heart almost turned over. He had only to look at her like that for her to forget completely how perverse and cold he could be. He could cast a spell over her with a glance, and it was a very sweet spell indeed. She was trembling a little as she said good night.

He took her hand suddenly, raising it to his

128

lips and kissing it. 'Good night, Miss Meredith.' For a moment he looked into her eyes, then he walked away.

In the seconds while the touch of his lips still burned on her hand, she knew that, perversely enough, she loved him.

11

Roslyn, Sir Owen, and James were among the very few to be up at breakfast the following morning. The wedding feast had gone on until well after dawn, and now the villa was quiet.

On the sunny terrace even the canaries seemed subdued after the long night. Sir Owen had gladly discarded his formal clothes for something a good deal more comfortable, but James was as correct and elegant as ever, in a brown coat and beige trousers. His waistcoat was of brown-and-white striped marcella, and there was a plain gold pin in his equally plain neckcloth.

Roslyn wore her apricot seersucker gown and matching silk reticule, and there was a brightly patterned shawl over her arms. She'd dressed her hair into a loose knot on the top of her head. She'd come down rather nervously, hoping that the fact that she now knew she was in love with James wouldn't make her behave any differently toward him. She didn't want him to guess, it would be too embarrassing. As they all sat at the table talking about the previous day's festivities, she hoped her manner was as light and carefree as her conversation.

It was while they were enjoying a final cup of coffee that they heard hoofbeats approaching from the direction of the town. James got up immediately and watched the solitary horseman urging his tired, sweating horse toward the house. It was the courier from Athens. Without a word James left the terrace.

Roslyn glanced at her uncle. 'It must be the news he's been waiting for.'

'I can't think what else it would be. Do you know what it's about?'

She shook her head. 'I presume it's something to do with his wife. At least . . . well, I don't know what else it could concern.' She sat back, gazing at the wonderful view. 'I shall miss this place when we leave.'

'I shall too. Still, we have three more days.'

At that moment James returned, carrying a sealed letter that he placed before Sir Owen. 'I'm still waiting in vain. This is addressed to you and appears to be rather urgent.'

As James sat down again, Sir Owen picked up the letter and looked rather apprehensively at the writing. 'It's from my lawyer. I suppose I must brace myself, for it can't be good news.'

The others watched as he broke the seal and unfolded the paper. He read the few brief lines and his face grew pale. 'It's as well we leave in three days' time, *cariad*, my financial affairs are once again in utter chaos.'

Roslyn stared at him in dismay. 'Oh, no,' she breathed. 'The investments Lord Elgin recommended — ?'

'Have proved as unwise as all the others. I'm advised to return to London as quickly as possible to salvage what I can.'

James looked at him in concern. 'Surely things cannot be as bad as all that.'

'Read it for yourself.' Sir Owen handed him the letter.

James glanced at it and then drew a long sympathetic breath, nodding. 'Your lawyer is right, you must return as quickly as you can.'

'The *Hydra* leaves soon.'

'Sooner than you think, tomorrow night to be precise. The messenger told me. It seems Mrs Macri charged him to see that you and Miss Meredith were told. There's been a last-minute change of sailing date and you will have to leave here first thing tomorrow morning.'

Sir Owen rose heavily to his feet. 'Not a very cheering note upon which to end our stay. I'm sorry, Roslyn, my dear.'

She got up quickly and went to hug him.

'It's not your fault, Uncle Owen.'

'But it is, *cariad*. I'm a financial disaster. We'll have to leave tomorrow as James says.'

'Maybe it would be wiser to go today?'

'And forfeit our last few hours here? No, *cariad*, I wouldn't hear of it. I intend to go up to the temple again to draw what I *like* to draw before I have to return to London and fashionable physogs like that of Lady Ferney.'

Roslyn couldn't help glancing at James, remembering that Lady Ferney, a very lovely and stylish lady of rather forceful personality, was Benedict Courtenay's sister.

James merely gave Sir Owen a sympathetic look. 'You have my commiserations, sir, for the lady is a she-cat if the first order.'

'She is indeed. She pursued me relentlessly before I left London. I was glad to escape. She was quite set that I was going to do a performance of her, and I was the proverbial maggot on a hook, squirming to no avail. Now I suppose I'll have to oblige her. I'm not in any position financially to refuse her.'

Roslyn couldn't bear to see him weighed down again after having been so carefree. 'Oh, Uncle Owen, I'm so sorry.'

'Don't look so sad, *cariad*. We'll manage somehow. Now, then, I must prepare for my excursion to the temple. Do you want to join me?'

She shook her head. 'No, I've too much to do here if we're leaving tomorrow.'

'Too much to do? There isn't all that much, sweetheart.'

James looked at her. 'Actually, I was rather hoping to claim your company myself today, Miss Meredith.'

'You — you were?'

'I realize that it mightn't be quite the thing, but I was toying with the notion of inviting you to join me on the caïque I've hired.'

'Caïque? Oh, of course, now I remember. Mr Niphakos's cousin.'

He nodded. 'Would it be very improper of me to invite you to come to Helena with me? We could walk to the monastery and picnic there. We'll be accompanied, the caïque cannot sail by itself.'

She wanted to accept, oh, how she wanted to accept. She glanced at her uncle. 'Do you think I could go?'

He smiled. 'I cannot see why not. You'll be chaperoned.'

Her eyes brightened and she turned to James. 'I'd love to join you.'

'Excellent. I'll see that the picnic basket contains enough for two.' He got up.

'When do you wish to leave?'

'I think as soon as you're ready, don't you? Why waste precious time?'

'I'll go for my bonnet,' she said, looking again at her uncle. 'You really don't mind if I go?'

'Of course not, sweetheart. Hurry along now.'

She gathered her skirts and went swiftly back into the house. Maybe this was unexpectedly her last day in Ayios Georghios, but she was going to spend it alone with James Atherton. Soon both he and the place would be part of her past, but she would have one wonderful day by which to remember them both.

*   *   *

Shortly afterward, they walked down to the town, with James carrying the basket of food. Roslyn was doubly aware of everything around her. Colors seemed clearer, and sounds had a sharpness she hadn't noticed before. Small scenes caught her attention, and she knew that she was subconsciously comitting them to memory. A woman was in a garden dyeing skeins of wool in a caldron over a fire, and the drying blue skeins were draped in the branches of an olive tree. The blue was almost vibrant and the caldron bubbled audibly. Nearby, the woman's husband was seated on the doorstep of the

135

little whitewashed house. He was mending a fishing net that rustled on the stone flags as he pulled it around to reach a new part. A little farther on, where the way was steep and narrow between high walls, she heard the rumble of a millstone and the little pattering steps of the two donkeys driving it.

The harbor square was very quiet now, after the riotous celebrations of the night before. The cobbles were littered with flowers and rice, and there was even a garland still caught on the topmost branches of one of the trees, where it had been thrown in the excitement. The caïques that had left first thing had returned with their catches of lobster, which were being loaded into the panniers of the donkeys waiting to take it to the surrounding villages before the sun was too hot.

Mr Niphakos's cousin, seen so fleetingly the night before, was a short, muscular man with a swarthy complexion and tightly curled gray hair. He wore a blue fisherman's cap and rough but serviceable clothes, and evidently didn't enjoy anywhere near the wealth of his important relative. His face was disfigured by an ugly scar; he took great delight in telling Roslyn that it was the result of a recent skirmish with Corsican pirates. James hastened to reassure her that by 'recent' the man

136

had meant the year before last and that the pirates hadn't been seen in the vicinity of Ayios Georghios or the nearby islands for some months now because of the Turkish presence in the next bay.

The *Andros* was moored where it had been the night before. It was about fifteen feet long and painted white with a handsome frieze of red, green, and blue. Its single mast sported a red sail, and there was a marmalade cat reclining on the cushions placed in the prow for the comfort of passengers.

The fisherman carried the picnic basket on board, placing it next to the cushions, and James assisted Rosyln on to the swaying boat. She sat next to the cat, which began to purr when she stroked it. She was told it was called Mauolina. When James was seated next to her, the fisherman nodded to a small group of boys on the quay. They untied the mooring ropes and as the caïque slid out on to the water, James tossed them a handful of coins.

Soon Ayios Georghios was slipping away astern as the little craft skimmed over the crystal water toward Helena. The ribbons of Roslyn's straw bonnet fluttered and the hem of her seersucker gown lifted in the breeze. James discarded his top hat, and his golden hair was swiftly ruffled. His eyes seemed as blue as the sea.

She looked ahead as Helena loomed ever closer across the wide channel. James glanced at her. 'Shame on you, Miss Meredith, for you're looking at a view you've been seeing all week when you could be looking at Ayios Georghios as you've never seen it before.'

She looked back and saw that he was right. Now she could see the little town clinging to the steep land in the lee of the cliffs. The houses spilled down to the water, and above them was the villa and the church. On the headland the temple of Poseidon had never looked more dramatic and white than it did from the sea. Gazing at the row of columns, she wondered if her uncle was there yet, or if he was still toiling up through the valley. She couldn't see him, but she waved just in case he was looking at the caïque.

James smiled. 'Do you think he'll see you?'

'I don't know. Maybe.'

He looked at the view again. 'A memorable scene, you'll agree?'

'Yes.'

'Is that all you have to say? Where's your poetic Welsh blood?'

'Would you have me recite the *Odyssey*? Or maybe you prefer the *Iliad*?'

'You don't have to go that far; I'll settle for something more modest.'

'Poetic Welsh blood finds it impossible to

be merely modest.' She struck a heroic pose. '*Heddychol tlws golygfa, nef eich enw*,' she intoned. 'There, will that do?'

He grinned. 'I don't know if it will do or not, because I haven't the slightest idea what it means. I trust it was polite?'

'Sir, would *I* say anything impolite?' She smiled at him. 'All I said was 'peaceful, beautiful view, heaven is your name'.'

'Ah. Then yes, it will do.'

Helena was much closer now and Roslyn turned to look ahead. The island was about two miles long and half a mile wide, and the monastery could be seen quite clearly on the rising land in the center. There were many trees inland, but the shore was rocky and without beaches.

The *Andros* sailed into the shelter of a small, rock-fringed bay from where it seemed that there was no way up from the water, but as the sail was furled and the little boat slid toward the rocks, Roslyn saw that steps had been hewn from the stone, leading up to the wooded land above. The scent of lilac was very strong as the caïque's prow nudged the shore, and when Roslyn looked up at the top of the steps, she saw several trees in full bloom.

Mr Niphakos's cousin jumped ashore and made the ropes fast, and then James put the basket on the rocks before assisting Roslyn. As she shook out her skirts and retied her bonnet, he turned to speak to the fisherman, who immediately shook his head and began to point to his foot. She watched in astonishment as the two argued for some time and at last she couldn't bear not understanding for a moment longer. 'What on earth are you talking about?' she inquired.

James turned to her, looking rather exasperated. 'He says he can't possibly accompany us to the monastery because he has blisters after dancing so much in his new wedding shoes yesterday. It means we'll have to picnic somewhere within sight of the caïque and forgo the monastery.'

She looked at him in dismay. He quite obviously didn't believe the Greek's excuse, and when she thought of how lithely he'd moved around the caïque during the voyage, she was inclined to disbelieve it as well. Without him, however, etiquette would be offended. She sighed. A pox on etiquette! Then an almost defiant look came into her eyes as she looked again at James. 'I was alone with you once before, at the temple,' she pointed out, 'and no one even knows about it.'

He raised a wry eyebrow. 'Miss Meredith, are you suggesting — ?'

'Why not? I'm sure I'll be quite safe with

you, sir, for you've promised to save me from dragons, not feed me to them. And I do so want to see the monastery,' she added on a wistful note.

'Then who am I to deny you your wish? We'll go, and to the devil with etiquette.' He spoke again to the Greek who looked quite relieved as he returned to the caïque and made himself comfortable on the cushions next to the still-slumbering Mauolina.

James picked up the basket and offered Roslyn his arm. Together they proceeded up the steps.

12

A barely discernible path led inland from the top of the steps, sweeping down into a shallow valley filled with wild flowers. It was a place of arcadian beauty, somewhere where Roslyn could well imagine Helen of Troy, the lovelist woman in the world, gladly giving herself to the embrace of her handsome warrior prince, Paris.

They entered some woods, and the land began to rise perceptibly toward the hill in the center of the island. At last they emerged on to open grassland, and the monastery was in front of them. They didn't speak as they walked toward it, passing through an ancient archway into what was left of a cloistered courtyard where there was a stone spring shaded by an almond tree. It was a leafy place where the old stones provided refuge for plants of all description. And for birds. As Rosyln and James entered, a cloud of startled white doves rose noisily into the flawless blue sky.

Roslyn gazed around. 'It's beautiful,' she breathed, 'a romantic landscape come to life. My uncle would *adore* it.' She thought about her uncle. 'I wish he didn't have problems with money. He was so happy here in Greece, but now it's been spoiled for him.'

'You love him very much, don't you?'

'Yes.'

'Something may turn up.'

'I doubt it. He was hoping against hope that these investments of Lord Elgin's would be lucrative.' With a sigh she untied her bonnet and hung it on one of the almond tree's branches, where it swung to and fro in the soft breeze.

James changed the subject for one a little lighter. 'Where shall we partake of our banquet?'

'On the sofa, of course,' she replied, pointing to a fallen piece of masonry that bore a strong resemblance to such an item.

He smiled. 'What more could we want? Except perhaps a butler to serve.'

She laughed and sat down. He joined her, placing the basket on the stone between them and beginning to take out the contents. There was a clean white cloth, some fresh bread, a large portion of cheese, some fruit, and two glasses with a corked earthenware jar of good red wine.

As he poured the wine, she smiled at him. 'Do you think Helen and Paris did as well as this?'

'Probably, even though they definitely didn't deserve it.'

She looked at him a little curiously. 'Didn't deserve it? Why? Because they were responsible for the Trojan wars?'

'No, because she was already married to Menelaus when she took Paris as her lover. My sympathies lie entirely with the injured husband, and they do so because I suspect that I too have been wearing horns of late.'

She didn't know what to say, the statement was so unexpected and personal that it caught her off guard. Slowly she accepted the glass he held out to her. 'I — I know it's not my business, but if it would help to talk, well, I've been told I'm a very good listener.' She colored a little, wondering if such an offer might be perceived as forward.

He smiled a little self-consciously. 'Forgive me, Miss Meredith, I should not have spoken as I did. As to you being a good listener, well, I've no doubt that you are, but I'm afraid that I'm the world's worst confider. I trust I haven't offended you, either by my earlier remark or by turning down your offer?'

'No. Of course not. I wish I could help, though; it makes me sad to see you so troubled.'

'Troubled? That's one way of putting it, I suppose.' He smiled, putting his hand to her cheek. 'You've helped me already, Miss Meredith, by coming to Ayios Georghios and making me behave in a civilized manner again.' It was a warm smile, matched by the warmth of his touch.

She felt the color intensify on her cheeks. She wanted so much to tell him that she loved him, but knew that she must not.

He studied her. 'The man who wins you will be very fortunate indeed. You have looks, spirit, charm, and compassion, and on top of that you're very good company.'

She lowered her eyes. 'You've very gallant, sir, but you've left out the most glaring of my faults.'

'Faults? You couldn't possibly possess such low things.'

'It's a fortune that I don't possess, sir, and that's the criterion by which gentlemen judge prospective wives, is it not?'

'Not all gentlemen. I didn't, for instance.'

'No, but you chose a bride of matchless beauty. I can hardly claim to be that!' She looked away, not having intended to turn the conversation back to Vanessa, but somehow it had happened.

He didn't say anything for a moment. 'Beauty is in the eye of the beholder, Miss Meredith, and I doubt now whether I'd still find my wife beautiful.'

'Of course you would.'

'Why? Because you think I still love her?'

'Don't you?'

'I don't know.' Slowly he got up, swirling his glass and watching the dark-red wine revolve. 'Maybe too much has happened now for me ever to find her fair to look upon again. She just stepped out of my life and I don't know why, or whether she'll return. I don't even know where she's gone, or who she's with. Oh, at one time I thought she'd gone to Courtenay, for I know that there was a great deal between them before I came along. Maybe enough for her to have seen him after the marriage, who can say? I fear it, though. Yes, I fear it. But I don't think he knows where she is now; his conduct suggests that he's as mystified as me.' He turned to look at her. 'I seem to be confiding in you, after all.'

'You don't need to say anything more if you don't wish to.'

He looked away again, taking a long breath. 'I've been hoping to hear from her. I left word with her fox of a lawyer, knowing that she was due to be in touch with him. I told her through him that if she wanted to mend the rift between us, then I was agreeable and that I could be contacted through the British representatives in Athens.' He smiled wryly. 'I don't know why I still came here. We'd intended to come together originally, and when she left, well, I allowed the plans to carry me along, I suppose.'

'You might still hear.'

He shook his head. 'No, not now. If she'd had any desire to save our marriage, she would have written straightaway. I'd arranged for couriers to be ready and waiting; the news could have been with me within days. There's been nothing. It's as if she no longer exists, except that for me she does so very much. So there you have it, Miss Meredith, the reason for my extraordinary silence about my wife's disappearance — I haven't said anything because I don't damned well know anything! I've had to run the gauntlet of London chatter, and then that of Athens. I've faced my justifiably furious aunt, who abhors anything even remotely touched with scandal, and not once have I been able to say anything at all. I feel I'm the original fool. The original fool!' He repeated the phrase savagely, suddenly hurling his glass against a wall, shattering it like his wife's miniature.

Roslyn stared at him, shaken by the fury that had suddenly burst from him. Trembling a little, she put her own glass down and got up to go to him. She placed a hesitant hand on his arm. 'You aren't the fool, James Atherton,' she said quietly, her voice shaking because she was close to tears for him. 'If anyone's the fool in all this, it's your wife for having turned away from you in the first place. And if she's done it because of someone like Sir Benedict Courtenay, then she's an even bigger fool. Believe me.' She wanted to hold him close, to whisper her love and kiss away his anger and hurt.

He knew he'd distressed her and immediately his fingers closed apologetically over hers. 'Forgive me, I shouldn't have spoken like that.'

'I'm glad that you did.'

'Glad?'

'Because now I understand so much more.'

His blue eyes searched her face for a moment. 'You have a tender heart, Miss Meredith,' he said softly, 'and that is yet another sweet quality to offer the man lucky enough to win you.' He hesitated, then suddenly bent his head to kiss her on the lips. He didn't draw her into his arms, but his fingers were still warm and firm over hers. His lips moved slowly and gently.

Her senses reeled wildly within her. She'd already stepped over the precipice into love, now she was lost forever in the abyss. It was all she could do not to respond to the fire that flared into life within her at the touch of his lips. She mustn't; he was beyond her reach. The kiss didn't mean to him what it meant to her.

He drew back then, smiling with a little embarrassment. 'Forgive me, I shouldn't have done that. I trust I haven't offended you.'

She strove to remain outwardly composed. 'Of course not.' Her voice was light and she even managed a smile. 'Besides, we have two excellent things to blame.'

'We do?'

'A certain Greek gentleman's blisters and the shades of Helen and Paris.' She smiled again. 'Now, then, shouldn't we consider finishing our picnic? I promise not to make you drink from the jar but will allow you to share my glass.' She didn't know how she was able to behave like this, but somehow she was finding the guile. Her lips still tingled from the kiss and her heart was pounding in her breast, but she sat down again, and when she picked up her glass, her hand didn't give the slightest sign of trembling.

He hesitated for a moment and then accepted the glass from her, smiling. 'Miss Meredith, I once accused you of not being a lady. I don't think I was ever more wrong in my life.'

'Thank you, sir.'

'You mentioned your uncle's financial difficulties earlier. Something will turn up, you know.'

'I wish I could feel as certain.'

He smiled a little, raising the glass to her. 'Your health, Miss Meredith.'

⋆ ⋆ ⋆

She didn't want that day to end, but end it did, and the *Andros* returned to the mainland late in the afternoon. She attended to the packing of her things and then those of her uncle, and in no time at all it was time to dress for their last dinner at the villa.

The meal was almost at an end and they'd been discussing the Turkish occupation of Greece when the conversation took an unexpected turn.

Sir Owen sat back, exhaling slowly. 'There's a depth of feeling just below the surface in this land, and it is going to explode to the surface someday soon.'

James nodded. 'The Turks aren't the force they were. The time's going to be right for revolution before very long.'

With a chuckle, Sir Owen picked up his glass and surveyed the contents. 'I wish to God my debts weren't the force they are,' he declared simply, 'for then I could look forward to achieving my freedom as well.'

'Do you have much work in hand?' asked James, an odd note in his voice making

Roslyn look quickly at him.

Sir Owen shrugged. 'I have work, and my order book is full, but it's strung out over a period of time. I need something exceeding lucrative right now. The only two commissions of note are at Chatsworth at the end of the summer, and Castle Howard in the autumn.'

James met Roslyn's glance for a moment before addressing himself to her uncle again. 'I couldn't help noticing the sums your lawyer mentioned in his letter.'

'They're substantial enough for a blind man to see,' replied Sir Owen glumly.

'I have a proposition to put to you.'

'If you think to kindly bail me out, James, then the answer must be no. I wouldn't dream of accepting.'

'You don't know what the proposition is yet.'

'I don't need to.'

'Your pride is misplaced in this particular instance, for I'm not offering to bail you out in the way you think.'

'What are you offering, then?'

'A commission as remunerative as you need to put you in the black.'

Sir Owen stared at him. 'I can't imagine any commission that rewarding.'

'This one is, I promise you.'

'What is it?'

'I want you to substantially alter the portraits you performed for me two years ago at Foxcombe.'

Sir Owen sat forward with a slightly incredulous laugh. 'With all due respect, James, if you're dissatisfied with them, then I feel obliged to alter them free of charge under the terms of our original agreement.'

'This has nothing to do with dissatisfaction.'

'But what on earth do you want done to them?'

'A considerable amount of work, I promise you, and important enough to me to warrant offering you the sort of sum involved. And please don't think I'm offering charity, because I'm not. I've come to a decision and wish to see that decision implemented as quickly as possible. Are you interested?'

Sir Owen studied him for a long moment, evidently totally bemused, but then he nodded. 'Yes, my boy, of course I am. I'd be a fool not to.'

'It's settled, then. I must remain here until the end of the month. I left word in London that I would, and I'm a man of my word, but then I'll be returning to England. You'll be staying at Elgin House, won't you?'

'Yes.'

'I will call upon you there. The commission will naturally entail you coming to Foxcombe with me. I trust that will be in order?'

'Quite in order.'

James raised his glass. 'I think the commission will be to everyone's benefit.'

Sir Owen lifted his glass as well.

Roslyn, who'd remained silent throughout, hesitantly picked up hers as well. She didn't know what to think. James had decided upon this on Helena that afternoon, she could remember the moment. 'Something will turn up, you know . . . ' A gladness sang through her, not only because her uncle's difficulties seemed to have been solved, but also because she'd see James again.

He was looking at her. 'I trust you'll find Foxcombe to your liking, Miss Meredith.'

Her heart almost stopped. 'You — you wish me to come too?'

He smiled. 'I wouldn't dream of anything else.'

13

They left Ayios Georghios early the next morning, and the whole house came to say goodbye. James stood on the terrace as they rode down the drive and out onto the track. She glanced back and he waved. She waved too before the view of the house was suddenly cut off by the greenery edging the track.

She was sad as they rode through the steep streets of the little town. The *Andros* was moored in the harbor and she saw Mauolina sitting sleepily on the deck. Caïques returning from the morning tide were unloading their catches just as they had been the previous day when she and James had set off for Helena.

All too quickly the last houses were slipping away behind and they were riding toward the steep grove of broom and the pineclad slopes ahead. The Greek guides were in cheerful moods, singing in unison so that their voices echoed all around, and the pack horses swished their tails as they toiled up the long climb. They paused at the same place at the top of the escarpment, and Roslyn looked back for the last time at the magnificent view. She saw the temple, where she'd been at sunset with James, and the church, where Christina and Theo had married and where James had ridden her down. She saw the lemon grove, where during the wedding feast he'd speared a greengage with his fork and handed it to her. 'Pax, Miss Meredith?' Lastly, kept until the final moment, she looked across the glittering sea toward Helena, where he'd kissed her. Then she turned her back on it, urging her horse on over the top of the escarpment and down the other side through the long pass that led to the rich rolling land spreading north toward Athens.

The weather began to change as the day wore on, and as evening fell and they at last saw Athens ahead, it began to rain. They returned to Mrs Macri's house to change into dry clothes and picked up the remainder of their baggage, then a carriage arrived to convey them in the gathering gloom to the *Hydra*, which lay at anchor in Piraeus.

The transport ship was an ugly craft, lying low in the water because of a heavy cargo that included Lord Elgin's last shipment of antiquities. It was still raining heavily as Roslyn and her uncle were rowed out across the gray, dismal water, and the horizon was lost in a haze of low cloud.

Gathering her already damp muslin skirts,

155

Roslyn stepped from the swaying boat on to the rope-edged gangway against the side of the ship. She was glad of her sturdy linen cape and wide-brimmed bonnet as she made her unsteady way up toward the deck above. The noise of the rain hissed all around and darkness was already almost complete. A sailor assisted her onto the ship, and as she stood on the deck, shaking out her skirts, she saw that the cargo had spilled over from the hold to clutter the deck as well. There were all manner of crates, cases, and sacks, to say nothing of cages containing various animals, including a very excitable greyhound. Seeing her astonishment, the sailor explained. 'It all belongs to Lord Byron, miss. He arrived on board with more servants and baggage than Ali Pasha himself.'

At that moment, just as Sir Owen stepped on the deck, Lord Byron himself emerged from the doorway leading to the captain's quarters. He was as flamboyant as ever in his Albanian costume, but he didn't look at all well; he was pale, with shadows beneath his handsome brown eyes, and he had a hacking cough. He bowed gallantly over Roslyn's hand, ignoring the steady downpour. 'Welcome aboard, Miss Meredith.'

'Thank you, my lord.' She eyed him warily.

'Don't attempt to flatter me by saying how

well I look, for I know that I look wretched. I'm sad to say that you'll only be enjoying my company as far as Malta because my many recent excesses have taxed my health and I've been persuaded I must see the British leech there.' He turned to Sir Owen. 'How were Poseidon's ruins, sir?'

'Splendid, my boy, splendid,' replied Sir Owen, pulling his wet cloak more firmly about his shoulders.

'And have you, like your rapacious Scottish friend, robbed Greece of her treasures?'

'Am I to understand that you're looking for a good argument all the way to Malta?'

'You are,' replied Lord Byron with disarming candor.

Sir Owen gave a wicked grin. 'Very well. Yes, I've robbed Greece of every antiquity I could find, and I strongly uphold my right to do so and the wisdom of my actions. There. Will that do to set the ball rolling?'

'It will do excellently. I look forward to many stimulating discussions.'

Sir Owen nodded. 'I'll give you a run for your money, sir, but for the moment I'm getting rather too wet for comfort, so if you will excuse me . . .'

'By all means.' Lord Byron bowed, indicating the door to the captain's quarters.

As Roslyn made to follow her uncle, Lord

Byron spoke softly in her ear. 'And how was handsome Lord Atherton, sweet lady?'

She turned, her breath catching, but his face was bland, as if he hadn't said anything. 'Please walk on in, Miss Meredith,' he murmured. 'Otherwise you'll catch your death of cold and then we'll be reduced to fighting for the attentions of the leech.'

She didn't say anything more, but hurried along the slippery deck between the piles of crates and cages, at last reaching the doorway and stepping thankfully out of the downpour. She glanced back at him. She had to know why he'd seen to it that she and her uncle went to Ayios Georghios, and why he was apparently so interested in her dealings with James Atherton. Before they reached Malta, she intended to find out what the handsome, clever poet was up to.

★　★　★

She didn't have long to wait, she found out before the lights of Greece had vanished in the gloom astern of the *Hydra*. It was still raining as the ship sailed on the night tide. Ignoring the endless downpour, Roslyn put on her cape and bonnet and went outside to stand at the stern watching the land fade away in the darkness. Dinner had proved very lively, both Sir Owen and Lord Byron enjoying themselves hugely arguing for the sake of it and forming a healthy respect for each other's talents in the process. But the conversation had frequently been punctuated by the poet's bad cough.

Roslyn had stolen away as soon as she could, and now stared back through the mist and darkness. A few lights were just visible. Behind her the greyhound began to bark again, and the sound startled her. She turned quickly.

Lord Byron was approaching, his scarlet costume vivid in the swaying light of the lantern. 'I'm sorry if my dog frightened you, Miss Meredith.'

'The poor thing looks dreadfully cooped up.'

'I promise to exercise it each day, I'll take it for jolly perambulations around the deck. Will that ease your heart?' He was laughing at her.

'I'll hold you to your promise, sir.'

'I've no doubt,' he replied, leaning on the rail beside her and gazing at the ship's wash.

'I'm glad of the chance to speak to you, sir.'

The brown eyes swung knowingly toward her. 'Should I be flattered and hopeful?'

'Not particularly.'

He pretended disappointment. 'Alas, she's indifferent to my charms.'

'She is.'

'But you're still glad to speak to me? I wonder why?' He coughed a little.

'I think you know, sir.'

'Do I?'

'Yes.'

He straightened, folding his arms and looking into her eyes. 'You have me at a disadvantage, Miss Meredith.'

'The day that happens, sir, pigs will take to the air on wings.'

He laughed. 'Now I *am* flattered.'

'To be honest, sir, I'm not particularly well-disposed toward you at the moment.'

'No? What have I done to offend you?'

'You connived to see that my uncle and I went to Ayios Georghios.'

'I must correct you, Miss Meredith. I connived to see that *you* went there; your uncle, delightful as he is, was purely incidental.'

She stared at him. 'So you admit it?'

'Oh, yes. I'm not ashamed of my actions. In fact, I'd be rather proud of them — if they'd worked. Unfortunately they don't appear to have come to the conclusion I'd hoped, which makes the whole thing rather pointless.'

'What are you talking about?'

'You and James Atherton, of course.'

Her lips parted and she was at a loss for words.

He smiled. 'Correct me if I'm wrong, but you are attracted to the gentleman, aren't you?'

'I've no intention of answering such an improper question!' Her eyes flashed.

'You just have. If you were indifferent to him, you'd say so, but instead, you look the picture of righteous indignation and decline to answer.' He studied her. 'I owe you a proper explanation, and so I shall tell you. The first time I met you, I found you interesting, not because you are so very attractive, which heaven knows you are, but because I detected your interest in Atherton. I happened to be near you when conversation turned to Vanessa Atherton's mysterious disappearance. You were intrigued by the matter, and not because of the mystery but because of James Atherton himself. I could see it in your eyes, in the light flush that touched your cheeks.' He reached out to place his fingers against her rain-dampened skin, and he smiled as she drew sharply back. 'Don't look so alarmed, Miss Meredith, I'm not about to pounce upon you, I'm feeling too fragile and sorry for myself to do that. Now, then, where was I? Oh, yes, your obvious interest in Atherton. I decided I must be certain of my judgment, so I observed you closely whenever we attended the same function.'

'So that's why you followed me around,' she cried angrily.

'You noticed? I wasn't as subtle as I'd thought.' He coughed again.

'Sir, I'd have to have been very dense indeed not to notice that you were constantly at my elbow.'

'My persistence paid dividends in the end, Miss Meredith, for I soon discovered that in you I'd found my perfect champion.'

She looked blankly at him. 'Your what?'

'My champion. My gallant defender, ready to ride into battle on my behalf.'

'I haven't the slightest idea what you're talking about.'

'I've been waiting to have my revenge upon Chienne Atherton, and you gave me what seemed to be a splendid opportunity. You're the ideal woman, Miss Meredith, the perfect temptress to steal James Atherton's bruised heart and snatch him up from the *chienne*'s vicious claws. He's vulnerable at the moment, and you're so sweet and innocent, so enchantingly original, that he'd be a fool indeed not to be drawn to you. The rest I thought I could leave up to you. However, I can tell that it didn't work, that Atherton is still dismally bound to the *chienne*, and your poor little heart has been broken.'

She'd been listening with increasing anger and outrage. 'You had no right. No right at all!'

'I know, and I'm truly sorry. I didn't want my manipulations to cause you any hurt, Miss Meredith. Indeed, I was convinced that the very opposite would be the case. I still think — '

'I don't want to hear any more!'

'I was just going to say that I don't think all's lost yet. Sir Owen said at dinner that you and he have been invited to Foxcombe.'

'Do you honestly imagine that I'm going to behave with complete abandon and fling myself at Lord Atherton? If you do, then you're a very poor judge of character, sir. And not only that, you're also breathtakingly insulting.'

'I don't mean any insult at all, Miss Meredith. Please believe me. And can I really be wicked to want you to defeat the *chienne* and vindicate my awesome genius?' He smiled charmingly at her.

'You don't charm me, sirrah, I find you and your actions totally abhorrent.'

'You don't mean that.'

'Oh, yes I do!' She was trembling.

'Maybe I was wrong to interfere — '

'There's no maybe about it, you were completely wrong!'

'My actions weren't entirely selfish, you know. I honestly think that you and James Atherton would do very well together. You do love him, don't you?'

She didn't reply.

He smiled a little. 'I can tell that you do, Miss Meredith. Before Ayios Georghios you were attracted and intrigued; now you've crossed over into love, and there's no going back.'

In the darkness her cheeks were flushed. She looked away from him.

'Don't give up hope, Miss Meredith. After all, he has seen to it that you go to Foxcombe, hasn't he?'

'He was merely being polite.'

'Was he?'

'Yes.' She turned completely away. 'Please leave me alone, sir.'

'Not until you accept that if I acted with any malice, it wasn't directed at you but at the *chienne*.'

'Please go.'

'I promise faithfully to promenade the greyhound every single day.'

She didn't reply.

'And every night too if that's what you wish.'

Unwillingly she looked into his teasing

brown eyes. She was justifiably angry with him, but it was impossible to remain so when faced with his determination to win her over. 'Yes, that's what I wish,' she declared. 'You must exercise that poor creature twice a day.'

'And I'll be forgiven?'

'No, sir, but I'll accept that you meant no malice toward me.'

'Never toward you, Miss Meredith,' he said, drawing her hand to his lips. 'But toward the *chienne*? Oh, toward her I meant every mischief imaginable.'

'To no avail, sir, for it's my belief that he still loves her and that nothing will change that.'

'Time will tell, Miss Meredith.'

He left her then, strolling away along the cluttered deck and vanishing through a doorway.

She turned to look astern again. Well, at least she now knew what had been behind it all. She should have guessed, really; she'd been told twice about his animosity toward Vanessa Atherton. She only wished that Lord Byron had been proved correct in every detail, but he hadn't, and she knew that her love for James Atherton was without hope and must never be revealed.

Behind the *Hydra* all was darkness and rain, and the lights of Greece had been extinguished.

14

The *Hydra* reached England at the beginning of June, after calling at Malta to leave Lord Byron to the tender mercies of the British doctor there. The poet had looked far from well; his cough had worsened, added to which the weather on the island was oppressively hot with the sirocco blowing. His stay didn't promise to be at all agreeable, but he'd been as incorrigible as ever as he took his private leave of Roslyn, telling her that he still regarded her as his champion and he expected her to vanquish the *chienne* for him. She had replied that he should be ashamed of himself for encouraging a young lady of impeccable character to pursue a married gentleman, and all because that gentleman's absent wife had once had the temerity to criticize his scribbles. Lord Byron had smiled at this, drawing her hand to his lips and wishing her bon voyage, to say nothing of *viel Glück* in her pursuit of happiness. Then he'd left the ship, entered a waiting carriage, and had been driven away.

When the morning of the nineteeth of June dawned, Roslyn and Sir Owen had been in residence in Elgin House for nearly two weeks. London was still rumbling about the Atherton mystery, and Lady Gallermayne was in residence in her nephew's Grosvenor Square home, having decided not to return to Yorkshire until the scandalous whispers had subsided. It was widely felt that her ladyship was in for a very long stay in the capital, because the odd affair of Vanessa Atherton's disappearance showed little sign of going away, and even promised to occupy conversation at the grand fete at Carlton House on the evening of the nineteenth. The fete was ostensibly in honor of the exiled royal family of France, but was in reality a celebration of the Prince of Wales's elevation to the regency. He'd been wanting to hold a grand ball ever since he'd been confirmed in the rank in February, but discretion had been forced upon him because at any time the king's health might conceivably improve enough for him to understand that his eldest son wished to joyfully celebrate becoming king in everything but name. Now, however, the king's health was so poor that it was felt once and for all that he'd never recover, and so invitations to the fete had been sent out. Over two thousand had been invited to arrive at nine, but by eight the streets of London were a horrid crush of elegant vehicles containing increasingly irritable, magnificently dressed guests. The corner of Piccadilly and Park Lane was no exception: it was a jam of superior carriages all anxious to reach Carlton House in time for the commencement of the famous ball.

Roslyn stood watching at her bedroom window over-looking Park Lane and Lord Elgin's 'stone shop' at the rear of the house. It was almost dinnertime and she wondered if her uncle would be able to return through all the traffic from his studio in the Strand. Notwithstanding James' promised commission at Foxcombe, Sir Owen had thrown himself into his work from the moment he'd returned. He was anxious to complete as many portraits as possible in order to stave off the more pressing of his debts, and what time he did not spend at the studio was spent instead in disagreeable interviews with his lawyers and accountants, who were justifiably unimpressed by his insistence that Lord Atherton had promised him an assignment that would put an end to his problems in one fell swoop. Roslyn was worried about her uncle's health. He was working far too hard, and in spite of the prospect of his difficulties soon being at an end, he was fretting a great deal. She wished he'd stay at home from time to time, just to relax. Now he was late returning, and with such a terrible crush of traffic it was likely to be some time yet before he arrived. He'd make himself ill at this rate. Oh, if only James would return from Greece, but so far there'd been no news from him; they didn't even know if he'd left Ayios Georghios.

Thinking about her uncle, she wondered if the reason for his being late was Lady Ferney, who'd waylaid him at the theater the night before, imploring him to perform her likeness before she and her husband returned to their Irish estates in less than a week's time. It was a tall order, and one that Sir Owen had rather rashly promised to undertake. The visit to the theater had been his first real relaxation since arriving back in the capital. He and Roslyn hadn't only been given the use of the Elgin's town house, but also their private box at the Theater Royal, and from the moment they'd taken their seats they'd been the object of much interest from the Ferneys in their box opposite. During the intermission the two made a point of coming to the Elgin box, Lady Ferney being determined to beard Sir Owen about her portrait. She was a lovely woman with titian hair and hazel eyes, but her loveliness was spoiled by her waspish tongue and sly Courtenay nature. She didn't resemble her brother outwardly, but inside they were very alike indeed.

She'd sat down in a rustle of golden taffeta, her painted fan wafting to and fro before her exquisite face as she'd glanced rather dismissively at Roslyn's demure white satin and gauze gown and plainly dressed hair. Lady Ferney did not care for other women, and women didn't much care for her; Roslyn was no exception on either count, and the two formed an instant mutual dislike for each other. Lord Ferney, a rather ineffectual, weak-chinned young man who was very much under his forceful wife's thumb, had taken up his position behind her chair and offered no contribution whatsoever to the ensuing conversation.

Initially Lady Ferney's purpose had been to browbeat Sir Owen into agreeing to paint her portrait, but she'd become most interested when she learned the reason for his recent absence from the capital. The fact that he and Roslyn had been staying not only in Greece, but in Ayios Georghios in particular, seemed to interest her ladyship very much indeed, and the glances she'd subsequently given Roslyn had been oddly speculative. The intermission had ended and the Ferneys had retired to their own box again, but throughout the remainder of the performance, Roslyn had been very aware of Lady Ferney's thoughtful glances.

Roslyn held the lace curtain aside to look out at the stationary crush of carriages still blocking Park Lane below. Behind her her new maid, Lizzie, was busily tidying the dressing table after having dressed her for dinner. The room was prettily decorated in pink-and-white, with silk walls, a velvet-hung four-poster bed, and muslin-draped tables. On the floor was a fine rose, gold, and gray Axminster carpet, echoing the design on the ceiling plasterwork. The warm evening sun glittered on the drop-crystal chandelier and cast Roslyn's shadow over the floor as she leaned a little forward to look down through the roof lights of the museum directly below where she stood.

Lord Elgin's antiquities received many visitors, those of rank and fashion calling at the front door of the house to be conducted through the museum by the Elgins' efficient butler, Fellows. The more vulgar were admitted through the smaller Park Lane entrance directly into the museum. There were several of the latter category of visitors there now, gazing in wonder at the huge array of statues, pieces of frieze, broken columns, and exquisite busts, to say nothing of the impressive collection of sketches executed by the talented and industrious Lusieri. The museum was supposed to close at half-past eight each evening, and that hour was fast approaching. Fellows looked at the clock on the wall, his thin, rather sallow face bearing a sour and impatient expression beneath his powdered wig, and as the large hand touched the six, he ushered the unfortunate visitors quickly out, closing and bolting the door behind them. Then he withdrew from Roslyn's view into the house, leaving the museum deserted and rather forlorn.

Almost immediately the clock on the mantelpiece behind Roslyn struck the half-hour as well, and she turned from the window, her pink watered silk gown whispering a little. It had a low neckline and fitted very high beneath her breasts, and its sleeves were daintily puffed. There were matching ribbons in her hair, twined around the ringlets hanging down to the nape of her neck, and she wore her mother's golden locket on a black velvet ribbon around her throat. It was time for dinner to be served, but there was no sign yet of her uncle.

'Lizzie, will you tell the cook that I'm afraid dinner will have to be delayed?'

'Yes, madam.'

'And if I'm needed at all, I'll be in the library. I have a letter to write.'

'Yes, madam.' Lizzie curtsied and hurried

out, a rather dumpy figure in unbecoming pale-blue linen, her sandy hair tugged severely back beneath a large mob cap. But appearances were deceptive, for she was a very efficient and resourceful maid, far better than the one Roslyn had lost before leaving for Greece.

Roslyn picked up her shawl and reticule, glancing for a last time at her reflection in the cheval glass across the room. Oh, how she wished that she was going down now to find James waiting. She missed him so, he was never far away from her thoughts. With a sigh she left the room, her little satin shoes making no sound on the deep Wilton carpet in the passageway. Past members of the Bruce family gazed solemnly down from their canvases on the brocade-hung wall, and her image moved in the elegant gilt-framed mirrors above the marble-legged console tables on either side.

She emerged at the head of the great double staircase that swept regally down to the black-and-white tiled vestibule far below, past Corinthian columns and dazzling chandeliers. As she began to descend, she was startled to a halt by the loud, impatient rapping of a gentleman's cane on the front door. She stared down in surprise, wondering who on earth it could be. It wasn't her uncle, he had far too much respect for other people's front doors to treat them so badly.

Remaining where she was, she watched as Fellows emerged grumbling from the kitchens, adjusting his powdered wig and smoothing the full skirt of his brown coat. His black, buckled shoes echoed on the gleaming tiles as he went to the door, where the impatient rapping continued unabated.

As the door opened, Roslyn tried to see who was there, but she couldn't. She heard a gentleman's voice. It sounded vaguely familiar, although she couldn't place it.

'Is Sir Owen at home?'

'Er, no, sir, he hasn't returned yet.'

'Then is Miss Meredith at home?'

Roslyn stared down in astonishment. Who could possibly want to see her? She wished she could place the voice; she knew it from somewhere.

Fellows opened the door more fully and bowed. 'Miss Meredith is in, sir. If you will please step inside.'

The gentleman entered, his face in shadow from the tricorn hat he was wearing because he was in full court dress for the fete. He was of medium height and slender build, and was quite obviously a man of rank and fashion. His dark-green velvet coat was embellished with fine embroidery, and the frills of a particularly elegant shirt protruded above the low-cut lines of his satin waistcoat. His white breeches were of a very costly silk, his stockings were white, and his silver-buckled shoes shiny black patent leather. His hair was concealed beneath the powdered bag-wig that was *de rigueur* for court occasions, and try as Roslyn would, she couldn't make out his face at all.

She watched as he handed his cane to Fellows, and then at last he removed his hat and she saw his face. It was Sir Benedict Courtenay.

15

Fellows placed the hat and cane on a nearby table. 'I will inform Miss Meredith that you are here, sir.'

She spoke then. 'That won't be necessary, Fellows. I was just coming down anyway.'

'Yes, madam.' The butler bowed and withdrew.

Benedict had turned swiftly the moment he heard her voice. His practiced glance raked her from head to toe, coming to rest at last on her face. He was darkly handsome, almost to the point of beauty, and his brown eyes had an inviting warmth that he used to devastating effect upon the fair sex. He had long been accepted as the most attractive man in society, but he didn't impress Roslyn at all; he paled into insignificance beside James Atherton.

He didn't know this, however, and there was a confident smile on his lips as he came to meet her, taking her hand and drawing it slowly to his lips, lingering over the moment in a way that suggested that he was very confident of his effect upon her.

She pulled her fingers away. 'Good

evening, Sir Benedict.'

'Ah, you remember me. I'm flattered.'

'You wished to see my uncle?'

'I did, but it seems he hasn't returned from his studio yet.'

The studio? How did he know that? Fellows hadn't mentioned it. 'He could arrive at any moment, Sir Benedict, so if you would care to wait?' She moved toward the library door.

'There's no need, Miss Meredith, for I'm sure you'll make an admirable deputy.'

'Deputy? I don't understand.'

'I came to examine Elgin's collection of stones before I dash off to the country, and I was hoping that your uncle would act as a guide — a rather informed one, since he's just returned from Greece. But I'm sure you'll do just as well.'

'I'm afraid that I know very little about Greek antiquities, Sir Benedict.'

'Then you know more than I do, sweet lady, for I know nothing at all. Please say you will oblige me.' He smiled warmly, offering her his arm.

He made it sound as if he was inviting her to dance a wicked waltz with him. 'Sir — '

'Please, Miss Meredith.' The words were uttered softly and accompanied by a winning smile.

The last thing she wished to do was go anywhere with him, but there was little she could do but accept. Very reluctantly she accepted his arm.

As they proceeded toward the museum, she wondered why he'd come. A man like Sir Benedict Courtenay wasn't in the slightest bit interested in Greek antiquities, and yet he'd called on his way to Carlton House. And he knew that her uncle was at his studio. She supposed it could be an educated guess, but somehow she didn't think it was. He was certain where her uncle was, which meant that he'd come purposely to find her on her own. Why? Somehow she couldn't help thinking of Lady Ferney at the theater the night before. There was a connection, her every instinct told her there was.

The museum's roof lights caught the evening sun, but there were dark pools of shadow where the assembled statues, busts, and pieces of column stood in careful rows. The smell of dust and old stone hung in the stuffy air, and the sounds of Park Lane were muffled beyond the closed doors and windows.

Determined to appear as if the antiquities were his prime object, Benedict circulated the room with Roslyn on his arm. He admired first this item and then that, exclaiming at the beauty of a frieze and the immaculate elegance of a statue's robes.

She smiled politely, nodding when it seemed appropriate, but all the time she was wondering when he'd come to the real point of his visit. She wondered too about Vanessa Atherton. This man had been her lover before she married James, and maybe afterward as well. Was he her lover still? Did he know where she was?

He came to a halt in front of a particularly fine urn. 'Is that not a pretty thing, Miss Meredith?'

'Very.' The word sounded more terse than she'd intended.

He turned to her. 'Am I imposing upon you?'

'Not at all, sir.' She colored. 'I — I was just wondering if you're making yourself late at Carlton House.'

'My peacock garb gives my destination away, does it?'

'I cannot imagine that you'd be wearing court dress for any other reason tonight.'

'I thought I'd toddle along and see how much like Lunardi's balloon Prinny looks in his fancy new uniform.' He smiled.

She endeavored to return the smile, but it was very difficult. She didn't like him and was finding it hard to hide the fact. She cleared her throat. 'Did you say earlier that you're leaving London?'

'Yes. As you are, I understand. Foxcombe, is it not?'

How very well informed he was. Now she *knew* he'd been speaking to his sister, for Lady Ferney and her husband were the only people who'd been told about the visit to Foxcombe; Sir Owen had mentioned it in passing. 'Yes, Sir Benedict, it is.' His lips parted to ask another question, but she quickly spoke again. 'I take it you're returning to your country seat. I believe it's in Devon, isn't it?' She had no intention of discussing her plans with him.

A light passed through his dark eyes. 'My country seat is in Devon, but it isn't my destination on this occasion.'

'Oh?'

'Oh.' For the first time the charm was less than winning.

'I'm sure the crush of traffic will be clearing now, sir. Shouldn't you be thinking of Carlton House?'

'All in good time, Miss Meredith.' He glanced at the urn again. 'Did you like Greece?'

'Yes.'

'I'm told the weather there is particularly agreeable in the spring.'

180

'It is.'

'Did you stay in Athens?'

He knew perfectly well where they'd stayed; he'd been talking to his sister. 'And in Ayios Georghios, Sir Benedict, but then you probably know that already from Lady Ferney.' She looked challengingly at him. Wouldn't he ever get to whatever the point was?

His smile was all innocence. 'Did you say Ayios Georghios? That's in the south, isn't it?'

'Yes, in Attica.'

'I'm told it's a place of great natural beauty.'

'It is.'

'Perhaps I should toddle there myself one day. Where did you stay?'

At last he seemed to be coming to it. 'At the house of Mr Constantin Niphakos,' she said.

'Really? Isn't that where — ?'

'Where Lord Atherton was also staying? Yes, Sir Benedict, it was.'

'Upon my soul, what a coincidence! No doubt he was charmed to have such agreeable company.'

'You'd have to ask him that, sir.'

'But I'm asking you.'

'And I'm saying that I cannot answer.' She held his gaze rather coldly. There was no doubt at all now that this man had come for very different reasons than a professed interest in Lord Elgin's stone shop.

'Come, now, Miss Meredith, don't tell me that a lady as lovely as you has no idea how exceeding agreeable a gentleman would find her company.'

She'd had enough. 'I don't care for your sly innuendo, sirrah.'

'Sly innuendo? My dear, Miss Meredith, nothing was further from my mind.'

'Then what were you saying?'

'Merely that it's always pleasant when far from home to find one's countrymen — and women — beneath the same foreign roof.' He smiled disarmingly. 'I wouldn't dream of implying that you and Lord Atherton were anything other than acquaintances.'

'Wouldn't you?' She made no pretense about her dislike or suspicions about his motives.

'No, Miss Meredith, I wouldn't, although your reaction is rather strange. To be sure, I begin to wonder if I've accidentally touched upon your guilty secret.'

'I don't have a guilty secret,' she replied icily, but there was color in her cheeks that she knew must look telltale.

'You're not very convincing, Miss Meredith. I rather think you were more than James

Atherton's acquaintance in Greece and that you intend to continue your intimacy at Fox-combe. Am I right?'

'How dare you! Please leave immediately.'

'You haven't denied the charge.'

'Nor have I confirmed it. If you don't leave straightaway, I shall have the servants eject you.'

'My, my, how very sensitive you are, and how unguarded. You've told me what I wish to know. You have notions of becoming the second Lady Atherton, don't you, Miss Meredith?'

With a furious gasp, she struck him, her fingers leaving angry lines on his pale cheek. His head jerked back and he gave a sharp curse. 'You'll regret that, madam,' he breathed, his eyes as cold as flint.

'Please leave this house.'

'I was going to deal kindly enough with you, but now I'll see to it that you suffer as much humiliation and disgrace as possible. You can forget any notion of sinking your ambitious little claws in James Atherton, for your affair with him is already a thing of the past. The whole sordid tale is about to be spread all over Town, and Lady Gallermayne is going to hear. She shudders at scandal, and her dear James has already been at the center of far too much. When she hears about your escapades in Greece and your plans to continue indulging in them at Foxcombe, she's going to put a stop to it, believe me. And James is a dutiful nephew, when it comes down to it; he places great store by his family. Forget Foxcombe, my dear, for you won't be going there, and the most you can hope for now is to be installed somewhere as his mistress.' He gave a cynical smile. 'And to be sure, you aren't fit for anything else anyway. *Adieu*, Miss Meredith. Oh, and thank you for your, er, kind assistance.'

Fighting back the tears, she remained where she was. As she tried to compose herself, she struggled to see beyond her distress to his motives. Of what possible concern was it to him whether she and James had indulged in a liaison? What difference did it make? Even if he was keeping Vanessa somewhere, it didn't make sense. Vanessa had left James. Roslyn hesitated then. There was only one circumstance that answered the question: if Vanessa intended to return to her husband, it would matter very much if her husband now had a new love. Was that it? But where did Benedict Courtenay fit into it?

'Miss Meredith?'

She looked around as Fellows appeared in the doorway of the museum. 'Yes?'

'Sir Owen has returned.'

'Thank you. Has Sir Benedict left?'

'Yes, madam.'

She found her uncle taking a glass of cognac in the library.

He smiled apologetically as she entered. 'I'm sorry I'm so late, *cariad*, but Lady Ferney called at the very last minute and simply wouldn't leave. She's all of a lather that her portrait shall be completed before she and her husband leave for Ireland.'

So that was why Benedict Courtenay had been so sure of Sir Owen's whereabouts; no doubt it had been planned that Lady Ferney would call and delay him.

'Are you all right, Roslyn? You look a little strained.'

'I've had a disagreeable visitor.'

'Ah, yes, Fellows told me. What did Courtenay want? Surely it wasn't really an interest in antiquities.'

'No, it was an interest in my liaison with James.'

'Your *what*?' He almost choked on the cognac.

'He chooses to believe that James and I were lovers in Ayios Georghios and that we intend to continue our affair at Foxcombe. He says he's going to disgrace me throughout society and see that Lady Gallermayne puts pressure on James to prevent me from going to Foxcombe.' She was still close to tears.

Sir Owen stared at her. 'Good God, he's taken leave of his senses. Oh, pay him no heed, *cariad*. He's a venomous little fop without any gentlemanly qualities, and no one's going to believe his vicious lies.'

'Aren't they?'

'No, because there's no truth in them. Now, then, let's see a smile on your lips, for I have some good news.'

'You do?'

'Yes, sweetheart. James is back in London and has sent word that he'll call tomorrow night at eight.'

16

But Sir Owen was wrong. Society did give credence to Benedict Courtenay's story, and while Roslyn slept that night, Carlton House talked of little else. It was Lady Ferney who spread the tale, doing it with a feline delight that added even more spice to this latest episode in the continuing Atherton scandal. The two thousand guests were shocked to learn that, with Vanessa Atherton still mysteriously disappeared, her husband had apparently commenced a liaison with as unexpected a new love as Sir Owen Meredith's far-from-wealthy niece. Carlton House rang with it, not even Lady Gallermayne's furiously disapproving presence stemming the talk.

It was raining the following morning and Roslyn rose from her bed not knowing that her name was already very much attached to the Atherton scandal. It was her intention later that day to visit the exhibition of Oriental porcelain on display at Ackermann's Repository of Fine Arts in the Strand, an establishment not far from her uncle's studio. He had told her about it over dinner the night before, encouraging her to go to take her mind off her worries about Benedict Courtenay's threats.

Anxious to complete Lady Ferney's portrait in the few days before she left for Ireland, Sir Owen took a very early breakfast and departed immediately for his studio. Roslyn breakfasted in her room and then Lizzie came to dress her to go to the exhibition. The rain was heavy and the June air unexpectedly cool, and so she decided to wear a peach-and-white sprigged muslin walking gown and matching three-quarter-length pelisse. Her hair was pinned up beneath a high-crowned straw bonnet with peach ribbons. As she looped her reticule over her wrist and drew on her gloves, she went to the bedroom window and looked down over the museum to the traffic in Park Lane.

A line of elegant carriages was drawn up at the curb, causing more than the usual congestion at the busy junction with Piccadilly. Tradesmen and hackneymen, never renowned for their even temper, were exasperated by the immobile private carriages and their imperturbable coachmen. Roslyn watched with some bemusement as another carriage halted at the end of the line, its occupants alighting into the rain and hurrying along the pavement beneath a large black umbrella, evidently intent upon calling at the house to visit the museum. 'How very strange,' she murmured.

'Madam?' Lizzie came to join her.

'I would have thought that after Carlton House last night, society would still be in bed, not calling here at this hour to visit Lord Elgin's marbles!'

'A lot have called already, madam. Mr Fellows was saying earlier that he couldn't understand the interest.'

A footman came to inform Roslyn that her carriage was at the door, and when Lizzie had put on a cape and bonnet, the two went down to the vestibule, just as two more callers arrived to visit the museum. As Roslyn and the maid went out, the lady nudged her gentleman companion. 'There she is! That's her!'

Roslyn's steps faltered and she turned to look at them, but the rain was falling heavily and she had to hurry on into the waiting carriage. The lady and gentleman made no secret of their curiosity, staring after her in the few moments before Fellows closed the door of the house.

Feeling rather uneasy, Roslyn sat back on the blue leather upholstery of Lady Elgin's town barouche. Why had they been so interested in her? A feeling of apprehension began to creep through her and she could only think of what Benedict Courtenay had threatened the night before.

The team of matched bays drew the handsome carriage eastward along Piccadilly, the wheels splashing through the puddles that collected everywhere. It was a thoroughfare of inns, shops, coach booking offices, and fashionable new hotels, and there was so much traffic that it was some time before the barouche turned south into the Haymarket. Moving into Cockspur Street, they passed the rather bleak royal mews into Charing Cross, before driving due east into the Strand itself past the elegant and immense facade of Northumberland House.

Ackermann's Repository of Fine Arts occupied numbers 96-101 on the south side of the street, almost opposite the Exeter Exchange, where a collection of wild beasts was kept and shown to the public. As Roslyn and Lizzie alighted into the rain, they could hear the roar of lions above the noise of the traffic and the weather. Ackermann's emporium stood on the corner of a side street, and was a very impressive building, with handsome windows set on either side of a discreet door with a polished nameplate and letterbox. Above the door, gracing the sill of a huge pedimented window, was a handsome coat of arms supported by heraldic animals, and in spite of the dullness of the morning, the colors and gilding of this fine decoration were dazzlingly bright.

Ignoring the alluring display of superior prints in the window, Roslyn and Lizzie hurried inside. The bell tinkled loudly over the quiet interior, and a young gentleman assistant hurried over. He wore a brown coat and beige trousers, as did all the assistants, and he spoke in hushed tones, as if afraid of disturbing the silence. 'May I help you, madam?'

'I wish to see the Oriental porcelain.'

'Very well, madam. If you will come this way.'

He led them through the premises, past ladies and gentlemen who were examining the prodigious display of prints for which the establishment was primarily known. A great glass lantern roof threw dull light over the green cloth covers on the counters, and countless unframed prints adorned the walls on all sides. Portfolios and prints rested on stands, and a selection of frames was displayed to one side as Rosyln and Lizzie followed the assistant. No one paid any attention at all to the newly arrived lady and her maid.

The porcelain exhibition was in a large,

airy room with tall windows overlooking the side street. It had columns and a marble-slabbed floor, and around its walls were glass cabinets filled with items of such exquisite Oriental workmanship that Roslyn could immediately understand the exhibition's success.

There were several large circular tables down the center of the room, laden with so much porcelain that Roslyn marveled they hadn't collapsed. A group of ladies and gentlemen were examining them, and to her dismay she saw among them none other than Lady Ferney.

Benedict Courtenay's sister was dressed in an orange silk tunic gown and matching wide-brimmed hat that looked almost vibrant with her titian hair. She was very eye-catching and lovely, and she carried a small dog in her arms.

Hoping she hadn't been noticed, Roslyn began to leave, but it was too late; the feline hazel eyes had espied her straightaway. 'Why, Miss Meredith, how very pleasant it is to see you again.' Her voice rang out clearly over the room, and everyone turned immediately to look at Roslyn. There were even some quizzing glasses raised.

'G-good morning, Lady Ferney.'

Pushing the little dog into the rather

unwilling arms of the gentleman next to her, Lady Ferney came toward her quarry, her orange silk skirts rustling. 'I *do* hope you aren't in a rush, for I'd so like to talk to you.'

'Indeed?' The sense of misgiving that had stolen over Roslyn on leaving Elgin House now increased rapidly. This definitely had something to do with Benedict Courtenay's threats.

'I trust the weather isn't *too* tedious for you after the sunshine of Greece.'

'Not at all.' Roslyn glanced around. Everyone was listening.

'Tell me, did you lack for good conversation while you were there? I mean, there isn't exactly an abundance of English society in . . . where was it, now? The name escapes me for the moment.'

Roslyn drew a long breath. 'Ayios Georghios,' she replied.

'Ah, yes. Well? Did you have company there?'

Rolsyn met her gaze. 'I was with my uncle.'

Lady Ferney gave a tinkling laugh. 'Oh, my *dear*, how very droll you are. One cannot regard an *uncle* as company, if you follow my meaning.'

A ripple of amusement passed through the room, and Roslyn felt the color entering her cheeks.

Lady Ferney smiled. 'Do tell, Miss Meredith, we're all agog to know.'

'Know about what, Lady Ferney?' inquired Roslyn, anger beginning to stir within her. This wasn't fair, it wasn't fair at all.

'Oh, I think you know, my dear.'

'Yes, I know, Lady Ferney, because I've already had your unpleasant, ill-mannered brother making similar comments. It would seem that you and he share the same vulgar traits.'

There were some shocked gasps at this, and Lady Ferney's hazel eyes flashed. 'Well, no doubt you know all about vulgar traits, Miss Meredith. Come, now, be sensible and tell us whether the rumors circulating at Carlton House last night are true or not. Is James Atherton your lover?'

Roslyn was trembling. 'No, my lady, he is not.'

'But you and he stayed beneath the same roof, didn't you?'

'You were beneath the Prince Regent's roof last night, my lady. Is he your lover?'

'If that's the standard of your wit, Miss Meredith, I marvel that James has even glanced at you.' Lady Ferney's eyebrow was raised disdainfully. 'Well, it doesn't matter what you do or don't say, for to be sure the little episode is well and truly over. Lady

Gallermayne wasn't at all amused last night, and I doubt now if either you or Sir Owen will see James again. Poor Sir Owen, now he'll have to look elsewhere for the saving commission he told me about, won't he? *Au revoir*, Miss Meredith, it was *so* pleasant talking to you.' She turned on her heel and strolled back to her companions, evidently pulling a face for their benefit, for they made little secret of their amusement at Roslyn's expense.

Taking a deep breath, Roslyn left the room, followed by Lizzie. As the barouche conveyed them back across London, Roslyn's thoughts were very despairing. If the talk at Carlton House had been so pointed and Lady Gallermayne had heard, it was now very doubtful indeed that James would still call at Elgin House that evening. It was even more doubtful that there would be a visit to Foxcombe or a commission, which meant that her uncle would once again have to face certain financial ruin. And all because of the inexplicable spite of Benedict Courtenay and his sister.

17

Eight o'clock came and went, and there was no sign of James. Fellows closed the museum and put a stop at last to the contant stream of callers. In the magnificent state drawing room. Roslyn stood at one of the tall balcony windows overlooking wet Piccadilly. The rain had fallen steadily all day and everything outside was dripping. The wrought-iron balcony extended across the whole of the front of the house and had a green roof that protected the windows from the weather, but pools of water had formed on the floor and were rippling in the cool summer breeze.

Behind her the room was quiet. It was a particularly fine chamber with an Italian ceiling coffered with exquisite gold-and-silver plasterwork and a deep, elaborate frieze. The walls were hung with damson silk and the floor was covered by a rose carpet. There were elegant cabinets, paintings and mirrors, and three beautiful chandeliers, and the furniture was upholstered in damson velvet. There were some particularly fine tables, but the most magnificent was a French writing desk with ormolu mounts and inlaid Sèvres panels. On it was Roslyn's half-finished letter to Mrs March in Chepstow. On the mantelpiece of the Adam fireplace the glass-domed clock struck nine.

Roslyn turned to look at it. James wasn't coming, it was pointless to go on pretending that he was. She glanced at her uncle, seated on a chair by the fireplace reading *The Times*. He'd been reading the same column for an hour now, pretending not to be worried by the way things seemed to have gone, but she knew him too well to be fooled.

She drew a long breath. 'He isn't coming, is he?'

'There's time yet, *cariad*.'

'I don't think so. Lady Gallermayne has seen to it that he's heard the rumors and he's staying well away from us. From me, anyway.'

'You can't be certain of that.'

'I think I can.' The frilled hem of her lavender silk evening gown swung as she left the window, and the fine silver ribbons twined in her hair fluttered softly. 'I've tried and tried to think of a sensible explanation for Sir Benedict's actions, but nothing really fits properly.'

Sir Owen folded the newspaper. 'Unfortunately I think I may have worked it out.'

'You have?'

'In my experience Courtenay never does

anything unless he can personally profit by it. I'm beginning to think that he and Vanessa have been playing a very clever game. Her disappearance cannot be connected with Courtenay, so she cannot be accused of adultery, but they could be hoping to prove James guilty of adultery.'

'With me?'

He nodded. 'Vanessa could divorce him and hope to gain financially.'

She was silent for a moment. 'Do you think that's what it is?'

'It's possible, and it's all I can come up with, although it's a little elaborate, to say nothing of risky. After all, she left James in the first place, the world and his wife knows that.'

'I wondered . . . '

'Yes?'

'If it was the very opposite. I thought perhaps Vanessa was hoping to return to James and was afraid that I presented an obstacle. If they made enough noise about James's supposed infidelities, they could reasonably hope to put an end to the so-called liaison, especially if Lady Galler-mayne puts pressure to bear on him. There's only one thing wrong with my explanation: it doesn't explain Sir Benedict's position. Why after all this time, if Vanessa has been with him, would he suddenly want her to return to

James? He'd have to want her to, otherwise he wouldn't be doing all this. So, why?'

Sir Owen had been looking at her for a long moment. 'I think you may have hit upon it, *cariad*. As I said, Courtenay doesn't do anything unless it's for personal gain, and he'd gain if Vanessa returned to James and once more had access to the Atherton wealth. There are whispers going the rounds that Courtenay's debts are catching him up again and that's why he's dodging off to somewhere secret in the country, to keep one step ahead of the duns. I can't believe that he ever wanted Vanessa to go in the first place; she was much more useful to him when she was with James.'

'This is all supposing that Vanessa is with Sir Benedict.'

'Agreed, but I think it's a very strong possibility, don't you?'

'Knowing him, yes.'

'So they'd be rather alarmed if they suspected James had fallen in love with someone else, wouldn't they?'

'Yes, I suppose they would.'

'And they'd do all they could to put a stop to it. That's exactly what Courtenay and his sister are now engaged upon, and they're doing it very well indeed, I fear. Except that there isn't a liaison to break, and the only outcome is likely to be my loss.'

She went quickly to him, putting a sympathetic hand on his shoulder. He patted her fingers fondly.

'Never mind, *cariad*, we'll manage somehow. You must forgive my selfishness, for I'm not the only one to suffer, am I? Your character will pay dearly.'

She smiled a little ruefully and returned to her place by the window. The rain lashed the cobbles of Piccadilly and the traffic splashed dismally through the puddles, the horses' heads low, their drivers huddled in cloaks and capes. Suddenly she noticed a particularly fine equipage, a dark-red town carriage drawn by a team of grays. It drew to a standstill at the curb in front of the house, and the footman jumped down from the back to open the door and lower the steps. If it was someone else hoping to view her under the guise of visiting the museum, then he or she was about to be disappointed, for Fellows wouldn't admit anyone now.

A gentlemen in evening dress alighted, pausing for a moment to adjust the lace spilling from his cuff. He glanced up at the lowering sky for a moment. It was James.

Roslyn's breath caught. 'Uncle Owen! James has called, after all; he's at the door now.'

'Well, I suppose it at least signifies that he's man enough to break the bad news to my face,' replied her uncle a little heavily, getting to his feet.

She turned agitatedly from the window. She went back to the writing desk and sat down, picking up her pen as if she'd been calmly writing.

A moment later Fellows opened the drawing room doors. 'Lord Atherton, Sir Owen.'

James entered. There were spots of rain on his indigo velvet coat, and he was still toying with the lace at his cuff. His white trousers were of superb cut and fit, and his white satin waistcoat was only partially buttoned, to show off the shirt lace. There wasn't a pin in his silk neckcloth, but there was a large ruby ring on his right hand. His face was still tanned from the Greek sun, and his tousled hair seemed more golden than ever. He was very formal and reserved as he bowed politely to them both. 'Sir Owen. Miss Meredith.'

She slowly put down her pen. 'My lord?'

Sir Owen cleared his throat, waving Fellows away. 'Good evening, James.'

'I'm sorry to be so very late, but to be perfectly honest, I hesitated about coming at all. You've no doubt heard the vile rumors?'

Sir Owen nodded. 'They have come to our

attention,' he said a little dryly.

'I've no doubt you find them as acutely embarrassing as I do. It seems that Lady Ferney originated them, at least, that is how it appears, although I've no doubt that her brother is the real culprit.'

'No doubt he is, but it makes little difference, the damage is done. I presume you've come to suggest a parting of the ways?'

'Parting of the ways?'

'I hardly imagine you still wish to proceed with the commission at Foxcombe.'

'Sir Owen, my honor and integrity have been called into question, and Miss Meredith's reputation has suffered grievously through no fault of her own, so the last thing I wish to do is give credence to the story by canceling the arrangement. Some precautions will have to be taken, of course, but I'm sure everything can go ahead as before — provided you are in agreement, of course.'

Roslyn was staring at him in disbelief. He still wished to continue?

Sir Owen was a little taken aback as well. 'You, er, mentioned precautions?'

'Miss Meredith's good name must not be exposed to further damage.'

'You think it would be wiser now for her to remain in London?'

'No, Sir Owen — unless that is what she wishes.' James looked at her. 'Is that what you would prefer, Miss Meredith?'

'Maybe it would be the most prudent course, sir,' she replied, unable to meet his gaze. She lowered her eyes to the letter.

'Perhaps you would reconsider if you knew that my aunt will accompany us, and you will therefore enjoy her considerable protection.'

Sir Owen was astonished. 'Lady Gallermayne has agreed to this?'

'Yes, Sir Owen, she has. Oh, I admit that at first her instinct was to cancel everything, but now she's persuaded to my point of view. As I hope you are as well. No one will believe there to have been any truth in the rumors if my aunt condones our acquaintance by joining us. Her reputation is such that the whole of society knows she wouldn't lend her name to any impropriety, no matter how remote.'

Sir Owen nodded. 'There's no gainsaying that. Very well, I'm certainly prepared to continue with our arrangements.' He smiled a little wryly. 'I'm still in no position to quibble financially, but as to what Roslyn wishes . . . ?' He looked at her.

'What should I do, Uncle Owen?'

'It's entirely up to you, *cariad*, but my advice is that you come with us. You can only benefit from Lady Gallermayne's presence. In two days' time Lady Ferney will be on her way to Ireland — without her portrait, I'm dashed if I'm going to finish it now — and I suspect that soon Courtenay will have to slink off to his dundodging retreat. It will all die down then, *cariad*, and you'll be protected by Lady Gallermayne.'

She nodded. But something else was on her mind and had been ever since her uncle had firmly declared that he believed Vanessa was on the point of returning to her husband. What if they were wrong about her and Benedict? What if Vanessa should wish to return to James because she loved him? How would she then regard the presence at Foxcombe of a woman whose name had been scandalously linked with his?

Her silence made both her uncle and James look a little curiously at her. It was James who spoke. 'Miss Meredith, is there something else concerning you?'

'Yes.' She had to say it. No one really knew why Vanessa had left him. It could have been an innocent misunderstanding that had got out of hand, and he had to see the implications of pressing ahead with the plans as they now were. 'I — I feel I should point out that Lady Atherton might not understand if I go to Foxcombe after all this talk. My presence might jeopardize your chance of a reconciliation.'

He seemed to find this faintly amusing, although he strove to conceal it. 'I doubt very much if my wife would misunderstand anything, Miss Meredith. She knows me far too well for that. Far too well.'

'I don't wish to be responsible — '

'You won't be responsible for anything, Miss Meredith. Please believe me.'

'If you're certain of that . . . '

'I am. Was there anything else concerning you?'

'No.'

'Then there is no reason why you should not come to Foxcombe if you wish to. You do wish to, don't you?'

'Yes, of course I do.'

'Consider it settled then.' He looked at Sir Owen. 'We'll leave in three days' time in my traveling carriage, if that's agreeable to you?'

'Perfectly agreeable.'

'Another vehicle will be provided for the maids and valets.'

Sir Owen nodded.

James hesitated. 'There's a drawback to these plans, and maybe it will make a difference to you. I'm afraid that my aunt has expressed a strong desire to accomplish the journey in one day. It's one hundred and ten miles from here to Foxcombe, but I'm afraid she has an absolute horror of inns, suspecting them one and all of harboring legions of bugs, and so she avoids them if at all possible. If such a lengthy journey daunts you, then I shall quite understand if you and Miss Meredith choose to do it in two days and follow us down.'

'My boy,' replied Sir Owen, 'I'm sure that if Lady Gallermayne is capable of withstanding such a journey, then so are we. Is that not so, Roslyn?'

She smiled. 'Yes. Of course.'

James looked at her. 'It isn't as arduous as it sounds, the roads are excellent and my horses the finest bloodstock. If we set off really early, and by that I mean about five in the morning, we'll be able to stop at Oxford for a leisurely luncheon and then travel on to Foxcombe and arrive at about six in the evening. That will give us all several hours to recover before dinner. We won't be dashing by any means, the stagecoach accomplishes the journey in ten and a half hours. If it rains, of course, then we'll be forced to stay overnight on the way, bugs or no bugs, but I trust that the weather will be lenient with us.' He turned to Sir Owen again. 'There is a consolation. My aunt never undertakes such a journey without seeing that she has with her one of Fortnum & Mason's very best hampers. She likes her creature comforts.'

'So do I, dear boy. So do I. Why, this journey begins to sound most agreeable indeed.'

'All the arrangements meet with your approval, then?'

'They do. A Fortnum & Mason hamper and a leisurely luncheon in Oxford? You'll not hear a single grumble from me, I promise you.'

'Excellent.' James looked at Roslyn again. 'There's just one more thing, Miss Meredith.'

'Yes?'

'Since you're definitely accompanying us, my aunt will wish to meet you before we depart. Will it be in order for her to call upon you?'

The thought filled her with trepidation, but she managed to smile. 'Yes, of course. But perhaps it would be more fitting if I called upon her?'

He smiled a little. 'My aunt enjoys calling.'

Sir Owen went to a table on which stood a decanter of cognac and some glasses. 'Will you take a drink with me, James?'

'I fear I cannot, Sir Owen, I have a great deal to attend to. I must ask you again to forgive me for having called so late, but now I must most regretfully bid you good night.'

'Good night, my boy.'

'Good night, Miss Meredith.'

'Good night.'

He withdrew, closing the doors quietly behind him. Sir Owen poured himself a generous glass of Lord Elgin's best cognac and then resumed his seat by the fireplace, sitting back with a long, comfortable sigh. 'My head is to remain above water after all, it seems. I confess I'm much relieved.' He glanced at her. 'I'm also much relieved that your good name is to be restored, and firmly protected from now on by Lady Gallermayne's chaperonage.'

She didn't reply. She was still going to Foxcombe, but she knew it was going to mean suffering a great deal more heartbreak. From the moment James had entered the room, her pulse had raced unbearably and her heart had pounded so much she was sure everyone must have heard it. Her love for him had grown, not diminished, and it could continue to grow each time she was with him.

If she had any wisdom at all, she'd decline to go. But she didn't have any wisdom, she wanted to be with him, no matter what the cost.

18

Lady Gallermayne called on the eve of their departure for the country. Sir Owen wasn't at home, and Roslyn was seated in the state drawing room with a newly acquired volume of Lord Byron's *Hours of Idleness* open on her lap. She wore a blue-and-white-spotted lawn gown and there were matching ribbons in her hair. Her mother's gold locket shone at her throat.

Downstairs the museum was still doing brisk business, as society continued to show a scandalized interest in Lord Atherton's new love, word of Lady Gallermayne's intention to accompany the party to Foxcombe not having got out over Town yet. But if anyone hoped to see Roslyn, they were disappointed. She hadn't stirred from the house since her unpleasant visit to Ackermann's and she didn't go downstairs when the museum was open.

The early evening was warm, the weather having improved considerably since the rain of a few days earlier. The balcony windows stood open and a light breeze wafted into the room. Outside, Piccadilly was still noisy, hooves and wheels passing constantly to and fro, but she was oblivious to everything as she turned another page of the book. She was glad she'd at last got around to reading some of Lord Byron's work because she found she liked it very much, but then she supposed she liked the poet himself. Was he still in Malta being administered to by the leech? She hoped his health had improved, for although he was guilty of unwarranted meddling in her life, she couldn't resent him.

She gave a start when the doors suddenly opened behind her and Fellows announced Lady Gallermayne. Hastily she closed the book and rose to her feet.

Lady Gallermayne was a widow of rather severe appearance. She'd worn black for fifteen years now, and it was a color that did nothing for her sallow complexion and pale eyes. Her gray hair was hidden beneath a black lace cap and black velvet hat, and her plain pelisse and gown were made of mourning taffeta. She wore black lace fingerless mittens and carried a parasol that she used as an elegant walking stick. Its silver tip gleamed against the rose carpet as she paused in the doorway for a moment, raising a lorgnette to survey the younger woman. 'So, you're Miss Meredith, are you?' Her voice was very precise and low.

'Yes, Lady Gallermayne.' Roslyn dropped a hasty curtsy.

It was met with disapproval. 'More haste, less grace. You should remember that in future, Miss Meredith.'

Roslyn lowered her glance. 'Yes, Lady Gallermayne.' She felt rather daunted, both by the other woman's presence and by her reputation as a stickler for absolutely every rule.

'Do you intend to invite me to sit, or are we going to stand throughout the interview?'

Color flooded Roslyn's cheeks. 'Oh, please sit down, Lady Gallermayne. Forgive me.'

'Forgive you? That remains to be seen.' The black taffeta rustled as Lady Gallermayne took her seat on an upright chair, her mittened hands clasped neatly on the handle of the parasol.

Slowly Roslyn sat down again. She felt most ill at ease and wasn't helped by having to look up into the older woman's eyes. Maybe Lady Gallermayne's choice of chair had been accidental, but it seemed very unlikely. Her ladyship did not appear to be a woman who did anything by accident, rather always by design.

Lady Gallermayne's glance fell upon the volume of poems. 'Lord Byron is to your liking, Miss Meredith?'

'Yes.'

'I would have thought him rather questionable reading for a proper young lady.'

'I don't find anything improper in his work, my lady.'

'That appears to be a sad failing with the younger generation as a whole, Miss Meredith, there is a universal lack of discretion. Which brings me to the disgraceful whispers that have recently been attaching to my nephew, and that now appear to encompass you as well.'

'The whispers are all untrue, Lady Gallermayne.'

'I'm sure they are, Miss Meredith, for my nephew would hardly invite my presence at Foxcombe if he intended to continue an immoral liaison with you. However, I am a little surprised to find you far from the plain creature the whispers have described. You are a very handsome young woman, very handsome indeed.'

Roslyn didn't know what to say to this.

'But you are also rather at fault in certain areas.'

'At fault?'

'To begin with I'm somewhat disturbed to find that you have discarded mourning when your father passed away less than a year ago. This seems to suggest a certain lack of respect.'

Roslyn drew a long breath. 'On the contrary, Lady Gallermayne, it shows very great respect. I've never worn mourning for my father, because he expressly wished me not to.'

'Indeed? How very radical. However, if that was his wish, then you were no doubt duty-bound to obey. There are other things, though. Proper young ladies do not travel without a maid, and they most certainly do not spend whole days unaccompanied with a gentleman they hardly know. I'm speaking of the day you went to an island with my nephew. I do not regard a Greek fisherman as a suitable chaperone, even if you, Sir Owen, and my nephew apparently do.'

Roslyn had to look away. Lady Gallermayne would be considerably more than disturbed if she knew exactly what had happened on that island; she'd be completely shocked!

'Have you nothing to say, Miss Meredith?'

Roslyn looked at her again. 'Only that as far as the maid was concerned, there was very little I could do. She left my employ on the eve of our departure. As to the visit to the island . . . '

'Yes, Miss Meredith?'

'I cannot defend my actions in that respect.'

'Well, at least you're honest about it.'

Roslyn was a little angry. She was being made to sound almost wanton!

'Are you an adventuress, Miss Meredith?'

The question stunned Roslyn. With an indignant gasp she rose to her feet. 'No, my lady, I most certainly am not!'

'You must admit that the question isn't entirely unreasonable.'

'Isn't it? Fogive me, Lady Gallermayne, but I find it not only unreasonable, but very offensive as well.'

'So I see. Please sit down, Miss Meredith. My neck aches with having to look up at you.'

Hoping that the ache was rather severe, Roslyn hesitated and then sat down again.

Lady Gallermayne's black-mittened hands clasped and unclasped on the handle of the parasol. 'Am I to believe your protestations of innocence, Miss Meredith? If you're speaking the truth, then I've insulted you and I beg your forgiveness, but if you're being deceitful, then you're not only an adventuress, but an actress as well. Are you an actress, Miss Meredith?'

'Yes, at this precise moment I am. My every instinct tells me to ask you to leave, but my upbringing and manners bid me remain polite in spite of your rudeness. I think that that makes me an actress.' Roslyn was too angry now to conceal what she thought.

Lady Gallermayne surveyed her for a long moment and then unexpectedly smiled a little. 'Yes, I suppose it does. You're quite justified in being angry, Miss Meredith, for I've tested you sorely. But I had to be satisfied in myself that all was as it should be. My nephew speaks very highly of you, very highly indeed, but it is my opinion that he is often a very poor judge of women — his misalliance is evidence enough of that. Lady Atherton is both an adventuress and an actress, Miss Meredith, and I dread the day when she reenters James' life, for she will make him as unhappy again as she made him before. But if my nephew proved an inadequate judge where his wife was concerned, I think he has redeemed himself now, for I think that you are everything he claims you are. I hope you will forgive my harshness with you.'

Roslyn was staring at her. 'I . . . yes, of course I forgive you, Lady Gallermayne.'

'But you must understand that I am going to be at Foxcombe to be your chaperone, to shield your character from malicious whispers, and that is precisely what I intend to do. Etiquette must be strictly observed at all times, you do understand that, don't you?'

'Yes, Lady Gallermayne.'

'I abhor scandal of any kind and will not

brook any more of it attaching to my family.'

'No, Lady Gallermayne.'

'I will leave you now. No doubt Lord Byron is much more congenial company than I am.' The black taffeta rustled as she stood. 'By the way . . . '

'Yes, my lady?' Roslyn rose too.

'This commission for which my nephew has engaged Sir Owen, I take it that it concerns the west and north views of Foxcombe?'

Roslyn looked at her in surprise. 'It doesn't concern views at all, Lady Gallermayne.'

'It doesn't? But I understood, at least, I presumed that that was what it was about.' The pale eyes held Roslyn's gaze. 'What is it about, then?'

'Lord Atherton wished to have alterations made to the portraits my uncle performed two years ago.'

Lady Gallermayne's lips twitched a little. 'Portraits? *Portraits*? Do you mean to tell me my nephew is insisting on all this mummery simply to have a few extra daubs made to those likenesses?'

'He — he did say that the alterations were quite considerable.'

'They had better be, Miss Meredith, they had better be. Good day to you.'

'Good day, Lady Gallermayne.'

Roslyn watched as the doors closed behind the black-clad figure. She heard the taffeta rustle away along the passage outside, then she sat thankfully down again, picking up the volume of poems and opening it. But then her eyes rose from the page. What exactly did James want done to the portraits? Why hadn't he told anyone, not even his aunt? Surely it was the most natural thing in the world to say that he wanted the background changed to a view of Foxcombe instead of a classical landscape, or something of that kind? Instead, he'd said nothing at all. She found it suddenly very curious.

19

Both Lady Ferney and Sir Benedict Courtenay had quit London when James's elegant dark-green traveling carriage conveyed the Foxcombe party west out of the capital at five o'clock the next morning, just after sunrise. Lady Ferney and her husband were on their way to Ireland, and Benedict *en route* for the secret destination that he hoped would protect him from the attentions of his duns. Roslyn trusted that the absence of all concerned would have the desired effect, and that by the time she and her uncle returned, the rumors would have died a natural death.

For the journey she wore her short-sleeved lilac muslin gown and a little matching straw bonnet with artificial flowers. There was a white cashmere shawl around her shoulders and a little silk reticule on her wrist. Beside her, Sir Owen wore his favorite coat, a garment more notable for its comfort than its style, but he had no intention of being trussed up in fashionably tight clothes for the 110-mile journey. Opposite them. Lady Gallermayne was again in unrelieved black — indeed she never wore anything else

— and next to her James looked as superbly turned out as ever, in a pale-blue coat with a high stand-fall collar, close-fitting gray cord trousers, gleaming Hessian boots, and a gray-and-white striped waistcoat. His starched muslin neckcloth was discreetly tied, and there was a golden pin in its knot. His top hat was tipped back on his head and he said very little as the carriage drove at a spanking pace along the Oxford road, the coachman under instructions to accomplish the journey in the allotted time.

The turnpikes were very good and they made excellent progress, passing through High Wycombe and reaching Oxford in good time for the promised early luncheon. Afterward they drove on westward, through Witney and reaching Northleach on the Cotswolds in the afternoon. The hamper from Fortnum & Mason proved to contain delicacies that were more than worthy of such an exclusive establishment, and Sir Owen enjoyed sampling everything. It was, he said, the only way to travel.

Soon Northleach was behind them and they were negotiating the long climb over the hills toward Cheltenham. It was a busy highway, conveying many stagecoaches and mails, and they frequently heard posting horns echoing over the countryside to warn tollgates of their approach.

The hedgerows were sweet with honey-suckle, elder flowers, and hawthorn, and the road verges swayed with the creamy lace of cow parsley. In the villages the houses and cottages were built of mellow Cotswold stone, with well-tended gardens and neat outbuildings, while in the closed fields there were sheep grazing on the lush June grass. Dry stone walls marked boundaries, and beech copses crowned hilltops, while through the valleys spread luxuriant green woods. There were many fine country houses presiding over noble parks and it was all very beautiful, fertile, and prosperous — England at its very best.

They broke their journey for the last time at the famous Frog Mill Inn on the hills above the vale where Cheltenham spa lay. The horses needed resting before tackling the final hilly stage. They were just over half an hour from their destination.

The Frog Mill's yard was busy as their carriage drew to a standstill, closely followed by the second vehicle carrying the maids and valets. Lady Gallermayne's maid was rather elderly and called Parrish, and was finding the pace of the long journey a little more wearying than her resilient mistress. While the horses drew breath, Roslyn and Sir Owen strolled along the banks of the little River Coln, which flowed past the inn. All too quickly it was time to drive on, but at least they knew now that the journey would soon be over. Their five o'clock departure from London seemed a lifetime away.

A new turnpike to Cheltenham was being built, but wasn't yet complete, so they had to use the old route, toiling up to the hamlet of Kilkenny and then over the edge of the escarpment down a very steep descent past Dowdeswell toward Charlton Kings, but before they reached the latter the carriage turned sharply to the right into a narrow lane, and began to climb the escarpment again toward Foxcombe. Soon a fine red brick wall rose alongside the lane, with above it the most splendid copper beeches Roslyn had ever seen. Their gleaming leaves whispered in the light breeze; she could hear them in spite of the noise of the carriage.

Ahead there was a lodge beside immense armorial wrought-iron gates, the stone posts of which were topped by proud unicorns, the badge of the Atherton family since the time of Richard the Third. The lodgekeeper swung the gates open and doffed his hat respectfully as the first carriage swept through, although he was quick to put the hat on again before the second passed by. He didn't salute maids

221

and gentlemen's gentlemen.

The wheels and hooves crunched on the freshly raked gravel drive leading up through a long valley that had been landscaped by Capability Brown. There were fine oak trees and rhododendrons as splendid as any Roslyn had seen. They were in full bloom, their heavy blossoms a riot of pale pink, mauve, and rose-crimson, and a small herd of red deer took fright as the carriages approached, leaping away across the park and vanishing into the beech woods covering the rising land to the left.

At the head of the valley stood the house, a rambling, beautiful building dating partly from the early fifteenth century but mostly from Tudor times. It had mullioned windows with Renaissance pediments, gables adorned with exquisite finials, and a stone-tiled roof with battlements. The second story was taken up by a long line of tall windows very close together, making the great gallery, which was nearly 180 feet long. The main entrance was beneath a great stone porch guarded on either side by heraldic unicorns, and abutting the porch were two immense oriel windows decorated with fine stained glass.

Roslyn looked out as the carriage approached. Immediately ahead the drive divided in two to pass around a low-walled garden that was laid out in the Tudor style, with ornately trimmed evergreen shrubs and trees that were master-pieces of the topiarist's art. Set between precise paths, with flower beds, fountains, and a cool summerhouse, it resembled a gigantic game of chess, with all the pieces the same match-ing green.

The drive swept together again in front of the house, and as the carriages came to a standstill James took out his fob watch. It was six o'clock. They were on time. A butler hurried out immediately to open the door, and James alighted, followed by Sir Owen. Then James assisted his aunt down and she immediately proceeded into the house beneath the great porch. James held his hand out to Roslyn. Their eyes met for a moment and then his fingers were steady around hers, assist-ing her gently down.

'Welcome to Foxcombe, Miss Meredith. Sir Owen.'

She looked around. The house stood at the head of two valleys, the one up which they'd driven, and another that swept toward the north and a beautiful lake fringed with beeches. She could see a boathouse. It was now the studio where her uncle would work, she remembered him telling her about it. Beyond the beeches, shining white in the distance, was the neighboring house. Was it

Grantby Place, the estate Vanessa had coveted so much that she wanted James to 'improve' Foxcombe to be like it?

She smiled at James. 'It's very beautiful indeed, my lord. I envy you.'

He returned the smile, offering her his arm. 'Shall we go in?'

Slipping her hand over his sleeve, she proceeded into the house with him, entering an immense entrance hall, where all the servants had been gathered to greet them. It was a lofty chamber with a carved wooden ceiling and hammerbeams embellished with the Atherton unicorn. Paneled halfway up, the walls above were whitewashed and hung with tapestries and paintings. It was furnished with Tudor chests inlaid with marble, metal, and wood, and carved wooden chairs from the same period. Two carved stone fireplaces, painted with unicorns and red and white roses, stood at either end, and the doors leading off it evidently led into the main rooms. A dark wooden staircase rose from the far end, its newel posts topped with more unicorns, and the stone-flagged floor was spangled with color as the sunlight streamed through the oriel windows.

Lady Gallermayne had already been greeted by the servants, but now the same ritual was gone through again as they welcomed James and his two guests. The maids all bobbed neat curtsies and the men bowed politely.

The butler, whose name was Morris, was uncannily like Fellows, clad in the same brown coat and wig, with the same rather superior face. He was also just as efficient. He informed James that a pot of tea would be served in the library in half an hour, and that all the rooms had been prepared as requested.

Lady Gallermayne turned immediately on hearing this. 'I trust that that means I am to occupy the red-tapestry room. I refuse to sleep in the blue room again, it's too cold and never gets the sun.'

The butler bowed. 'The red-tapestry room has been set aside for you, my lady.'

'And where is Miss Meredith to sleep?'

'The north room, my lady. Sir Owen has the south.'

She nodded. 'Very well, that sounds suitable. Parrish, where are you?' She looked around for her maid, who had just entered with Lizzie and the two valets. 'Ah, there you are. Well, come along, then, I wish to refresh myself before taking a dish of tea.'

Parrish was a thin, elderly woman with sparse gray hair and a pointed nose. She had served Lady Gallermayne for as long as anyone could remember, and although she found the work and hours very tiring indeed these days, there was no question at all of her ever being replaced. Evidently very stiff from the journey, she hastened to follow her mistress up the staircase. Her mob cab bobbed as she went and her starched gray skirts crackled.

Morris led Roslyn and her uncle up the staircase, the walls of which were hung with more tapestries. At the top there was a paneled passageway leading away on either side, while directly ahead, across a small landing guarded on either side by impressive doors, another staircase led up to the great gallery on the floor above. The butler indicated one of the doors. 'That is his lordship's apartment,' he explained.

Roslyn glanced at the other door. 'Does that lead to the red-tapestry room?' she inquired.

'No, madam, that is the mistress's apartment.'

Vanessa's rooms. Roslyn looked at the door for a moment longer and then proceeded in the wake of the butler and her uncle along the passage to the left. There was a dark-red patterned carpet on the floor, and candles in iron holders on the paneling. The floor was uneven with age, and the boards squeaked occasionally. Passing one door, through which female voices could be heard, the butler turned to Roslyn again. 'The red-tapestry room, madam.' Then they walked on to the very end of the passage, where he opened the last door on the left. 'The north room, madam. I trust it meets with your approval.'

He and Sir Owen watched as she stepped into the room, which stood on the very corner of the house, with one window overlooking the drive and the topiary garden, the other facing toward the second valley, where the lake glittered in the late-afternoon sun. The bed was hung with gold-fringed green velvet, and had an elaborately carved headboard, and the highly polished wooden floor was strewn with Persian rugs of jewel-bright colors. There were two upright wooden chairs on either side of the stone fireplace, and a window seat at both windows. A carved wooden screen of considerable antiquity separated the main bedroom from the dressing area beyond. In this second area there was an oddly modern-looking muslin-draped dressing table, a cheval glass, a washstand, and a brooding, dark wooden wardrobe.

She turned to the waiting butler. 'It's very agreeable.'

'Thank you, madam.' He bowed, turning to

Sir Owen. 'If you will follow me, sir, I will conduct you to the south room.'

Roslyn smiled at her uncle. 'I will see you in the library directly.'

'You will indeed, *cariad*.'

They walked away just as Lizzie arrived with the portmanteau containing the apricot seersucker gown Roslyn had elected to change into as soon as she arrived. The seersucker traveled well, and packing it separately was so much more convenient than searching through all the baggage. As the maid put the portmanteau down on the dressing table, some men carried Roslyn's baggage in and then withdrew.

As the door closed at last, Lizzie smiled at Roslyn. 'It's good to have all those hours of traveling over and done with, isn't it, madam?'

'Very good indeed. Lord Atherton's traveling carriage may be the finest equipage on the road, but one hundred and ten miles is a horridly long way.' She sat thankfully before the dressing table, untying her bonnet and removing it.

Lizzie took a brush, comb, and covered dish of hair-pins from the portmanteau and began to attend to the rather flattened tawny-blond hair. The brush crackled through it and soon it was lively and shining again, twisting up glossily into a knot on the top of her head.

After a quick wash to refresh herself, Roslyn stepped into the apricot gown, shivering a little as the cool seer-sucker touched her skin. A few minutes later she was ready to go down to the library. But she was too early and had no desire to be the first to arrive. She decided to go up to the floor above to look at the view from the gallery.

Leaving Lizzie to unpack properly, she hurried along the passage past Lady Galler-mayne's red-tapestry room to the landing and the doors of James's and Vanessa's apartments. Gathering her skirts, she went up the second staircase, emerging at last to find herself halfway along the gallery. It was over forty feet wide and just twenty feet short of two hundred feet long, and the continuous line of windows down its one side allowed a dazzling amount of sunlight in over the polished wooden floor, the Tudor chests and chairs, and the magnificent display of paintings on the paneled wall opposite. The coffered ceiling was rich with painted plaster-work, and from it were suspended iron-rimmed candleholders like large horizontal wheels.

The view was breathtaking. She walked the full length of the floor, gazing down over the gardens and the park toward the vale and

Cheltenham in the distance. The fashionable spa shimmered in the haze of summer heat at the foot of the Cotswold hills, occupying land that in aeons gone by had been submerged beneath the sea. Reaching the far end, directly above her own room, she looked in the other direction, over the lake, the boathouse studio and the beechwoods beyond. From up here she could see the neighboring estate more clearly. The house was very large, and built in the highly fashionable classical style. It had to be Grantby Place, surely. Looking at it, Roslyn couldn't understand anyone finding such a stark, impersonal building preferable to the centuries-old delights of Foxcombe.

Thinking that it must by now be time to go down to the library, she retraced her steps to the stairs and went down. Reaching the landing below, she hesitated, glancing at the door of Vanessa's apartment. There was no sound from James's rooms opposite; indeed, there was no sound from anywhere, the house was silent.

Hesitantly she went to Vanessa's door, turned the knob, and pushed it slowly open. Beyond there was a small but luxurious antechamber, furnished and decorated in very much the latest style. The paneling had been removed and the walls hung with rose-patterned Chinese silk, and there was a sofa and chair covered with rose velvet. The white marble fireplace was topped by an ornate mantelpiece on which stood two graceful silver candlesticks and a porcelain Buddha with a very rotund body and a heavily jowled, smiling face. Its head, fixed by a hidden spring, moved slightly in the draft caused by the opening of the door.

As Roslyn's glance was drawn toward the tiny movement, there was a sudden crash from the room beyond, a sound only too reminiscent of the breaking of Vanessa's miniature in Ayios Georghios. She froze, her heart almost stopping. Someone was in there.

20

She drew sharply back, her eyes wide. She was about to close the door and hurry away when something made her stop. Who could it be? Was it James? She listened. The other room was silent again. Maybe it was a maid.

'Is someone there?' The question slipped out almost before she knew it.

There wasn't a reply. Everything was still. Maybe she'd imagined the noise. She dismissed the thought immediately, it had been too loud to be imagined.

'Is anyone there?'

The silence continued. Slowly she approached the door, hesitantly putting her ear to it and listening. There wasn't any movement. Her heart thundering, she turned the knob and pushed the door open.

There was a sumptuous pink-and-gold bedroom beyond, and it was empty, as was the boudoir leading off it. She looked nervously around, and her glance fell on a little bonbon dish lying where it had just fallen on the polished floor. There was an odd scent in the air. It was familiar, but she couldn't quite place it. A breath of fresh air wafted through the room then, stirring the curtains at the tall windows. Someone had opened one of the casements. Slowly she went toward it and found herself looking out over another walled garden, this time at the rear of the house. Laid out very elegantly in the Dutch style, it boasted a fine formal canal lined by rows of ornamental trees, with a beautiful pavilion closing the superb vista. It was a perfect view for the mistress of the house to gaze upon from her bedroom. Roslyn gazed all around, but there wasn't a sign of anyone; besides, there hadn't really been enough time for anyone to —

There was another crash behind her and with a frightened cry she whirled about, expecting to see she knew not what; she was just in time to glimpse a large black cat darting through into the antechamber after knocking a silver candlestick over on the mantelpiece. A cat! It was only a cat! She almost laughed out loud with relief. She didn't know who or what she'd been afraid of seeing, but it certainly hadn't been anything as ordinary and reassuring as a cat. She closed her eyes for a moment to try to compose herself, and when she opened them again, her frantic heartbeats had begun to subside.

Bending, she retrieved the bonbon dish

and replaced it on the little inlaid occasional table from which the cat had dislodged it, then she straightened the candlestick before pausing to look properly at the room.

It was beautifully furnished and very feminine, with a wealth of soft draperies and frills. The walls were hung with pale-gold brocade, and the immense gilded four-poster bed had rich pink velvet hangings with golden fringes and tassels. There were elegantly upholstered French chairs and graceful little tables, and the pink marble fireplace had a frieze of gray-and-white cherubs. Two pot-pourri jars of rose petals stood before the shining fender, and on the mantelpiece, as well as the silver candlestick, there were more of the porcelain Buddhas, their heads moving in the draft from the window.

She was drawn inexorably toward the boudoir, with its dressing table draped with frilled muslin, its gilded washstand, and its row of fine wardrobes. The dressing table was laden with neatly arranged jars and dishes, a silver-handled brush and comb, and a large jewelry casket. Filled with curiosity and a need to learn more about James's absent wife, she opened the doors of the first wardrobe. Vanessa's beautiful clothes hung there as if soon she would come to choose from them. An array of pelisses, gowns, dressses, spencers, mantles, and shawls swayed on their hangers as she ran her fingertips along them. The colors were modish and the materials costly. Vanessa, Lady Atherton, hadn't lacked for clothes, that was certain. The second wardrobe had shelves containing hat boxes, shoes, bootees, and slippers, and a selection of the most exquisite and fashionable of accessories. The third was filled with more clothes.

Slowly Roslyn closed the doors. She shouldn't be looking around like this, but she couldn't help herself. Turning, she went to the dressing table. Everything had been polished. Someone came in daily to attend to the apartment; there wasn't any dust and everything was as fresh and tidy as anyone could wish. Vanessa would be able to return here and not find anything to complain about . . .

Roslyn looked at the jewelry casket. Hesitantly she reached out to open it. Inside lay box after box bearing the name of Messrs. Mayhew & Son, jewelers of Bond Street. She picked one up, opening it to find herself gazing at an emerald necklace with rectangular stones of matchless color and depth. Unbidden, her uncle's voice echoed in her head. ' . . . She did her damnedest to persuade James to 'improve' Foxcombe, but to his eternal credit he denied her such a sacrilege. She sulked, but was consoled by the gift of a very fine emerald necklace . . . ' Was this that necklace? Closing the box, she picked up another, opening it to see a topaz necklace lying on a bed of black velvet. Another snatch of the Elgin House dinner conversation returned to her. 'That's why she accepted James, so that she could dip into the Atherton thousands to help Benedict settle his debts . . . She became worked up about it out of all proportion. With hindsight, I think that her reason for behaving like that was that the topazes were no longer in her possession, but had been given to her lover . . . ' But they hadn't been given to Benedict, they were still here. Roslyn closed the box and replaced it in the casket, closing that too. They'd been wrong about Vanessa.

Taking a long breath, she gathered her skirts to leave, but as she walked through the bedchamber, she again became aware of the fragrance she'd noticed earlier. What was it? Glancing around, she suddenly saw what it was. There was a little dish on a table beside the head of the bed, and in it was a recently stubbed-out cigar. It was James's, she recognized the brand and the way it had been put out. She stared at it. He'd come here immediately on arriving, and he'd stayed long

236

enough to smoke a cigar. Why had he come? What had his thoughts been? Her glance moved unwillingly to the bed. Had he remembered the joy and happiness of lying there with Vanessa in his arms? Had he hoped that soon they would lie there together again. Turning, she hurried on out, closing the apartment door softly behind her.

Reaching the hall, she paused. Where was the library? There wasn't a footman to ask, but as she hesitated, she heard voices coming from a doorway at the far end. The door stood slightly ajar. Crossing toward it, she recognized one of the voices as belonging to Lady Gallermayne. As she peeped inside, she saw that it was indeed the library. Shelves of gold-embossed books stretched from floor to ceiling, and there was carving everywhere: on the sides of the shelves, around the door and windows, and above all around the fireplace. It was carving of such exquisite workmanship that it could only have been by Grinling Gibbons himself.

A Jacobean chandelier was reflected in the mirror above the fireplace; also reflected in it were James and his aunt. His blond hair was ruffled, as if he had but a moment before run his fingers irritably through it. Lady Gallermayne, now in black crepe, seemed concerned about something. 'James,

237

if what Morris says is true, then this is a most disagreeable situation.'

'I couldn't agree more.'

'This wretched scandal isn't going to go away, is it?'

'Which scandal, Aunt?' he inquired with heavy irony. 'My wife's mysterious vanishing act? Or my exceeding immoral and carnal affair with Miss Meredith?'

Roslyn drew back. She couldn't go in.

'Don't be facetious, James. It's far from becoming. Vanessa's absence has been haunting this family for months now, but that isn't what's concerning me now, it's this business with Sir Owen's niece.'

Outside the door Roslyn stepped back. She shouldn't be eavesdropping. But as she moved away, the voices were still audible.

'James, under the circumstances I think it would be wiser to return to London and avoid all possibility of — '

'No.' It was said quietly, but with great firmness.

'Do you want to court scandal? That man didn't leave Town to avoid his duns; he came here to be right on your doorstep in order to continue causing you as much embarrassment as possible! Now that we know that Sir Benedict Courtenay is the new tenant of Grantby Place, I urge you most strongly to return to London and deny him the opportunity of causing trouble here.'

Roslyn had halted in her tracks, turning to stare at the open door. Benedict Courtenay was at Grantby Place?

James spoke again. 'No, Aunt, I will not change my plans because of him.'

'You're being deliberately mulish.'

'It isn't mulish to conduct my life as I wish to.'

His aunt was very displeased. 'There's no reasoning with you at times, James. I shall take my tea in my room.' The black crepe swished as she approached the door.

Roslyn glanced desperately around, not wanting to be seen. She saw a heavy curtain beside the door and hurriedly stepped behind it just as Lady Gallermayne emerged briskly from the room, walking crossly to the staircase.

As the black figure vanished from sight, James spoke rather dryly from the doorway. 'You can come out now, Miss Meredith.'

Her heart sank with mortification. How long had he known she was there? Unwillingly she came out of her hiding place, her cheeks flaming. She could hardly meet his eyes. Did he think she'd been deliberately eavesdropping? 'How . . . ?' she began.

'Mirrors have a habit of reflecting — at

least they do in this house.' It was hard to tell from his eyes or voice what he was thinking.

'I didn't mean to listen, I was walking away when I heard — '

'My aunt mention Courtenay's presence in the vicinity?'

'Yes.'

'I can imagine how disquieting you find the information. Please come in, Miss Meredith, we do not need to stand out here.' He indicated the library.

Still very embarrassed, she walked past him. He closed the door behind them. 'Grantby Place changed hands some months ago, but no one knew the name of the new tenant. Courtenay was seen arriving last night. My gamekeepers have been having trouble with poachers recently and they were watching the boundary in the belief that the poachers were entering Foxcombe from Grantby Place. Courtenay's face was recognized as he drove past. My aunt is of the opinion that all the talk about fleeing from his duns was incorrect and that he's coming here for the express purpose of continuing to stir up the mud he and his sister set in motion in London.'

'Do you think so too?'

He looked away for a moment. 'I don't know. He's quite capable of it; he has more than his fair share of spite and he's always loathed me. I should add that the feeling is mutual.' He smiled a little. 'But then you already know what I think, don't you? I told you on Helena.'

'Yes.'

'Do you share my aunt's view that a return to London would be advisable?'

'I . . . don't know. I haven't given it any thought.'

'Then do so now. I'm afraid I didn't really pause to consider anything when I refused to do as my aunt wished. Your reputation could continue to suffer after all if you remain here.'

'Do you wish me to leave?'

He met her eyes and shook his head. 'No, Miss Meredith, I don't, but my wishes must not be allowed to enter into it. You must consider yourself.'

'I don't wish to return to London.' I want to stay here. With you.

'Are you quite sure?'

'Yes.'

'If it's because you fear such a move would adversely affect your uncle, let me assure you that it wouldn't. I'll honor my word to him.'

'I know you will. That isn't my reason. I admit that in spite of Lady Gallermayne's kind agreement to offer me her protection, I was still immensely relieved when Sir

241

Benedict and his sister departed from the scene, for I felt that their absence would mean an even speedier fading of all the talk. The fact that Sir Benedict is apparently here, after all, doesn't really alter anything. I still have Lady Gallermayne's protection. And so do you, if it comes to that.'

He smiled. 'I wasn't aware that I needed protection, Miss Meredith.'

'If her presence means I cannot be accused of impropriety with you, sir, then the reverse must also apply and you cannot be accused of impropriety with me. I still cannot help fearing that if Lady Atherton wishes to return to you, then there should not be any risk at all of her misinterpreting my presence.'

'I've already said, Miss Meredith, that my wife will not misunderstand anything.'

'How can you be so certain?'

'Because I know.'

She was silent for a moment, then she looked at him again. 'Of course, if Lady Gallermayne intends to leave because of what's now happened, the situation would be altered — '

'She isn't leaving. She said she would remain here and that's what she'll do. So, it's settled. We all remain here as originally planned, and Sir Owen can proceed with the commission first thing in the morning.'

'May I ask you something?'

'That depends what it is.' He smiled again. 'It's about the commission.'

'Yes?'

'What exactly is it?'

'I've already said. I wish the portraits to be substantially altered.'

'How?'

'Is it so very important?'

She colored again. 'No. I suppose not.'

'Forgive me if I seem deliberately mysterious, Miss Meredith, but it's something that's very important to me. I must be absolutely sure of everything, there mustn't be a shadow of any doubt that I'm doing the right thing.'

She stared at him. 'I don't pretend to understand, but — '

'Your uncle will know exactly what I require before this day is out.'

She didn't say anything more, for at that moment Sir Owen himself entered, looking splendidly proper again after his rather crumpled appearance on the journey. He beamed at them both. 'Am I late? I do hope not. I swear I could annihilate a whole pot of tea.'

21

It was dark four hours later when James at last told everyone the truth about the mysterious alterations of the portraits. They'd all dined well and were seated with fruit and liqueurs in the candlelit dining room.

Lady Gallermayne had recovered from her displeasure with her nephew by the time the dinner gong sounded and had come to the table wearing a handsome beaded black taffeta gown with long sleeves and a high neckline. There was a black plume gracing her hair, and a cashmere shawl of particular delicacy around her shoulders. Sir Owen had squeezed himself into his tight evening clothes, and his face was rather pink because he was uncomfortably hot on such a warm evening. Roslyn had chosen to wear the figured French gauze and white satin gown she'd first worn at the fateful Elgin House dinner party in January. Her tawny hair was pinned up into a knot at the back of her head from which several ringlets tumbled to the nape of her neck, and her mother's locket was on its ribbon around her throat.

Opposite her, James wore an indigo

evening coat with velvet facings and silver buttons. There was a sapphire pin in his complicated cravat, and lace on the front of his shirt where it protruded from his white satin waist-coat. His hair was very bright in the candlelight and throughout the meal he'd put himself out to be an attentive and amusing host.

The dining room was at the back of the house directly below Vanessa's apartment, and its windows stood open onto the Dutch garden. Outside the light had long since gone, but the lilies and irises at the edge of the canal could just be made out in the darkness. The pavilion was a vague shape in the distance, the eye led toward it by the silvery line of water and avenues of shadowy trees. There was honeysuckle growing against the house and its perfume was sweet and heady.

The room itself was so perfectly Tudor that Queen Elizabeth herself might have dined there. Paneled, with a coffered plaster-work ceiling and iron-rimmed chandeliers like those in the gallery, it boasted a range of magnificent carved livery cupboards, and on a long side table there was a display of gold plates that had once belonged to Sir Walter Raleigh. The great oblong oak table at which they sat could have graced Hampton Court itself, and the silver cutlery and large goblets they'd used went perfectly with it. The candlesticks illuminating the room were all supported by silver Atherton unicorns, and the same emblem was repeated in the heavy carving of the chairs.

Lady Gallermayne was in good humor, having dined on her favorite beef steak and asparagus, followed by pineapple tartlets made with fruit from the Foxcombe pinery. This, together with a fine wine and James's entertaining conversation, served to dismiss the thought of Sir Benedict Courtenay's close proximity temporarily from her mind.

Sir Benedict wasn't far from Roslyn's mind, however; her thoughts constantly returned to him and his possible reasons for taking the lease of Grantby Place. Was he really intent upon stirring up as much scandal as he possibly could? And if so, why? Could he really despise James so much that he'd go to such lengths?

James was just pouring them all a last glass of liqueur when the butler, Morris, came apologetically into the room. 'Begging your pardon, my lord.'

'Yes? What is it?'

'Some more information about the gentleman at Grantby Place has come into my possession.'

Silence fell over the table. Sir Owen had

been regaled with the news about Grantby Place, and so knew as well as everyone else who the 'gentleman' was.

James glanced at them all and then nodded at the butler. 'What have you learned, Morris?'

'It seems that one of our grooms was returning from visiting his sick mother in Charlton Kings when he was approached by two, er, gentlemen requesting directions to Grantby Place and inquiring if Sir Benedict was in residence at the moment. The groom directed them and informed them that as far as he was aware, Sir Benedict was indeed in residence. The two rode on.' The butler cleared his throat. 'The groom says they were debt collectors, my lord.'

'How does he know that? Did they tell him?'

'Er, no, my lord, but as a rather devoted follower of Cheltenham races, he knows a dun when he sees one. It has been his misfortune to be pursued by them himself from time to time.'

'Has it indeed?' James smiled a little. 'And he's in no doubt about these two?'

'None at all, my lord.'

'Thank you, Morris.'

'My lord.'

As the door closed behind him, James

glanced around the table. 'It seems the original story about friend Courtenay was correct, after all: he was leaving Town to slip the duns.'

'And has been singularly unsuccessful,' said his aunt, her smile showing no sympathy at all for Sir Benedict Courtenay and his problems. 'I hope they haul him off as ignominiously as possible.'

Sir Owen was faintly amused. 'Where's your charity, my lady?'

'In tatters from the moment that odious fellow and his equally odious sister commenced their campaign.'

'It was tatters long before that,' said James. 'You've disliked him ever since his name was mentioned in the same breath as Vanessa's.'

His aunt raised an eyebrow. 'Very well, if honesty is the order of the day, I admit it. I also admit that I've disliked Vanessa all along as well. She was never right for you, and everyone in Town knew it except you. Still, love is blind, or so they say.'

Roslyn glanced at James, wondering how he would take such remarks. He was smiling a little. 'If that is the case, Aunt, you'll be very pleased indeed to hear of a certain decision I've made.'

'And what decision might that be?'

'Perhaps it would be best if you all came

with me now. There's something I wish to explain concerning Sir Owen's excellent portraits.' Getting to his feet, he picked up one of the unicorn candlesticks and then smiled at Roslyn, offering her his arm. 'Miss Meredith?'

Slowly she rose, slipping her hand over his sleeve.

Lady Gallermayne grumbled as she too got up. 'James, is it really necessary to be so wretchedly secretive?'

'Yes, Aunt, for I must look at her as I say it.'

'Look at her?' Lady Gallermayne was startled.

'At her likeness,' he qualified.

With a disapproving breath, his aunt accepted Sir Owen's arm, and with James lighting the way, they proceeded through the dark house, up the staircase to the landing, and then up to the gallery floor above.

The candlelight flickered and danced on the paneling, and their reflections looked back at them from the lantern of windows overlooking the front of the house.

Roslyn was rather surprised when he paused at last, holding the candlestick aloft so that the pale light fell on the three portraits, for she hadn't even noticed them when she'd been here earlier, but then she'd been more interested in admiring the magnificent view of the valleys and park.

The portraits were very fine indeed, among the best Sir Owen had ever done. The first was of James and Vanessa on horseback, with Foxcombe house in the background. Vanessa was almost brazen in a scarlet riding habit, her face turned challengingly toward the front. She was very lovely, and seemed haughtily aware of it. Her heart-shaped face was tilted a little, and her lustrous dark-brown eyes gazed almost scornfully out of the canvas. Mounted on a large black horse at her side, James was leaning over to rest his gloved hand on hers. It was a tender, protective gesture, except that the Vanessa Sir Owen had captured did not need protecting at all.

The second portrait was set in the library at Foxcombe. Vanessa reclined on a sofa, with James standing behind. She wore white with a lace overgown. Her dark, shining curls had been pinned up almost casually on the top of her head, and the emerald necklace Roslyn had seen earlier was at her flawless throat. There was a little dog on her lap, and a brightly colored cashmere shawl spilled down to the floor. One hand was raised to her shoulder, to touch James's as he bent over her to look at the dog.

The final portrait was set in the little

summerhouse Roslyn had noticed in the topiary garden at the front of the house. Yellow roses climbed over the little building and James and Vanessa were seated inside. She carried a posy of them, and James was in the act of handing her another bloom. She wore a mauve silk gown and a diamond necklace. Roslyn remembered what her uncle had said about Vanessa's refusal to wear the topaz necklace James had wanted for this portrait. The topazes would have been perfect had Vanessa agreed to change her gown for something cream or white, for with so many yellow roses all around, it was the obvious thing for any woman of taste. But Vanessa insisted on mauve silk and diamonds, and the portrait lost. Roslyn lowered her glance. Why had Vanessa refused to wear the necklace? She still had it, it was in her apartment even now.

Lady Gallermayne had been studying the portraits. With a sniff she nodded with grudging admiration. 'You've a very deft hand, Sir Owen, a very deft hand indeed.'

'Thank you, my lady.'

'And I suppose I must admit that Vanessa is a gloriously beautiful creature, although, to be sure, the real woman has been captured very well in the scarlet riding habit. That look in her eyes says everything one should need to know about her.'

James nodded. 'Yes, it does. She's vain, arrogant, scheming, deceitful, and shallow.'

Even his aunt stared at him. Roslyn's lips parted in surprise and Sir Owen cleared his throat a little uncomfortably.

James smiled at them, his eyes very dark in the candlelight. 'They say it's better to realize something late than never to realize it at all, and I've realized at long last that the woman I married was unworthy in every conceivable way. I wish to forget that she ever existed, which is why, Sir Owen, I must have the portraits changed. I don't wish to get rid of them because I think they're very fine, so if I want to continue hanging them here at Foxcombe, Vanessa's likeness must be removed. She must be erased. Absolutely.'

As he spoke, he looked at the equestrian portrait, directly into his wife's eyes. It was as if she could hear every word he said.

22

The following morning James remained firm in his decision, and Sir Owen left the house directly after an early breakfast to go to the boathouse studio and prepare for the work. He arrived to find men already carrying the three paintings inside.

Wearing her primrose-and-white striped lawn dress, Roslyn went down to a later breakfast. She found Lady Gallermayne still seated at the table with a newspaper, and James on the point of leaving for an appointment with his lawyer in Cheltenham.

He smiled at Roslyn as she entered, his glance sweeping her quickly from head to toe. 'Good morning, Miss Meredith,' he said.

'Good morning, my lord. Lady Gallermayne.'

Lady Gallermayne looked over her newspaper, her eyes owlish behind a pair of thick-lensed spectacles. 'Good morning, Miss Meredith.'

James indicated the silver-domed dishes on the side table. 'I do hope you aren't fond of smoked fish for breakfast, Miss Meredith, because if you are, I'm afraid my aunt has consumed it all.'

Lady Gallermayne darted him a disapproving look. 'Are you suggesting that I've made a pig of myself, James?'

'Well, where smoked fish is concerned — '

The newspaper rustled crossly as she returned her attention to it.

Roslyn smiled quickly. 'I — I like a little crisp bacon for breakfast, my lord.'

'You'll find that in abundance under that dome there.' He pointed. 'By the way, it's my custom to drive around the estate each time I return, and I've already invited my aunt to join me. Would you care to come too?'

'I'd like that very much. Thank you.'

'Excellent. We'll set off after luncheon, which will be served in the summerhouse, as it's such a fine day. But now, if you'll excuse me, I really must leave. Lawyers and estate business wait for no man.' He drew Roslyn's hand quickly to his lips and then bent to kiss his aunt on the cheek. A moment later he'd gone.

Roslyn helped herself to some bacon and a crisp roll, and then Morris drew out a chair for her and poured her some coffee. Lady Gallermayne was evidently a poor conversationalist at breakfast, for she remained buried in the newspaper without a word until Roslyn was sipping her second cup of coffee. At last the newspaper was folded, the spectacles removed and replaced in their case in the reticule on the table beside her, and she surveyed Rosyln. 'Did you sleep well, Miss Meredith?'

'Yes, thank you. Very well indeed.'

'That's more than I can say. I spent a most disagreeable night.'

'I'm sorry to hear that.'

'It was James's fault, of course. It's quite obvious that he's decided to rid himself of Vanessa completely, which can only mean a divorce. Divorce is a vulgar, shameful thing, and there's never been an instance of it in the family before. It really is too much. First there was the endless scandal of Vanessa's disappearance, and now this. It gave me a very disagreeable headache and robbed me of any ability to sleep. I feel quite fatigued this morning, quite fatigued, and that isn't at all to be recommended after a long journey. It will be the death of me, I swear.'

Roslyn didn't quite know what to say. 'Perhaps if you returned to your bed you'd be able to sleep now?'

'Possibly.' Lady Gallermayne considered it for a moment. 'Yes, maybe I could indeed sleep now,' she said with sudden decision. 'I shall return directly to my room. I trust that you will be able to amuse yourself in my absence, Miss Meredith.'

255

'I'm sure I can, Lady Gallermayne. I'll go for a walk.'

Lady Gallermayne nodded approvingly. 'A most creditable notion. I will leave you, then, my dear.' Her black skirts rustling, she got up and left the room.

As Morris stepped forward to pour Roslyn another cup of coffee, there was a sudden cry from the hall, followed by a dull thump. Then a maid's tearful voice rang out. 'Lady Gallermayne! Oh, my lady, are you all right?'

Alarmed, Roslyn and the butler hurried out to see what had happened. Lady Gallermayne had fallen at the foot of the staircase and a frightened maid was standing over her as she struggled to sit up. The maid had been carrying a pile of freshly laundered hand towels, and these lay scattered on the stairs and floor.

Pulling herself up by the staircase newel post, Lady Gallermayne looked furiously at the maid. 'Don't just stand there, you foolish chit, help me up!'

The maid hastened to obey, but as she did so, Lady Gallermayne's ankle buckled beneath her and she gave a grimace of pain. 'No! Put me down again!'

Roslyn crouched anxiously beside Lady Gallermayne. 'What is it? What happened?'

'This idiotic creature was coming down the

stairs and she dropped those wretched towels. I tried to step aside, lost my footing, and fell. I think I've sprained my ankle; I may even have broken it.' She gave the maid a dark look that reduced her to helpless weeping.

Morris nodded quickly at the girl, who thankfully retrieved the towels and rushed away. Then the butler cleared his throat. 'Shall I have some men carry you up to your room, my lady?'

'Unless you imagine I wish to lie here for the rest of the day,' snapped Lady Gallermayne. 'Have someone go to Cheltenham for that fool of a leech. What's his name?'

'Dr Eggerton, my lady.'

'That's the one.'

'Yes, my lady.' He hurried away.

A few minutes later Roslyn followed the footmen carrying her ladyship up to the red-tapestry room, and a rider was on his way to Cheltenham to bring the doctor.

Lady Gallermayne's ankle was giving her a great deal of pain and she complained constantly as the men carried her as carefully and gently as possible to her bed, laying her down as softly as if she was made of eggshell. Her elderly maid, Parrish, had come running the moment she heard of the accident, and now she waved everyone away except Roslyn. Piling pillow after pillow behind her mistress, she began to unbutton the high-throated black crepe dress.

Lady Gallermayne was extremely irritable. 'Oh, do stop fussing, Parrish, you'll give me the vapors.'

'Very well, my lady. Shall I bring you a cup of tea?'

'Please do.'

Roslyn had been looking around the room, which earned its name, for the bed was hung with wine-red velvet and the floor was carpeted in a rainbow-hued Wilton the predominant shade of which was crimson. On the walls were fine Belgian tapestries depicting medieval hunting scenes. The room overlooked the topiary green at the front of the house, and a light breeze came in through the open casements. This did not meet with her ladyship's approval.

'Close the window, if you please, Miss Meredith, or I'm sure I'll contract pneumonia.'

Roslyn hurried to obey, and then she sat quietly by the bed while Lady Gallermayne lay back on the pillows. It seemed an age before Parrish returned with the tea, and a positive lifetime before at last the doctor arrived.

To everyone's relief the doctor quickly ascertained that the ankle was only sprained, not broken, and he bandaged it most carefully, with Lady Gallermayne making a great deal of noise about the pain. Prescribing a mild dosage of laudanum to ease the pain and assist in making her sleep for a while, the doctor departed soon afterward.

With the dutiful Parrish remaining at the bedside, Roslyn was at liberty to go for the walk she'd decided upon. With a white shawl over her arms, she set off to walk down to the boathouse. There was a wide, much-used gravel drive leading down toward the lake. It curved down through the park in such a way as to command a fine view over the water and valley, but there was a path leading down more directly, passing through a magnificent grove of rhododendrons. She hesitated only for a moment before taking the path.

The heavy, brightly colored clusters of blooms were quite breathtaking, and they were at their full June glory. In the distance she could hear a woodpecker, while close to she was startled when a cock pheasant broke from the undergrowth, flying off with a great deal of noise and commotion. Behind her the rhododendrons soon hid the house from view. The path descended swiftly, and suddenly the lake was before her, with the boathouse studio in the foreground.

Once for the shelter and protection of a

fine pleasure barge, it was now a long time since a craft of any kind had been moored within its confines. Its roof now sported large window lights, and its mooring bay had been completely covered over to provide the studio floor. Recently repaired and improved, it had been painted a discreet shade of blue that looked particularly well on a bright, sunlit day like this. The water sparkled and reflected the brilliance of the sky, and around the little building's watery foundation grew some fine, tall reeds and yellow irises that swayed to the gentle motion of the lake.

She tiptoed along the little stone path leading to the door, intending to leave again without interrupting her uncle if he was particularly involved in his work. But as she gingerly pushed the door a little ajar, he heard immediately and came over to her, a broad smile on his face.

'Hello there, *cariad*. Have you come to see that I'm keeping busy?' He kissed her on the cheek.

'I'm just going for a walk and I thought I'd say hello.' She glanced around. The roof lights allowed an almost blinding light into the boathouse, and sunbeams danced in the still air. Stacks of canvases of all sizes rested against one wall, while another was lined with cupboards containing drawers of paper.

Tables of jars, paints, oils, pencils, charcoal, and everything else an artist needed stood in the middle, surrounded by easels and stools, while the wall behind Roslyn boasted a fine dais and draped curtains of every texture and color, ready for the next portrait.

The three paintings of James and Vanessa rested on their easels, and the equestrian one had already been worked upon; Vanessa was vanishing behind a cloudy sky.

Sir Owen followed his niece's glance. 'He wanted her erased from his life, and that's precisely what she'll be — from the portraits, at least.'

'How will you remove her from the others?'

'They're a little more difficult. I think I shall be able to extinguish her from the summerhouse and replace her with a plethora of yellow climbing roses, but the library poses a problem.'

'Why?'

'Well, James may well be given to sitting alone in the summer-house, but is he also given to bending over sofas reaching out to nothing? No, I think not. I was hoping that perhaps Lady Gallermayne would consent to replacing Vanessa.'

'Oh, that reminds me, Lady Gallermayne has sprained her ankle and is confined to her bed for the moment.'

'Dear me, I hope it isn't serious?'

'No. The doctor is of the opinion that she's making a great deal of noise for nothing. I think he's a little unkind, for she's obviously in pain, but she *is* making a fuss. At least, she was. He's prescribed laudanum and she was asleep when I left.'

'A sprained ankle can be a very disagreeable thing. I shall call upon her as soon as I return to the house.'

'Which will be when?'

'With all the work I've got to do, not until dinner-time.' He grinned and then pointed to a nearby wall. All his sketches of Christina and Theo's wedding had been pinned there. 'I thought I'd put them up so I could keep glancing at them. They'll gradually form into a whole in my mind's eye.'

'Will it be a masterpiece?'

'All my paintings are masterpieces, you cheeky minx. Now, then, off with you, I must get on with things.' He accompanied her to the door. 'Where are you thinking of walking?'

'I don't know. I didn't think of asking anyone which way was the best.'

'Well, the fellows who brought the portraits down earlier told me that the boundary with Grantby Place is quite close in that direction.' He pointed northwest along the shore of the lake. 'Apparently there's a stream feeding the lake somewhere over there, and it forms the dividing line between the estates. They told me about it because it's said to be very picturesque and they thought I'd be toddling off with my sketching pad.'

'And will you?' she inquired with a smile.

'I'll let you do a preliminary reconnaissance for me. If it meets with your approval, I'll consider an excursion or two; if not, I'll have saved myself the exercise.'

She was smiling as she walked away, following the edge of the lake in the direction of the boundary stream. The beauty of Foxcombe folded over her. The air was warm and sweet-smelling, the sunlight danced on the water, and the rich greens of the Gloucestershire scenery seemed to fade into an indistinct haze on the horizon, merging with the peerless blue of the sky.

The boundary stream entered the lake beneath a rustic bridge. Weeds waved sensuously in the clear water, and jeweled damselflies hovered over the surface. Alders and willows lined the water's edge as the stream meandered toward the lake, the water sometimes shallow and babbling over stones, and sometimes silent in deep pools where minnows flitted in sun-dappled shoals. She disturbed a kingfisher and paused to watch a heron wading toward the shade of an immense weeping willow on the opposite bank. The willow grew on Grantby Place land.

She walked on for a while and then sat on a flower-dotted, mossy bank to rest for a while before retracing her steps. She'd been sitting there for a few minutes watching a family of moorhens when she heard hoofbeats approaching the clearing on the opposite bank. She could hear raised voices, a man and woman arguing.

They rode in the clearing. It was Sir Benedict Courtenay and his sister, Lady Ferney. He wore a dark-green riding coat and tight buckskin breeches, and his handsome face was as dark as thunder. His titian-haired sister wore a rust-colored riding habit and was probably as angry as he was, but her face was concealed by the little net veil attached to her beaver hat.

Dismayed, Roslyn hoped they'd ride by without seeing her, but something made him glance straight at her. Startled, he reined sharply in. His sister broke off in midsentence, bringing her horse to a standstill and staring across the stream at the figure in primrose-and-white-striped lawn.

Benedict maneuvered his horse right to the edge of the water, leaning foward on the pommel, a rather unpleasant smile curving his fine lips. 'Well, well, if it isn't little Miss Meredith. I confess I didn't expect to see you in these parts.'

'No, I don't suppose you did.'

'You persuaded him to let you come, after all, did you? How taken with your charms he must be to go against his aunt's wishes like that.'

'It might interest you to know that Lady Gallermayne is at Foxcombe as well.'

The news caught him off guard for a moment and he turned quickly to glance at his motionless sister. Then he looked at Roslyn again. 'How very fortunate for you,' he murmured, 'or unfortunate, as the case may be.'

'Unfortunate?'

'Her presence will no doubt be an, er, damper on the proceedings.'

Roslyn's cheeks reddened at the implication and she got up from the bank, intending to walk away.

His mocking voice followed her. 'Don't think he's yours, Miss Meredith, for that would be a sad mistake. He's still in love with his wife, as you'll soon find out.'

'Soon find out? What do you mean?'

'You'll see, my dear. You'll see.' He turned his horse's head, looking briefly at his sister.

'Come,' he said abruptly, kicking his heels and riding swiftly out of the clearing again.

Lady Ferney remained where she was, staring across into Roslyn's eyes for a long moment, then she too turned her horse and rode away.

Roslyn gazed after them. There was only one thing she could think now: Vanessa was about to return to her husband.

23

James had returned from Cheltenham when she reached the house again, and she joined him as he sat with his aunt, who was awake again. Being temporarily confined to her bed did not improve Lady Gallermayne's temper and she was proving to be a very difficult patient. She was demanding and occasionally unreasonable, and poor Parrish was beginning to look very harassed indeed as she was sent scurrying to and fro on all manner of unnecessary errands. It was with no small relief that everyone left the room when her ladyship at last announced that she wished to sleep again.

It was time for luncheon to be served in the summerhouse, and as James escorted Roslyn out to the topiary green, she wondered how to broach the rather delicate subject of Benedict Courtenay and his cryptic remark about Vanessa.

They crossed the wide gravel area before the house and entered the garden through a wrought-iron gate set in the low surrounding wall. The path to the summerhouse led between rows of shrubs clipped to resemble the neatly stacked weights of a huge pair of scales, and the air was very warm and still. There were flowers everywhere, from the delicate little crimson-and-purple fuchsias nodding over the edge of the path, to the stately spikes of white and light blue Canterbury bells. Snapdragons, wallflowers, candytuft, and columbine basked in drifts of sweet-smelling color, and the tinkling splash of water came from the playing fountains.

The summerhouse was a charming little wooden building, painted white and covered with the magnificent yellow climbing rose Sir Owen had painted in his portrait of James and Vanessa. A table had been set in its shade, the cutlery and glasses gleaming where the sunlight pierced the foliage and open woodwork. James handed Roslyn to her place, and she found herself occupying the position Vanessa had had in the portrait.

Some footmen appeared from nowhere to serve a delicious cold chicken salad and to pour a bottle of excellent chilled white wine, then they withdrew and Roslyn was quite alone with James.

He glanced at her. 'There's something on your mind, isn't there?'

'Well . . . ' Her voice died away on the single word. She didn't know how to begin.

'If it's the lack of propriety we might be showing — '

'Lack of propriety?'

'Eating alone together like this.'

'Oh. No, I hadn't even thought of that.' She looked at him. 'Lady Gallermayne would disapprove, wouldn't she?'

'Probably, but please don't let that spoil our enjoyment of the meal. It's hardly likely that the *beau monde* is going to descend upon Foxcombe and catch us in the very act of sharing a wicked chicken leg together.' He smiled. 'So, it isn't the breach of etiquette that's concerning you. What is it, then?'

'When I was out walking this morning, I had the misfortune to encounter the new tenant of Grantby Place.'

'Courtenay?'

'And Lady Ferney.'

He was surprised. 'I thought she'd gone to Ireland.'

'So did I, but she's here.'

'I take it that the meeting was far from congenial.'

'Very far from it. He made some very disagreeable remarks about my being here.' She could feel the color entering her cheeks. Should she tell him exactly what he had said?

'What remarks?'

She met his eyes. 'Well, first of all he

commented that Lady Gallermayne's presence might be putting a frustrating check upon our affair.'

'Did he indeed?' he murmured, his blue eyes very piercing and cold.

'And he warned me not to cherish hopes that I'd won you, because you were still in love with your wife, as I'd soon find out.'

He sat back. 'What do you think that meant?'

'All he'd say when I asked was that I'd soon see what he meant, but my guess is . . . '

'Yes?'

'That he was implying Lady Atherton would soon be returning to you.' Her cheeks were fiery and she could no longer meet his eyes.

He was silent for a long moment. 'Do you really think that's what he meant?'

'Yes. What else could he have meant?'

'What else indeed,' he murmured. 'And what did Lady Ferney have to say?'

'Nothing.'

He didn't conceal his surprise. 'Nothing at all?'

'No.'

'How very unlike her.'

'Yes, I suppose it was, although . . . '

'Yes?'

'They had been arguing, so her silence

270

could just have signified her displeasure with him.'

'Yes, I suppose it could.' He still sat back, his face very thoughtful as he toyed idly with the stem of his wineglass. After a while he smiled at her. 'Enough of such a disagreeable subject as the Courtenay family, they one and all render my digestive system incapable. Tell me, are you really not disturbed that we may be breaking all manner of laws by dining alone like this?'

She stared at him, taken by surprise by the abrupt change of subject. Wasn't he going to say anything else about Vanessa's possible return? 'My lord — '

'Please, Miss Meredith, I don't wish to discuss Courtenay, his sister, or my wife. I'd much prefer to talk about what you and I should or should not be permitted to do. Now, then, how bothered are you at what my aunt might or might not say about this sinful chicken salad we've shared with such wild abandon?'

She couldn't help smiling. 'I really don't know what to think,' she admitted. 'To be perfectly honest I fail to see what is so reprehensible about us sitting alone out here, when nothing at all would be said if we sat similarly in the dining room. Etiquette has some very dubious rules, for if we were going to be tempted into disgracefully immoral conduct, I've no doubt we'd be more likely to indulge in the relative seclusion of the dining room, which has a door to lock, than out here in the garden, which is overlooked by every window at the front of the house.'

'What a very entertaining picture you conjure in my base male imagination, Miss Meredith.'

'Nevertheless, what I say is true, isn't it?'

'Perfectly true. So by the same token we're quite likely to indulge in our insatiable passion when we drive out alone around the estate this afternoon, aren't we?'

She was almost lost for words. 'I, er, suppose we are.'

'Which means forcing restraint upon those same passions by the presence of a chaperone, and since that cannot be my aunt, it will have to be your maid.'

'Yes.'

'Do I take it then you'll still accompany me?'

'Yes.'

'Good.' He smiled a little roguishly. 'Although how I shall contain my beastly desires, I really don't know. Drink up your wine, Miss Meredith, you look all of a fluster.'

'That's because I *am* all of a fluster,' she replied, doing as she was told.

* ⋆ ⋆

Roslyn sat for a while reading to Lady Gallermayne before she and James set off on their drive around the estate. Before leaving, she was quizzed at length by Lady Gallermayne, who was determined to see that all was as it should be. She even sent for Lizzie, to see that the maid was suitable.

At last Roslyn and James emerged from the house to the waiting carriage, a very handsome equipage with dark-blue lacquered panels and gleaming lamps. Drawn by a team of finely matched dappled grays, it was driven by a young coachman who appeared to find Lizzie rather eye-catching, for he gave her a broad wink that made her blush a great deal.

The window glasses were lowered as the carriage drew away, for the weather really was far too fine to leave them closed. They drove down to the lake and Roslyn glanced out to see the path she'd taken that morning through the rhododendrons. They passed the boathouse, where Sir Owen had worked continuously since morning, his luncheon having been taken to him in a wicker basket. James looked at the studio as they drove by. Roslyn wondered what he was thinking. He hadn't ordered the work to stop now that it seemed likely that Vanessa would return.

Indeed, he hadn't mentioned his wife once since the summerhouse. It was almost as if nothing had been said to him about the meeting with Benedict Courtenay.

They drove along the lakeside for a while before the road climbed up through a fine hanging beechwood where the shivering song of wood warblers echoed through the high canopy of leaves. Red squirrels darted up to safety as the handsome carriage rattled by, the coachman urging the grays to greater effort up the long incline.

They paused for a while at the home farm, where James's land agent was the tenant. It was a fine, prosperous farm, well managed and profitable, and Roslyn remained in the carriage with Lizzie as James discussed various items with the agent. The coachman alighted from his box for a while, under the guise of checking the traces, and it was some time before Roslyn happened to glance at Lizzie and saw her exchanging a smile with him as he passed the open window.

From the home farm they drove on past stone walls, flocks of sheep, and another farm before the road began to curve sharply to the north along a shallow wooded valley where the way was edged with dogwood, spindle tree, and hazel. Wild roses arched over the carriage, their pink and white blooms reminiscent of the Ayios Georghios rose, and yet not really like it at all.

The road climbed steadily now toward a hilltop crowned with a copse of fine Scots pines. As they reached the summit, James ordered the coachman to halt and rest the horses. Alighting, he handed Roslyn down and then Lizzie. A sea of waving grasses and flowers stretched away on all sides from the pine copse where they stood, and the throb of grasshoppers filled the sweet, resin-scented air.

Roslyn shook out her skirts and retied the ribbons of her gypsy hat. She'd been sitting in the carriage for some time and was glad to be out of it for a while.

James glanced at her. 'I'm afraid carriages can be rather fatiguing, can't they?'

'Just a little.' She smiled.

'Perhaps a short promenade would be agreeable?' He offered her his arm, and as he did so, he looked at Lizzie. 'We won't be out of sight, so you may remain here. I'm sure you and Frederick can find something to converse about.'

The maid looked uncertain, but Roslyn nodded at her before slipping her hand over James's sleeve and strolling with him through the pine trees. The resin in the air reminded her of Greece.

'Are you thinking what I'm thinking, Miss Meredith?' James inquired suddenly.

'I was thinking about Greece.'

'Then we think alike. It seems a long time ago now, doesn't it?'

'Yes. Actually I've thought about it twice since we left the house. There was a rose by the roadside that reminded me of the Ayios Georghios rose.'

'Was that the flower you wore on your bonnet at the wedding?'

She was surprised that he should remember such a thing. 'Yes.'

He smiled. 'I am known to be occasionally observant, Miss Meredith.'

They emerged from the pine trees. Behind them the carriage was clearly visible on the road. Lizzie and the coachman were engrossed in conversation. In front the land sloped away and the upper reaches of the lake were just visible along the valley, but directly opposite, and very clear now because they were so close, was Grantby Place.

The house seemed very white, its wings and immense columned portico facing the hill where they stood. Roslyn could see the drive curving up through the open park and some gardeners engaged upon raking the gravel. The pine trees seemed to still the air, so that when the gardeners laughed together at some shared joke, the sound carried with almost startling clarity.

James was gazing across at the house. 'What do you think of Courtenay's new abode, Miss Meredith?'

'It seems a little cold.'

'Cold?'

'Remote and without character. I much prefer Foxcombe.'

He smiled. 'I always knew you were a lady of exceptional good taste.'

'I don't understand how anyone could fail to love Foxcombe, my lord.'

'My name is James. As to not liking Foxcombe, my wife managed it from the outset. That is her ideal.' He pointed across the valley.

'But it's to Foxcombe that she'll be returning,' she replied, quietly, very aware that he'd invited more intimacy.

'She won't be returning, Roslyn, you have my word on it.' He looked at her. 'In the absence of any comment from you, I shall take the liberty of calling you by your first name. I trust you do not disapprove of such forwardness.'

'I don't disapprove at all.'

'What of etiquette?' he murmured.

'I'm becoming rather tired of etiquette; it has a very disagreeable way of thrusting itself into everything.' She smiled at him, loving him so much that it was all she could do not to blurt it out.

His glance moved over her face and suddenly he put his hand on her cheek. 'Roslyn, you have a way of looking at me sometimes that makes me forget that I'm a gentleman.' Bending his head, he kissed her on the lips, and this time, unlike on Helena, he drew her into his arms, pressing her close and moving his lips over hers in a way that was far from chaste. This wasn't an affectionate kiss, it was a full-blooded demonstration of the desire she'd never realized she'd stirred in him.

Her senses began to spin with a wild joy and her whole body was alive with him. The blood coursed warmly through her veins, flushing her cheeks as she returned the embrace, her lips responding to his. Her inhibitions deserted her, denying her the will or strength to conceal the love she'd kept secret for so long. The truth poured out in her silent but ardent response. He wasn't indifferent to her! He wanted her. There was no mistaking it in the way he held her against him, as if he would make her part of him, and as his lips continued to move over hers, she could taste the sweet passion he had so suddenly and completely acknowledged.

Her senses sang with an outburst of happiness, and she wanted the moment to go on forever, but then, with an abruptness that shattered her newfound joy, something made him release her. There was rejection in the way he drew sharply back, turning to look quickly across at Grantby Place as a woman's laughter carried clearly on the motionless air. Lady Ferney was riding with her brother again, and it was her laughter that had cut through headily aroused passions to stifle desire as completely as a candle flame can be extinguished. Gone was the lover who'd thrown caution to the winds by taking her in his arms and kissing her into the revelation of her innermost feelings, for James Atherton was now a man who had been suddenly and poignantly reminded of the wife he still loved, no matter how much he tried to deny it.

Shaken and confused, Roslyn stared at him and then at the two distant figures riding down through Grantby Place's elegant park. She knew that Lady Ferney's laughter had brought Vanessa back to him; she didn't need to be told. She felt as if ice-cold water were washing over her, freezing the fires that a moment before had burned through her veins. Had he slapped her face he could not have hurt her more than he had in that brief moment. She'd made an utter fool of herself.

Her every instinct had warned her all along that her love must never be revealed; she'd gone against her better judgment, she'd shown him exactly how she felt, and almost immediately she was paying the price.

With a stifled sob she gathered her skirts and hurried away, her shoes making little sound on the cushion of pine needles. She heard him call her name, but she didn't look back.

At the sound of his voice, Lizzie and the coachman had turned quickly to look, and seeing her obvious distress, they exchanged quick glances.

Blinking back the tears, she climbed quickly into the carriage, and Lizzie followed her. The coachman hesitated for a moment, but then saw James approaching as well and resumed his place on the box.

James reached the carriage door and looked in at Roslyn. 'I must speak with you.'

'We have nothing to say, sir. May we please return to the house?'

'Roslyn —'

'We have nothing to say,' she repeated stiffly, hurt beyond all reason.

Glancing at Lizzie, who was endeavoring to look as if she couldn't hear a word, he instructed Frederick to drive home, then he climbed in and slammed the door behind him. A moment later they were driving swiftly back toward Foxcombe.

The journey was accomplished in an embarrassing silence. Roslyn couldn't meet his eyes. She felt humiliated and more wretched than ever before, and as the carriage swayed to a halt before the house, she climbed quickly out first, hurrying away before James could say anything.

'Roslyn! For God's sake, let me explain,' he cried.

She didn't look back. She'd reached the head of the stairs when he entered, but before he could follow her, Morris approached him. 'Begging your pardon, my lord, but Mr Barraclough has called. He says it's important estate business.'

'What does my damned lawyer want now? I only saw him this morning. Very well. Oh, and Morris, see that a man is ready to ride with an urgent letter.'

The butler bowed and withdrew. James glanced at the staircase again, hesitated, but then strode away across the hall.

From the top of the staircase, hidden from view, Roslyn watched him, then she gathered her skirts and hurried on to her room, locking herself in and then flinging herself weeping on the bed. Her heart was breaking with misery and shame.

24

It was a long time before Roslyn's tears subsided and she was composed again, at least as much as she could be under the circumstances. Lizzie came several times to the door, knocking anxiously but discreetly in case Lady Gallermayne should hear from the nearby red-tapestry room, but Roslyn asked her to go away. It was evening and the shadows were lengthening when at last she admitted the maid.

'Are you all right, madam?'

'Yes. Thank you. Has Sir Owen returned from the studio yet?'

'No, madam. He's expected to come back in time for dinner.'

Dinner. The thought filled Roslyn with dread.

As if she knew what her mistress was thinking, Lizzie volunteered the information that James was still closeted with his lawyer. 'They've been discussing something important all this time, madam, and they stopped just long enough for his lordship to dispatch an urgent letter. Frederick took it.' She blushed at mentioning the young coachman who'd paid her such marked attention.

'Do you know who it was for?'

'No, madam. Frederick didn't say. What shall you wear for dinner?'

Roslyn had no desire to attend dinner, but she knew she must. She had to put on the best face she could and behave as if nothing had happened, it was the only way to salvage her pride. 'I think I'll wear the pale-green silk.'

'Very well, madam.'

There was another tap at the door. Roslyn turned nervously, fearing that it might be James, but it wasn't, it was Parrish.

'Begging your pardon, madam, but her ladyship would like to speak to you.'

'Very well, I'll be along directly.' Roslyn sat quickly at her dressing table for Lizzie to make her rather crumpled hair look respectable again, and then smoothing her primrose-and-white-striped skirts, she hurried along the passage to the red-tapestry room.

To her astonishment Lady Gallermayne was seated in a comfortable chair by the window, and she was dressed in her beaded gown, as if she had every intention of going down to dinner. 'Oh, my lady, should you be out of your bed?' she asked in concern.

Lady Gallermayne raised an eyebrow. 'Do you imagine that I intend to remain cooped up any longer than I have to? My ankle is still painful, but it isn't incapacitating.'

'No, my lady.'

'Come here.'

Roslyn went unwillingly closer.

'You've been piping your eye, Miss Meredith. May I ask why?'

'It was merely some dust, Lady Gallermayne. I wasn't crying.' Roslyn met the other's shrewd eyes. She wasn't going to admit to crying, she was going to behave as if nothing had happened.

'Indeed? A rather troublesome speck of dust, it kept you snuffling for an hour or more.'

Roslyn colored a little but still didn't admit to anything.

'I was seated in my window when the carriage returned earlier. It seemed to me that you left it somewhat precipitously and that my nephew was rather anxious to speak to you about something.'

'Oh?'

'Yes, Miss Meredith. Am I to understand that your hearing has become defective?'

'Hearing?'

'He called after you, even I could hear him, but you appeared not to be aware of anything.'

'I, er, didn't hear.'

'Are you in love with my nephew, Miss Meredith?'

Roslyn stared at her. 'No, Lady Galler-mayne, I'm not.' She answered in a level voice, hoping she sounded convincing.

'You aren't a very good liar, Miss Meredith.'

'Lady Gallermayne, I really don't wish to discuss this.'

'But I do, young lady. It's very important.'

'That's the one thing it isn't, my lady. Whatever my feelings may or may not be, Lord Atherton still loves his wife. I know that beyond any shadow of a doubt, and when Lady Atherton returns, as seems very likely indeed, it will not matter in the slightest what state my heart is in.'

'I don't think you understand — '

'I understand very well indeed, Lady Gallermayne.'

'But — ' There was another knock at the door and Lady Gallermayne broke off irritably. 'Yes? Parrish, see to it.'

The elderly maid hurried to the door. It was Sir Owen. He came in with a very handsome bouquet of flowers he'd picked in the gardens. 'Dear Lady Gallermayne,' he said, bowing over her lace-mittened hand, 'I do hope that you are not too indisposed by your accident.'

'As you see, sir, I intend to come down to dinner tonight.'

'Excellent, then conversation will not wilt. Nor, I hope, will these.' He handed her the flowers.

She looked at them in some surprise and then smiled at him. 'Why, Sir Owen, what a charming thought. Parrish? A vase of water, if you please.'

The maid scurried away.

Lady Gallermayne beamed at Sir Owen. 'You, sir, are a wicked flatterer. You'd have me believe you're genuinely concerned about me.'

'But I am, dear lady,' he protested.

Roslyn seized her opportunity to withdraw. 'If — if you'll excuse me . . . '

Lady Gallermayne looked sharply at her. 'We haven't finished yet, Miss Meredith.'

'I asked for a hot bath to be prepared for me before dinner, Lady Gallermayne, so I really should go.' Aware of her uncle's astonishment at her haste, she gathered her skirts and hurried out. He was obviously wondering why she was so determined to avoid talking to Lady Gallermayne and why Lady Gallermayne was equally determined to see that such a talk took place. Well, Lady Gallermayne no doubt would explain, if she wished.

Reaching her own room again, Roslyn instructed Lizzie to say that she was taking a bath if anyone should ask to see her, and sure enough, a few minutes later her uncle called at the door. He hadn't questioned Lady Gallermayne, but was anxious to find out from his niece if something was wrong. Putting on a lighthearted voice, she spoke to him from behind the screen.

'I'm perfectly all right, Uncle Owen. I'll see you at dinner.'

'If you're quite sure . . . '

'Quite sure. Oh, and Uncle Owen?'

He turned in the doorway. 'Yes, *cariad*?'

'How are the portraits going?'

'She's vanished behind the clouds now, at least her top half has; the remainder poses more of a problem. Clouds can be daubed, detail must be taken care with.'

'Will the work take long?' She splashed her hand in the jug of water on the washstand, as if she'd moved in the bath.

'Long enough. Why? Don't tell me you want to leave already?'

'Let's say I won't be sorry to return to London.'

'Really? I thought you loathed the capital and longed for the country.'

'I've changed.'

He didn't say anything more, but went out,

closing the door quietly behind him.

The sun was sinking toward the horizon as Roslyn dressed for dinner in the low-necked, pale-green silk dress. Lizzie had brushed her hair until it shone, and now it was in a knot at the back of her head, one long curl tumbling over her shoulder. The knot was adorned with a green ribbon bow, and the falling curl twined with flutters of the same ribbon. There was rouge on her pale cheeks, and a little dab of white powder around her eyes, to conceal the traces of her tears.

At last the dinner gong echoed through the house. With a heavy sigh she draped her shawl over her arms and picked up her reticule, then with another deep breath, she went out.

Lady Gallermayne was still in her room as Roslyn passed, and there wasn't a sign of either James or her uncle. She reached the staircase and began to go down to the great hall, where the fading sunlight was casting bright colors through the stained glass of the oriel windows.

James came to the foot of the staircase. He'd been waiting for her. He was dressed in a tight black velvet coat with a high standfall collar, a white satin waistcoat, white trousers, and gleaming Hessian boots. His lace-edged neckcloth had been tied very intricately, and in its folds there was a fine diamond pin. He had never looked more handsome or elegant, and just looking at him sent a new shaft of pain through her. Putting a hand on one of the unicorns topping the staircase newel posts, he barred her way. 'Roslyn, I've been waiting to speak to you.'

'I don't think there's anything to say, sir.'

'But there is, there's a great deal. I understand my aunt tried to speak to you.'

She drew back a little. 'Yes, she did. I find it more than a little embarrassing to have my privacy invaded so directly.'

'I asked her to speak to you. Roslyn, I have something I must tell you — '

But before he could say anything more, there was the sound of a carriage at the door. He turned sharply, making no other movement as Morris appeared as if by magic to hurry out through the porch. A carriage door slammed. 'G-good evening, madam.' The butler's voice sounded shaken.

'Good evening, Morris. I trust his lordship is at home?' Roslyn didn't recognize the voice, but she knew who it belonged to. It was Vanessa.

'Yes, my lady. Welcome home.'

'Thank you, Morris.'

Roslyn stared at the doorway, her heartbeats quickening. At last she was going to see the absent wife, the woman whose disappearance had kept London gossip at fever pitch for months now.

Vanessa came slowly and dramatically into the great hall, her bluebell taffeta gown blushed to mauve by the dazzle of the setting sun behind her. There were sapphires at her throat and in her ears, and a white feather boa trailed carelessly along the floor behind her. Her almost black hair was piled on top of her head and adorned by a single white rose. Soft curls framed her matchlessly beautiful face, and her large, dark-lashed eyes were so magnificent that they must surely stop the heart of any man who gazed into them.

She saw James. 'Oh, my darling,' she whispered, 'I've been such a fool. Can you ever forgive me?'

He smiled at her. 'I forgive you everything,' he murmured, holding out his hand.

She came to him, her slender fingers reaching out hesitantly at first, but then curling around his. With a moan she came into his arms, her lips upturned to meet his kiss.

It was as if they were alone and Roslyn had ceased to exist. She wanted to move away, but she couldn't.

Vanessa drew back slowly, smiling up into his eyes. 'Do you want me to stay?'

'Of course I do, I never want to lose you again.'

Her maid had entered the great hall behind her and Vanessa turned to nod. 'You may return for my things.'

'Yes, ma'am.' The maid went out again and a moment later the carriage drove off once more, its wheels crunching on the gravel.

Vanessa turned back again and seemed to see Roslyn for the first time, although Roslyn sensed that she'd been aware of her all along. 'Why, James, you haven't introduced us.'

'Forgive me.' He turned apologetically, purposely avoiding Roslyn's eyes. 'Miss Meredith, this is my wife, Lady Atherton. Vanessa, this is Miss Meredith, Sir Owen's niece.'

Roslyn was cut to the quick by his formality, but she gave no hint of it as she smiled at Vanessa. 'Lady Atherton.'

'Miss Meredith.' Vanessa's beautiful eyes were full of malice, but her voice was warm and friendly. 'Sir Owen's niece? Is he here, then?'

James nodded. 'It's nothing all that important, just a daub or two.'

'What is he to paint? A likeness of your favorite horse?'

Lady Gallermayne's voice interrupted from the top of the staircase. 'No, Vanessa, he's

291

performing the north view of the house for me.'

Roslyn looked up in quick surprise. Why had Lady Gallermayne invented such a plausible lie? She didn't like Vanessa and had no reason to spare her feelings.

James's aunt came painfully to the head of the staircase, the beads of her black gown glittering in the shadows. She was leaning on Parrish's arm and using a walking stick. Her face was cold and haughty as she gazed down at Vanessa. 'So, you've decided to come back, have you? Courtenay's run out of money again, has he?'

Vanessa turned quickly aside, distress written large in her eyes. 'Oh, please, don't say that,' she whispered. 'I want to forget the past.'

James put a reassuring hand on her slender arm and then gave his aunt a dark look as he went up to her. 'Aunt Gallermayne, this is my house and I'll thank you to not speak to my wife in that tone.'

'Why not? Is she afraid of the truth?'

'She and I merely wish to put the past well and truly behind us. We're going to start again, and if you cannot accept that, then I think it would be better if you refrained from joining us at dinner.'

Roslyn stared at him and then glanced at

his wife's averted face. A faint smile touched Vanessa's lips, a cool, calculating, and unpleasant smile that was not for James's trusting, adoring eyes. A cold, sinking feeling passed through Roslyn. Oh, James, she's false after all. Don't believe her, don't put your faith in her.

Lady Gallermayne was very displeased with James, but had no intention of forgoing such a suddenly important dinner. 'It is my duty to join you, James, just as it is my duty to welcome dear Vanessa home again if that is what you really wish. I only trust that this is the end of the matter, for if there's any more scandal and talk, I will wash my hands of you. Now, then, assist me down the stairs, if you please.'

As James and Parrish helped her carefully down, Roslyn moved away to stand in the hall. She watched James. He hadn't been surprised when Vanessa's carriage had arrived; indeed, on reflection it was obvious now that he'd been expecting it. He'd been aware of his wife's plan to return that evening, and that awareness went far beyond any hint there may have been in Benedict Courtenay's remark earlier in the day. Suddenly it seemed that James had been being less than honest and had known far more about his wife's whereabouts than he'd ever admitted. Roslyn lowered her eyes. Now she knew what he'd been on the point of saying when Vanessa's return had interrupted him; he'd wanted assurance that the afternoon's embarrassing incident would never again be mentioned, so that his wife did not learn that there had been fleeting truth in the rumors about his friendship with Sir Owen Meredith's niece.

At the foot of the staircase, Lady Gallermayne insisted on James continuing to assist her to the dining room, which left Roslyn to walk with Vanessa.

The bluebell satin swished richly, and Vanessa's eyes flickered spitefully. 'I know all about you, Miss Meredith,' she whispered icily, 'and so I shall expect you to leave this house as soon as possible.'

Roslyn's steps faltered and she stared at the other woman. 'I — I beg your pardon?'

'You heard me. I won't have another woman making sheep's eyes at my husband, is that quite clear? James Atherton belongs to me.' She walked on, leaving Roslyn gazing after her in stunned dismay.

25

She turned then as Sir Owen hurried down the staircase and across the hall. 'Ah, so I'm not late, after all. My cravat took an absolute age, it *wouldn't* sit right. Shall we go in?'

Before she could say anything, he'd taken her arm and was steering her toward the dining room. They entered and he immediately saw Vanessa seated at the table. He halted in utter amazement. 'Good heavens!'

She smiled warmly at him. 'Why, Sir Owen, how very pleasant it is to see you again. Don't tell me you're at a loss for words, for I simply will not believe it.'

He recovered a little, escorting Roslyn to her place and then going to take Vanessa's hand and drew it gallantly to his lips. 'My dear lady, forgive me if I seemed so startled, it's just that I really wasn't expecting to see you.' He still looked a little shaken, but was striving to conceal the fact. His glance moved briefly to his niece's lowered eyes and then he took his place.

Because the dining room lay at the back of the house, facing east, the sunset did not illuminate it at all and already the unicorn candlesticks had been lit. An extra place had been hastily set for Vanessa and the cutlery and crystal shone as brightly in the candlelight as the sapphires she wore. The soft glow flattered her already breathtaking beauty, giving her a yielding warmth that Roslyn could see did not extend to her eyes. She smiled and gave James glances touched with emotion, as if she were struggling not to be overcome by the sheer joy of being with him again, welcomed and forgiven; if only James could see the truth, that she was acting a part. There hadn't been anything genuine or heartfelt about her from the moment she'd entered the house.

The footmen served the soup and poured the first wine.

Vanessa picked up her glass and raised it to James. 'To us, my love, may we never be parted again.'

Lady Gallermayne gave a rather disdainful sniff. 'Far be it for me to remind you, Vanessa, my dear, but if there was a parting it was because you chose to leave.'

'It — it was all a silly misunderstanding,' answered Vanessa, her lovely eyes lowered with fluttering regret.

'A misunderstanding of monumental pro-portions, it would seem,' declared Lady Gallermayne a little sourly.

James glanced disapprovingly at his aunt. 'I don't think this is the time or place for recriminations.'

'Recriminations? I was merely making an observation.'

Vanessa looked imploringly at her. 'Please, Lady Gallermayne, I understand your anger, but I don't wish to discuss my private affairs in front of . . . strangers.' Her glance briefly encompassed Roslyn.

Lady Gallermayne wasn't moved. 'James, I cannot allow this to pass without comment, no matter what your wishes are. Vanessa drove out of your life some months ago, without explanation. Now she capriciously returns and expects everyone to carry on as if nothing happened. I've yet to divine her real reason for returning, but I've little doubt it has nothing to do with her overwhelming love for you. She deserted you, sir, and she should not be treated as if she's blameless.'

His blue eyes were very angry. 'Aunt, this is my house and I am the master. I am quite content that Vanessa has returned to me, and I will not have anything more said on the matter. Is that quite clear?'

Again Roslyn noticed the gloating triumph shining secretly in Vanessa's eyes. Lady Gallermayne was being very firmly put down, and Vanessa was reveling in her old enemy's defeat.

Lady Gallermayne glanced at Vanessa and then at James. 'Yes, sir, it's unfortunately very clear indeed.' Picking up her spoon, she commenced to sip her soup.

Vanessa smiled gratefully at James, reaching over to rest her cool fingers over his. She didn't speak; her look said everything and it promised so very much — when they were alone.

Of the many disagreeable dinners Roslyn had endured in recent months, this one was by far the worst. Vanessa didn't miss a single opportunity for belittling the woman whose name she'd discovered had been salaciously connected with James's. Little barbs were there all the time, concealed very skillfully behind a sweet smile and charming air of interest.

'How very, er, healthy you look, Miss Meredith. Have you been abroad recently?' It was a way of pointing out that Roslyn's complexion had been a little too exposed to the sun.

James didn't seem to notice the unkindness behind the remark, but both Sir Owen and Lady Gallermayne did. No one said anything.

Roslyn met Vanessa's gaze. 'Yes, Lady Atherton, I was in Greece with my uncle.'

'Greece? How interesting.' Vanessa turned to James. 'Did you go to Ayios Georghios, after all?'

'I did. I met Sir Owen and Miss Meredith there.'

'Did you? Oh, my poor James, fancy having London follow you like that.'

James didn't look at Roslyn. 'It was hardly that,' he murmured.

When the main course was served, a magnificently presented leg of pork with all the trimmings, Vanessa looked at it for a long moment. 'What a very country dish, to be sure. I'll warrant it's the very best Monmouthshire pork, don't you, James?' She tinkled with laughter then, managing to look embarrassed and apologetic at the same time. 'Oh, forgive me, Miss Meredith, I didn't mean to suggest that everything from Monmouthshire was country.'

Sir Owen was a little angered, although politeness prevented him from saying anything. Lady Gallermayne's glance moved briefly to her nephew and then she continued to apply herself to her meal.

Vanessa smiled a little and said nothing more for the moment. She ate very sparingly, as if she was only too conscious of Beau Brummell's observation that women should never be seen eating as they looked so very unattractive when they did so. As the main course was being removed, she looked at Roslyn again. 'Tell me, Miss Meredith, did you bring your gown with you from Monmouthshire? I declare that it's very unusual, most eye-catching, in fact.'

Unusual implied unfashionable and rustic. Roslyn smiled, for here at last she had an opportunity to get her own back a little. 'Why no, Lady Atherton, the gown is from your own couturière in London. I'm surprised you do not recognize her touch.'

Vanessa's sweet smile faltered, but only momentarily. 'Why, to be sure, you're right. How strange that on you it should look so different.'

Roslyn fell resignedly silent. The point had gone to Vanessa, after all.

At last the dessert was served. It was a delicious confection of meringue, strawberries, and cream, and was greeted by Vanessa with another tinkle of laughter. 'Good heavens, I couldn't possibly indulge in such wickedness, I wouldn't have a waistline left to boast about.'

Sir Owen gave her a bland smile. 'I'm sure you'd manage somehow,' he said.

She looked uncertainly at him, not quite sure how to take the remark. Roslyn smiled a little. Her uncle had had enough of the lady of the house.

Vanessa's eyes flickered toward him again. 'I understand you're here to daub a little again, Sir Owen.'

Lady Gallermayne spoke up quickly. 'I told her that you were performing a north view of the house, Sir Owen.'

He cleared his throat uncomfortably. 'Er, yes. That's correct.'

'You must show me,' said Vanessa. 'I'd so like to see such a work. All I've ever seen before have been your portraits.'

There was a silence, broken by Roslyn deliberately dropping her spoon so that it fell with a loud clatter. She smiled apologetically. 'I'm so sorry, how very clumsy of me.'

Vanessa had winced a little, as if she found the noise not only gauche but also conducive of an instant headache.

The dreadful meal at last began to draw to a close, the liqueurs and fruit were removed, and Roslyn knew that soon it would be time for the ladies to adjourn to the drawing room while the gentlemen lingered over their port. She'd endured enough by now and the thought of being further exposed to Vanessa's venom was too much. Vanessa herself had given her an ideal excuse: she'd plead a headache and retire to her room.

Lady Gallermayne sent a footman to bring Parrish, and immediately Roslyn smiled a little self-consciously. 'Forgive me, Lady Gallermayne, but I'm afraid I have a dreadful headache and really feel quite unwell. Would you mind very much if I declined to join you and went straight to my room instead?'

Sir Owen was immediately concerned. 'Oh, *cariad*, why didn't you say earlier? Is there anything I can do?'

'Nothing at all. I'll be quite all right after a good sleep.'

James suddenly rose to his feet. 'I'm afraid that I have to cry off our port and cigar, Sir Owen. I have a rather urgent matter to attend to in Cheltenham.'

They all stared at him, taken completely by surprise by the announcement. He hadn't indicated by a single word that he wouldn't be joining them for the remainder of the evening.

Vanessa was suddenly a lot less confident. She looked pleadingly at him. 'Do you have to go on my first evening back?'

'I'm afraid so. It's urgent estate business and the wretched fellow's off to London in the morning.'

Lady Gallermayne smiled then. 'Of course you must go, James. I'm sure Sir Owen and I can entertain Vanessa during your absence. Can't we, Sir Owen?'

'Of course.' Sir Owen gave Vanessa another

of his rather unsettling bland smiles. She'd seriously offended him by her treatment of Roslyn, and he did not intend to allow her to emerge entirely unscathed.

Vanessa had no alternative but to accept that James intended to keep his appointment. She gave him a weak smile. 'You will hurry back, won't you, my love?'

'Of course.' He raised her hand to his lips, turning the palm uppermost at the last moment.

Roslyn rose to her feet. 'If — if you will excuse me, then. Good night, Lady Galler-mayne. Uncle Owen. Lady Atherton.' She looked at last at James. 'Good night, my lord.'

He met her gaze. 'Good night, Miss Meredith. I trust you are soon recovered.'

She inclined her head and then left, emerging with relief into the great hall and then gathering her skirts to hurry to the staircase. The sun had long since set now and the great iron-rimmed chandeliers had been lit. Their light was feeble and the hall was lofty and filled with shadows. Her skirts rustled as she went up the staircase, pausing at the top as she heard the dining room door open again.

James emerged with Vanessa on his arm. Her bluebell taffeta skirts were softened to a warm gray in the dim candlelight.

Morris entered from the porch, bowing to James. 'Your horse is ready and waiting, my lord.'

'Thank you, Morris. Is everything else in order?'

'Everything, my lord.'

'My instructions are to be followed precisely.'

'Yes, my lord.'

At the top of the staircase, Roslyn listened a little curiously. The exchange had been a little odd. What instructions were they that had to be followed precisely?

The butler withdrew and James turned to Vanessa, drawing her into his arms. 'I promise to return as quickly as possible, but I'm bound to be away for at least two hours.'

'Just hurry back,' she whispered, linking her lovely arms about his neck and drawing his lips down to hers.

Roslyn couldn't bear it. Drawing back from the stairs, she hurried on to her room. There was a dull ache deep inside her, the ache of loving so hopelessly. She didn't need Vanessa to tell her to leave, she knew she had to anyway. She had to return to London and do all she could to put James Atherton from her mind.

26

Roslyn sat in the moonlit window of her room. Below in the topiary garden the fountains played with silver softness, and the roses around the summerhouse were very pale, robbed of their rich yellow color. Everything was very quiet.

James had ridden away some time ago, and Vanessa's carriage had returned with her maid and belongings. Footmen carried Vanessa's belongings from the carriage into the house and the maid followed them. A few minutes later there had been a slight disturbance of some sort, the maid's voice had been raised, but then there'd been silence again. Puzzled, Roslyn had gone to the door and looked along the candlelit passage, but there was only silence from Vanessa's apartment.

Closing the door again, Roslyn was about to return to the window when the room seemed claustrophobic; in fact, the whole house seemed claustrophobic. She needed to escape from it for a while. She'd think more clearly in the fresh night air. Selecting a warm shawl from her wardrobe and changing her little satin slippers for shoes, she left her room and made her way along the passage toward the landing and the staircase.

As she neared the landing, a slender little figure suddenly appeared in the shadows before her. Roslyn's breath caught on a startled gasp and then she gave a relieved look. 'Parrish! Whatever are you doing standing there like that? You gave me such a fright.'

Lady Gallermayne's maid looked a little embarrassed. 'Forgive me, ma'am, I didn't mean to startle you. I'm waiting to be called by her ladyship.'

Roslyn looked at her in some surprise. When Lady Gallermayne required her, she'd send a footman, and meanwhile Parrish could be sitting comfortably in the kitchens with the other servants instead of standing up here in the darkness.

Leaving the maid still standing at the top of the stairs, Roslyn descended to the great hall. All was still very quiet. She slipped out into the night. She'd just crossed the gravel area and was walking along the wall of the topiary garden when a horseman approached at a gallop. Thinking that it might be James, she halted in dismay. But it wasn't James; it was a roughly-clad man she'd never seen before. He reined in before the house, and as if by magic, Morris emerged to see what he wanted. A letter was handed to the butler and then the man turned his horse and rode away again, the hooves scattering gravel over the hem of Roslyn's skirt as it passed.

When the butler had gone back into the house and the horseman had disappeared from view, Roslyn walked on. She didn't know where she was going exactly, but soon found her steps taking her the same way she'd gone earlier in the day.

Foxcombe's park was very lovely in the moonlight, the trees casting dense black shadows on the silvery grass. An owl hooted somewhere in the woods and she heard the grunt of the red deer. A breeze rustled the shining rhododendron leaves as she made her way along the path leading through them.

As she emerged at last with the boathouse lying down the slope before her, she suddenly felt that someone was watching her. It was a strong feeling and she halted, looking quickly all around. There was no one there, all was as quiet and peaceful as before. The feeling lingered and she hesitated about going on, but then with sudden resolve she continued down the path toward the boathouse and the lake.

She was going to walk as far as the rustic bridge over the stream separating Foxcombe from Grantby Park, but then something made her decide to go into the boathouse and look at the portraits again. She knew the building wouldn't be locked. Her shoes tapped on the stone path, and the door creaked as she went in.

The moonlight flooded in through the roof lights, making everything inside very clear indeed. Her glance was drawn immediately to the wedding sketches her uncle had pinned to the wall. He'd commenced a pochade of his intended painting, sketching in various figures and objects as the inspiration took him. The daubs of paint were in whatever color he'd been using to eliminate Vanessa from the portrait, a gray lemon tree, a mushroom dancer, a blue serving girl. She wondered how long it would be before he finished the painting and it was on its way to Christina and Theo. She hoped it wouldn't be too long, or they might think he'd forgotten all about them.

There was a stealthy sound from the end of the moonlit room. She turned immediately. She wasn't alone! But even as her lips parted on a stifled cry, there was another sound from the doorway behind her and she whirled about again as a man entered. It was James. The cry died in her throat and she stared at him, her whole body trembling with fright. 'James?'

He was looking angrily at her. 'What in God's name are you doing here?' he demanded, frightening her by seizing her arms and shaking her.

Her eyes were huge. 'I — I only came out for a walk.'

He relaxed a little. 'And you had to pick this place?' He glanced beyond her, nodding at someone. 'It's all right.'

She turned and saw two men standing by the tall cupboard they'd been hiding behind. She looked at him again. 'James, what's going on? What's happening?'

Before he could answer, the door opened again and one of the Foxcombe footmen looked anxiously in. 'There's someone coming, my lord. We think it's him.'

'All right, get back to your places, and don't make a move until I give the signal.'

'Yes, my lord.' The men hurried away again.

James looked at the two in the studio. 'You know what to do.'

They nodded and pushed into their hiding places again.

The sound of approaching hoofbeats carried clearly into the boathouse. James breathed in sharply. 'Damn! He's closer than I thought. Roslyn, you'll have to stay in here now, but one sound from you and it will all have been for nothing.'

'All what? James, please tell me!'

'There's no time. Come with me.' Grabbing her arm, he almost propelled her up to the dais and the swathes of draperies suspended from the ceiling high above. Stepping behind some heavy velvet, he drew her in with him.

She was frightened and unsure, her whole body shaking. He felt her fear and pulled her close, his fingers moving reassuringly in the warm hair at the nape of her neck. 'Hush now,' he murmured. 'If all this goes according to my plan, then my troubles will soon be over once and for all.'

Afraid she would somehow betray their presence, she pressed close to him, her face buried in the frills of his shirtfront. She could smell the costmary on his clothes. Her heart was beating loudly and so frantically that she knew he could feel it. She closed her eyes as she heard the horse halt outside the boathouse. There was a jingle of bridle and squeak of leather as whoever it was dismounted, then the horse was led into the dark shadows beside the boathouse, right at the water's edge. A man's boots sounded on the path and the door creaked as he pushed it open. James's arms tightened around her, his fingers still moving softly in her hair.

The steps came right into the studio and then halted somewhere in the center. James put a finger to Roslyn's chin, turning her head very slightly so that she could see out through a tear in the velvet. She looked slowly out and saw Benedict Courtenay standing there in the moonlight.

His riding crop was tap-tapping against his gleaming top boot, and he looked very elegant in brown riding coat and nankeen breeches. He'd removed his top hat and placed it on a table with Sir Owen's jumble of paint jars, and he glanced uneasily around and then at his golden fob watch. He seemed nervous and uncertain, and very much as if he wished he wasn't on Atherton land.

The minutes passed and still he stood there, his unease and impatience increasing all the time. He didn't glance once toward the three portraits. At last another sound broke the silence, the light, hurrying steps of someone else approaching the boathouse. They were the steps of a woman, and as she neared the door, they could hear the rustle of her skirts.

Benedict had turned the moment he heard her. The door opened and she came in, at last moving into Roslyn's view. It was Vanessa. With a glad cry she ran into her lover's arms.

27

'Oh, my love, my love,' she whispered, 'I don't think I can bear it away from you.'

'You must.' He gripped her arms and looked urgently into her eyes. 'There's no doubt about him taking you back?'

'Of course not. He adores me.'

'Have you brought any of the jewels?'

'No. I tried to go up to my apartment before coming here, but Lady Gallermayne's wretched maid was just coming down and told me my maid hadn't arrived yet. I learned my lesson with those topazes. I'm not going to take anything unless I can replace it immediately with the paste copies, and I can't do that until my things arrive.'

'I can't imagine why your maid isn't here yet. She left Grantby Place a long time ago.'

'Well, she's still on her way, that's all I can say.'

He drew away with an impatient, irritable gesture.

She looked accusingly at him. 'You're only interested in those jewels, aren't you? You don't care about me at all.'

He quickly put a reassuring hand to her

pale cheek. 'You know that isn't so, my love,' he murmured, 'but the duns have followed me and they're becoming very persistent. I have to satisfy them or I'm a dead man. You know that I didn't want to ask you to return to Atherton, but I'd been forced to even before you received his note this afternoon. There was no choice left then, sweetheart; you either had to return to him and save me, or he'd divorce you and we'd both be lost. You do understand that, don't you?' He tilted her face toward his.

Behind the curtain, Roslyn and James listened to every incriminating word. She was a little bemused. Nothing was as it had seemed to be. James wasn't taken in by his wife, after all . . .

Vanessa's fears were allayed. She smiled up at Benedict. 'I love you so,' she murmured.

'And soon we'll be together forever, I promise you, but in the meantime you have to help me.'

'I know, and I will, just as soon as I can. The moment my maid arrives I'll replace the rest of the jewels with the copies.'

'If you hadn't decided to leave him as you did, we'd have been able to do it gradually as originally planned, and none of this would be happening now.' He couldn't conceal the edge in his voice.

'James was suspicious after that business with the topazes. We argued. I was angry, and I didn't think, I just left.'

'And presented me with problems I did not need.'

She stiffened a little. 'I suppose you're going to accuse me again of being irresponsible for taking the lease of Grantby Place.'

'It wasn't exactly one of the wisest things you ever did. It's too costly for our present finances, and it's too damned close to this place. There was always the chance that Atherton would find out you were there, as he did this afternoon when he recognized your laugh. A red wig may make you look like my sister, but it can't make you sound like her. Now he's issued an ultimatum, the duns are pressing the very life out of me, and we still haven't got our hands on the real jewels. I only hope you have him as spellbound as you think.'

'Of course I have. Don't worry so.'

'The little Meredith isn't the milksop you take her to be, and he appears to have gone to considerable lengths to see that she accompanied him here. He even persuaded Lady Gallermayne to his way of thinking.'

'You've read far too much into that all along, Benedict. I've seen them together now, and although I admit that she's handsome enough and is quite obviously in love with him, he doesn't seem to hold her in any particular regard. I believe she's here simply to please Sir Owen, who's taken her under his wing since her father's death. She means nothing to James, you may take my word for it. You wasted your time stirring up all that talk in London, there wasn't a romance to break up.'

'If there had been and I'd failed, Atherton would want to be rid of you in order to marry her, and that would mean an end to my hopes of getting his jewels. I couldn't take the chance.'

'Well, you failed anyway, she's still here. And I've been right about her all along: she's of no interest to James. It's me that he loved and will always love.'

James' fingers stopped moving in Roslyn's hair for a moment, but then continued.

Vanessa was smiling up into her lover's eyes. 'We may not have another chance to be alone like this for a while,' she murmured. 'Can't we make the most of it?'

'Not now.'

She drew back petulantly. 'As you wish. Well, what did you want to see me for? I suppose you're only concerned about the jewels and I don't really count, no matter what you say to the contrary.'

He looked blankly at her. 'Did you ask me why I wanted to see you?'

'Yes.'

'Vanessa, you wanted to see me. I thought it was madness, but your note assured me that James was in Cheltenham and you'd be able to meet me here.'

She stared at him. 'I didn't write a note,' she said slowly.

'Nor did I.'

They gazed at each other, becoming suddenly wary as they at last began to realize that something was wrong.

Vanessa turned suddenly, her glance falling on the portrait Sir Owen had altered. Her face drained of all color. 'It's a trap, Benedict,' she whispered. 'James knows the truth. He knows!'

'What are you talking about?' He whirled about as well, staring at the portrait.

'I've been painted out, Benedict. He wouldn't have that done if he wanted me back.' Her voice rose on a panicky note.

Behind the curtains James released Roslyn and then slowly stepped out into the open of the dais. 'You're quite right, Vanessa, I wouldn't have had that done if I wanted you back.'

The two in the center of the studio froze. Vanessa's face was ashen and she was trembling so much that Roslyn could see as she too stepped out into the open.

Vanessa's eyes fled toward her. 'You!'

James gestured to Roslyn to stay back and then looked at his wife again. 'You and your lover were far too confident, my dear. Far too confident.'

'James, it isn't what you think.'

'It's all I think.'

'No! Truly!'

'I heard everything you said.' James' glance was contemptuous. 'What gullible fools you both are, falling neatly into a simple trap. I find it sad that after conducting your sordid little affair for so long, neither of you can apparently recognize the other's writing. Still, I suppose you can be excused, Vanessa, for I doubt very much if your gallant lover is ever unwise enough to put pen to paper. He's careful to hide his tracks if he can, ask any of the foolish women who've fallen for his superficial charm. As for you, Courtenay, well, no doubt your eagerness to seize my property blinded you to anything else. Greed is an overwhelming emotion, is it not?'

Vanessa was at her most persuasive. 'You're wrong about all this, James.'

'No, Vanessa, *you're* wrong. You've been taken in, can't you see it? He isn't interested in you, he's interested in what you can get for him. And my aunt and I duped you tonight — you really believed our little act, didn't you?'

Roslyn stared at him. Lady Gallermayne had been party to it?

Vanessa was shaken. 'You — your aunt knows about all this?'

'She does. It was her idea to station her maid on the stairs to tell you your maid hadn't arrived. I know about the copies you've been having made of the jewels, I've known about it since I took the rather belated precaution of having the topazes examined. I didn't want to believe it, I didn't want to believe that the wife I loved had been stealing my family's jewels in order to satisfy her lover's demands. Oh, I was fooled for a while by Courtenay's air of innocence, but in my heart I knew the truth. Vanessa, if you look at him now, you'll see the truth as well. He hasn't a thought in his head for you, he's only concerned with how he can extricate himself from this.'

She glanced unwillingly at her lover's still face and knew that James was right. With a gasp she looked at her husband again. 'James, I know that you still love me. I knew it when you kissed me tonight.'

'All you knew tonight was that, when I choose, I can be as consummate a deceiver as you. I don't want you anymore, Vanessa, and I haven't for a long time.' He looked at Benedict. 'The trap's closing on you, sir. The moment you were seen approaching, a man was dispatched to Cheltenham to bring the necessary authorities. You'll be under lock and key before the night is out.'

A sneer curled Benedict's fine lips. 'You've taken leave of your senses. Think of the scandal. You can't really want your wife's name dragged through the mire of my arrest.'

'I'm indifferent to my wife's name, Courtenay, as even she must know by now.'

Vanessa turned weakly away, steadying herself by resting a trembling hand on the easel supporting the altered portrait. The lover she'd risked everything for had proved cold and callous, and the husband she'd betrayed had seen through her and found nothing to cherish anymore.

Benedict was smiling a little. 'Have me arrested then, Atherton, but I'll make you pay for it. Nothing can be proved against me, unless it be adultery with your wife.' He spread his hands then. 'You won't find an Atherton jewel anywhere on me or at Grantby Place.'

'No, but I have a casket of fake jewels my wife intended to substitute for the real thing, and I have her maid, who is prepared to testify that you had the fake jewels made, and she can identify the very jeweler you went to.' James smiled coolly at Benedict. 'I think I have enough proof to have you locked away for some considerable time.'

'You'll have to detain me first, Atherton, and if you think I'm going to be fool enough to wait here to be arrested, then you're very much mistaken. Goodbye to you.' He turned and began to walk toward the door.

With a cry Vanessa hurried after him. 'Don't leave me, Benedict. I love you!'

Her answer was to be thrust forcefully aside. To save herself from falling, she snatched desperately at a table of paints and oils, but it tipped over and she fell to the floor, the paints splattering over her beautiful taffeta gown and staining it beyond all redemption. She lay there, huge sobs racking her body.

Benedict didn't even glance back at her but continued swiftly toward the door.

James drew a pistol from his coat and leveled it at him. 'Stay right where you are, Courtenay. Don't give me the excuse!'

Vanessa's sobs ceased and Roslyn stared in horror. With a loud click the pistol was cocked.

28

Benedict froze and then slowly he turned. 'It seems I must bow to your wishes, after all, Atherton.'

James looked toward the far end of the studio, where his two men had come from their hiding place. 'Hold him!'

They hurried across the floor and took Benedict's arms, thrusting him bodily back against the wall. James stepped down from the dais and went to where a long-handled window hook rested against a wall. Raising it, he tapped three times on one of the windows. It was a signal, and a moment later some more of his men had entered.

He turned to the footman who had warned him earlier of Benedict's approach. 'Has someone ridden to Cheltenham?'

'Yes, my lord, on the fastest horse in the stables. He'll be there by now.'

'Good. And the carriage?'

'Is waiting as you ordered.'

'Take Courtenay up to the house, lock him in the buttery until they come for him, and have the carriage come right up to the door here.'

'Yes, my lord.'

Benedict was bundled unceremoniously out, his hands tied. Two of the men hesitated, looking at Vanessa. James shook his head. 'I'll deal with her ladyship.'

They went on out then and the door closed. Slowly Vanessa struggled to her feet. James made no move to assist her. Her face was very pale as she looked at him. 'What do you mean to do with me?'

'You may be as guilty as your lover, madam, but you're still my wife and I won't have you arrested. I'm going to allow you to leave.'

A carriage drew up directly outside. Vanessa's eyes fled in the direction of the sound and then back to James's emotionless face. 'Where can I go?'

'As far away as possible, I suggest. You don't imagine that your lover is going to silently submit to being imprisoned, do you? He's going to incriminate you as well. Here, take this.' He drew a full purse from his pocket and held it out to her. 'You'll find enough there to take you out of the country.'

Her eyes widened. 'Leave England?'

'Stay, and Courtenay's evidence will see you in prison as well. You have a sister in Madras, I suggest you call upon family loyalty, if there is any in your family. The carriage is at your disposal.'

Vanessa had taken the purse and now she turned to throw a hateful look at Roslyn. 'It's her, isn't it? Benedict was right when he suspected you of being her lover.'

'I suggest you leave while you can, Vanessa.'

She tried to compose herself. It was all up, and she knew it. She looked at him again. 'Will you answer me one thing?'

He didn't reply.

'When did you really decide you wanted to be free of me?'

'Does it matter?'

'It does to me.'

'I decided that I had to do it when I found out that the topaz necklace that had been in my family for centuries had suddenly became a paste fake. I decided that I wanted to do it when I was in Ayios Georghios and there was no word from you.'

'Don't you mean when you met that Meredith creature? She's the real reason, and you can't fool me into thinking otherwise.'

'Please leave, Vanessa.'

Without another word she walked away. A moment later they heard the carriage door slam, a whip crack, and the team's hooves clatter on the dusty road as they took Vanessa out of James's life forever.

Roslyn came to the edge of the dais. 'I'm so

very sorry, James.'

'Sorry?'

'That it should have ended like this.'

'Well, I'm not sorry, just relieved that it's all over at last.' He held his hand out to her and assisted her down. He didn't immediately release her hand. 'There is something I'm sorry about, though.'

'There is?'

'I'm very sorry indeed that I hurt you today. I didn't mean to. When I heard her laughter and knew the truth, I just couldn't help reacting as I did. There wasn't any intention of spurning you, quite the opposite. I tried to tell you.'

'But I wouldn't let you.'

'I can't blame you, it must have seemed very damning. I would have insisted upon speaking to you when we reached the house, but my damned lawyer kept me talking for hours, and I had to write my ultimatum to Vanessa and then enlist my aunt's help in what I planned to do tonight. I needed to convince Vanessa that I'd even put my aunt down in order to give our marriage another chance, and I could hardly do that without my aunt knowing it was an act. I asked my aunt to speak to you on my behalf.'

Roslyn lowered her eyes. 'I refused to discuss anything with her.'

'I know. That's why I waited for you in the hall. Vanessa arrived before I could say anything. If I hurt you still more by my subsequent actions, believe me, I hurt myself as well.' He put his hand to her chin, raising her face a little so that the moonlight shone in her green eyes. 'Did I hurt you?'

'Yes,' she whispered.

He held her gaze. 'This afternoon I gave in at last to an emotion I've felt for a long time but have been denying. I haven't any right to want you, Roslyn Meredith, but from the moment you came to Ayios Georghios, I haven't been able to put you out of my thoughts. When I knew you were going to return to England and I'd probably never see you again, I moved heaven and earth to see that I did.'

She was staring at him. Time seemed to be standing still. Her heartbeats were the only sound she could hear. He was telling her he loved her. He loved her! James Atherton loved her! Her lips moved a little, but she couldn't speak, the joy was too great.

His thumb moved softly against her skin. 'Haven't you anything to say?'

She put her hand quickly over his. 'Oh, James, I've loved you since — since . . . '

'Yes?'

'Since a night at the theater when I looked

across the auditorium and saw you. I didn't know who you were, but I fell in love with you.'

He smiled then, bending his head to put his lips softly over hers. He kissed her tenderly, cherishing the moment, as if he would survive on the sweetness forever. 'Oh, my darling,' he whispered, his voice trembling, 'if you only knew how often I've dreamed of this.'

'We might never have met, had it not been for . . . ' She bit her lip. Perhaps she shouldn't tell him about Lord Byron's willful interference in their lives.

He cupped her face in his hand. 'Hadn't been for what?'

'Lord Byron.'

He gave an incredulous laugh. 'And how does the poet genius enter into it?'

'He told us about Ayios Georghios and persuaded my uncle that he should go there. He did it because he'd perceived how I felt about you and wanted to get back at your wife for daring to insult his work.'

'The devil he did!'

'He admitted it. He's quite incorrigible.'

James smiled a little. 'I take it you find him a wicked charmer. Should I be jealous?'

'Definitely not.' She looked up at him. 'Will you tell me again that you love me?'

He drew her closer. 'I love you, Roslyn Meredith,' he said softly, 'and when I'm free, I want you to do me the honor of marrying me. Will you be mistress of Foxcombe, my darling?'

Tears filled her eyes and she nodded. 'Oh, yes,' she whispered. 'Yes, yes, yes.'

He kissed her again. They stood wrapped in each other's arms, unaware of the sound of another carriage outside. They knew nothing until there was a heavy step at the door and Sir Owen looked tentatively inside. 'Ah, there you are! What on earth is going on?'

They'd jumped guiltily apart the moment they'd heard his step.

He looked from one to the other. 'First there's Lady Gallermayne asking the butler very odd questions about mysterious messages, then she's ordering carriages to come down here and see if all's well. She said you'd both be here, but I told her that couldn't be the case because one of you was in Cheltenham and the other in bed with a headache. It seems I was wrong.'

Roslyn smiled and went to him. 'It's a very long story, Uncle Owen. A great deal has happened.'

'So I can see.' He glanced at James. 'I trust I don't have to call you out to defend my niece's reputation?'

'My intentions are very honorable indeed, Sir Owen. I've asked Roslyn to marry me the moment I'm free.'

Before Sir Owen could respond to this startling information, a rather imperious voice called impatiently from the carriage outside. 'Well, Sir Owen? Are they there?' It was Lady Gallermayne.

He turned. 'Yes, my lady, they're here.'

They all went out into the moonlit night. James's aunt leaned out of the carriage door. The beads on her gown flashed in the light from the carriage lamps. She looked quizzically at her nephew. 'Morris told me that Courtenay was safely bundled up, so I imagine all went well.'

'It did.'

'And Vanessa is out of your life once and for all?'

'Yes.'

She smiled then. 'Good. Does it also mean that you and Miss Meredith have finally said all that should be said?'

'We have.' James took Roslyn's hand.

'Excellent. I never could abide Vanessa. I hate adventuresses and actresses, and she was both.' She looked at Roslyn. 'I trust that you're still not an adventuress or an actress, Miss Meredith.'

'I've never been an adventuress, Lady

Gallermayne, but I was once an actress. Now I leave that to you. I'm filled with admiration for your performance tonight. I'd never have guessed that you knew all about James's plans.'

Lady Gallermayne chuckled. 'You'll do, missy, you'll do. James, you've made a wise choice at last, I was beginning to despair of you. Don't let her escape, she's right for you in every way.'

James brought Roslyn's palm to his lips. 'I'll bear that advice in mind, Aunt,' he murmured.

★ ★ ★

Two days later a letter addressed to Roslyn was delivered at Foxcombe. It was from Lord Byron and had been written on the frigate *Volage*, which had sailed from Malta on the second of June. It had been posted in Portsmouth, where the frigate had called briefly before sailing on to Sheerness.

She took it out to the summerhouse, where the sweetness of the flowers filled the air and the climbing rose was in full splendor. The hem of her apricot gown lifted gently in the light breeze, and the matching ribbons in her hair fluttered softly as she sat down in the summerhouse and broke the seal.

My dearest Miss Meredith,

I trust that by now you're at last well on your way to making a happy man of friend Atherton. If not, then the cards are wrong, the stars are wrong, and so is my intuition — which God forbid! If I arrive in Albion and discover you still to be wilting with unrequited love, then I shall feel obliged to marry you myself, my unwarranted dabbling in your affairs having brought you to such a pass. But I think you're safe from such a dire prospect, because I have Minerva's promise that you'll be granted your heart's desire. Yes, Miss Meredith, I have Olympus' ear at last. I'm addressing this to you at Foxcombe, because if you aren't there yet, you soon will be. Be my champion now, sweet lady, and when the second Lady Atherton sets London alight with her refreshing charm, she won't have a more willing or gallant champion than your affectionate and admiring servant.

George, Lord Byron

She smiled and folded the letter again.